Shadows in the Pleasure Gardens

Regarding Robberies and Racehorses

Elaine Mary Griffin

Black Rose Writing | Texas

This is a work of fiction. Names, characters, businesses, places, events, and incidents are either the products of the author's imagination or used in a fictitious manner. Any resemblance to actual persons, living or dead, or actual events is purely coincidental.

ISBN: 978-1-68513-612-3
LIBRARY OF CONGRESS CONTROL NUMBER: 2025931953
PUBLISHED BY BLACK ROSE WRITING
www.blackrosewriting.com

Printed in the United States of America
Suggested Retail Price (SRP) $21.95

Shadows in the Pleasure Gardens is printed in Garamond Premier Pro

*As a planet-friendly publisher, Black Rose Writing does its best to eliminate unnecessary waste to reduce paper usage and energy costs, while never compromising the reading experience. As a result, the final word count vs. page count may not meet common expectations.

Praise for
Shadows in the Pleasure Gardens

"A richly detailed, character-driven story that captures the social nuance, layered moral choices, and language reminiscent of Charles Dickens. Chester Carter's reluctant coming-of-age amid early nineteenth-century scandal feels both timeless and refreshingly earnest."
–Cam Torrens, award-winning author of the *Tyler Zahn* mystery/suspense series

"*Shadows in the Pleasure Garden* by Elaine Mary Griffin is an engaging mystery set in the early 19th Century featuring Chester Carter, a charming young bank apprentice who finds himself embroiled in a small-town scandal when he witnesses a robbery at his bank."
–Clifford Garstang, author and attorney

"Anyone caught up in armchair time travel should check out Elaine Mary Griffin's *Shadows in the Pleasure Gardens: Regarding Robberies and Racehorses.*"
–Mary Ann Noe, author of the *Lynn and Alfred* series

"This is a great mix of historical fiction, coming of age, and a heady brew of bad guys, danger, and finding a way to do the right thing."
–Karen E Osborne, author of *Justice For Emerson* and *True Grace*

"Elaine Mary Griffin weaves her historical backdrop with the dialogues, personalities, and perspectives of characters whose motivations and interactions shine with realistic color."
–D. Donovan, Senior Reviewer, *Midwest Book Review*

"A very unpredictable story, my favorite kind! Compelling and thought-provoking."
–*Amy's Bookshelf Reviews*

To Mum

Acknowledgements

First, my most sincere and deep gratitude to my mother, my first reader, editor, and literary agent. She told me she liked this book, so then she had the pleasure of reading it five times more, back-to-back-to-back, looking for misplaced apostrophes. This book would never have been printed without her taking the reins and driving it there herself.

I appreciate the help of my Aunt Cat, who reads and critiques my various attempts at novels and says nice things about them.

Thanks to the horse people in my life, past and present, and my father, who has put up with my horse for so many years.

Finally, I would like to thank all the characters I've met along the way who ended up inside this book.

Shadows in the Pleasure Gardens

Regarding Robberies and Racehorses

Prologue

I asked the lad to write down an account of his understanding of the matter. That's all. An affidavit is as good as witness testimony to a judge, and there's no better way to refresh a witness's memory of the incident. So, as I said, I asked young Mr. Carter to prepare a written statement of what had happened regarding our case. To be sure, I interviewed and deposed him myself, and my clerk wrote up a tidy stack of notes which could attend to the foregoing purposes just fine. But I never hesitate to cause the creation of more paperwork, especially if it doesn't fall upon me to write it up. I find it only the proper course of due diligence to ask a witness—at least a material, and literate, and at least mostly mentally sound witness—to prepare his own written account.

No different in this case. I told him he could take his time, this Chester lad: no need to rush home and write it out at once, though I admonished him to have done with it before his memory was too far flown.

Well, I directed the lad as such and sent him on his way. The lad didn't come back, nor did he send me a written product. I left messages for him at the post, I sent my clerk after him, I even crossed his path in town and inquired personally about the state of his memorandum. Each time, he responded he was working on it, that it was coming along, that he hadn't forgotten and would present me with the manuscript at the instant it was finished.

As a professional who had, at the time, practiced law for longer than dear Chester had then been alive, I understood he hadn't started, nor even thought about the written narrative, that he'd forgotten about it, and that he simply could not be bothered to remember, much less to put pen to paper. I dismissed it as a losing claim, thinking perhaps I'd overestimated the mental capacity of this young witness. He'd certainly not proven himself to be the ambitious sort, though he was articulate enough, when I got him to speak.

I daresay now that I was wrong in my first impression of the lad, and even further from the truth in my subsequent assessment. For, lo and behold, the lad reappeared in my law offices one day, some two months later, looking much better than I remembered from our last meeting, with a stack of script-covered papers some two inches thick. Of course, I invited Chester inside and asked him what in the world he intended to do with such a document. The poor lad looked quite crestfallen. He told me 'twas the memorandum he had written, which I had been asking after, finally finished.

That did naught to assuage my surprise, for I couldn't account for how he managed to get so many pages out of a single incident, consequence notwithstanding. To be sure, I'd advised the lad to err on the side of over-inclusivity, to add all the details he could remember and allow me, doctor of the law, to decide upon their legal relevance. Well, the lad had taken me a mite literally, I suppose, for he'd gone and written what I'd take as a novel if I didn't have corroborating evidence.

Still, I don't take him for a simpleton. Nay. I think he, like any (who can throw stones), found it quite enjoyable to write a narrative account of his experiences, which, in normal circumstances, he alone would find interesting. Enjoying being the hero of his own story, he got quite carried away in the writing of it.

He did seem ever so pleased to hand over the document, a boyish grin across his whole face, even adding that he hoped I'd enjoy it. Enjoy it! What a juvenile idea, for when ever had I found enjoyment from my profession, unless grave satisfaction can be counted as enjoyment. Even that, mind you, is reduced to horror at the sight of the gallows.

I had no mind to read this document for myself. As soon as I dismissed Chester, I handed it off to my clerk with instructions to read and extract the relevant points—for I knew there could be only a page or two of relevant points within the encyclopedic record. But, much as it pains me to admit it, the tedium of tweaking minor points in trust and estates issues was becoming insufferable by the late afternoon. My eyes fell upon the manuscript, still unopened upon the clerk's desk, and I chanced to run my eyes across it.

I'll be, enjoy it, I did. So much that I fear dear Chester gave in to fancy and took artistic liberties that would make this document more a liability than an asset at trial. But it is no matter: the document was never used in trial. Instead, I do believe the document should serve as an entertaining history of the biggest scandal our town has yet seen. That, and as a cautionary tale against idleness, fancy, caprice, and drunken freedom for our up-and-coming generations. I returned the manuscript to Chester when it became clear I couldn't use it at trial with suggestions for the foregoing uses. I reckon he took the idea under advisement and then forgot about it for two decades. Then, a bolt from the blue, I received a letter to my door and a request that I write the foreword to this piece. I'm pleased he didn't think me already dead, or at the least too senile to write coherently. I was most happy to oblige, and I have endeavored to do so, in near as rambling and inefficient a fashion as I remember Chester's original narrative to be.

Now all that's left is for me to commend you to the following pages, imploring that you should pay special heed to the lessons therein.

Signed,

Counselor Lindsay Worthingham

Attorney at law and prosecutor for the Village of Fairmount

Chapter One

It was hot and muggy, and I was doing my darndest to keep to the shade as I meandered back from Mr. Willerson's house with the signed document, probably a loan of some sort. Mr. Tate was gladsome to extend a loan to Mr. Willerson, because Mr. Tate was glad to collect interest, and Mr. Willerson could be relied upon to make his payments so long as someone would go to collect those payments. I was glad to be sent on house calls to collect signatures, deliver promissory notes, and convey large sums of paper tender or small golden coins. 'Twas always a good day when my work allowed me to escape the dull roof of Tate's Banking and Loans.

I was in no hurry to get back to the bank. Though 'twas dim inside, the bank was stuffy and near as warm as the out-of-doors. All I ever did there was sort documents or other such dreary work. Much better to meander on back to the bank as slowly as I liked, mayhaps even avoiding showing up all sweaty. It was never any good to be sweaty there—too much in the way of paper and ink, and smudges can never be unmade.

Sheriff Hoogkirk rode towards me and dismounted in front of the general store, just across the street from Tate's Banking and Loans. He halloed to me and threw his reins over the hitching post.

"Yon' Chester. Out on business or a frolic this fine morn'?"

The Sheriff, I suppose, was an optimist, for 'twas hardly a fine day, thick and hot as it was, and I reckon 'twas after noon when we spoke, unless I am much mistaken.

"Business, Sheriff," I said. "I was calling upon a client for a signature. And what brings you into town?"

"Looking around, as per usual. Pete! How're ye doin', ol' man?"

Pete was just leaving the general store.

"Jus' fine," Pete said, sauntering over and looking pleased that someone asked. "The boys chopped up an old honey tree today."

"Ye don't say?"

"An' only got stung once or twiced, moreover."

"What luck!"

"Well hardly luck, really. The darned thing had fallen over the fence and the ol' heifer was halfway to Congress Hall by the time they caught up with her."

"Huh."

"But Johnny's missus got to jarrin' that honey, not before I got a hunk o' it fer meself, course. Reckon she'll be baking som'in up soon, too."

"I'll have to stop by," the Sheriff said. "Say, that's odd."

Sheriff Hoogkirk was looking across the street. A couple of men had dismounted in front of the bank and were walking inside, their horses standing dolefully with lowered heads, though they were tied to no post nor held by a groom. That's what I found chiefly interesting, for it's not every day you see a pair of horses with those kinds of manners, not in the city, anyhow.

But the Sheriff's eyes were following the two men. They were wearing breeches and boots, but no waistcoat, jacket, nor tie. Atop their white shirts hung fringed leather vests. Instead of respectable top hats, they wore headbands tucked with hawk feathers, their faces painted in garish streaks of red, black, blue, and white. They were clearly no gentlemen. Nor could they be humble farmers. Yet least of all were they Indians.

"Traders from the mountains?" Pete asked. Frontiersmen were known to come back wild. Pa said they did it to demonstrate their bravery for the ladies, though I don't reckon that would've given me any advantage in Alida's eyes.

"Journey a day or two west and it's lawless out there. Folk dressed like that, if at all."

"Johnny thought of goin' west, back 'fore he found his missus. Lot'o land. But what's all the land in the world worth without a civilization to cultivate it?" mused Pete.

The men had disappeared inside of the bank. I nearly wished I'd walked back from Mr. Willerson's a tad more spritely-like so I could've seen those men face-to-face. Instead, I'd have to rely on Casey's account. Casey wasn't much for talk, unless he could tell me something I didn't know. He'd be in high snuff to relay such an interesting event I had missed.

The men were back out only a moment later. It really must've been less than a minute, I reckon. The Sheriff, Pete, and I were still standing across the street, though I think we'd run out of chatting fodder.

The men walked out of the bank and let the door bang behind them. Each was carrying a new satchel. They went straight for their horses.

"Hallu! Yous two Injuns! Pray stop and chat a moment," Sheriff Hoogkirk yelled across the street. The men glanced over. One raised an arm in a salute, but they kept on towards the horses.

Casey burst out of the bank, his face ashen.

"Robbers! Robbers!"

Sheriff wasted no time. He turned to his horse, drew his rifle from the saddle, leveled it over the horse's back, and yelled "stop" as he pulled the trigger.

The two men poorly dressed as Indians turned and froze. The Sheriff pulled the trigger again. The rifle clicked again. The robbers were in their saddles the next moment, wheeling their horses around and kicking them into a gallop down Main Street.

The Sheriff aimed again. He pulled the trigger again. The rifle remained unloaded and offered only a dull, harmless click.

"Robbers! Catch those robbers!"

Mr. Tate was in the street now, too, as red in the face as Casey was pale. Mr. Tate ran after the robbers, waving his arms above his head, yelling, "Thieves! Thieves!" Casey started after him. Sheriff Hoogkirk thrust his rifle into my chest before putting a foot into the stirrup and swinging heavily onto his horse, Champlain, who spun a circle in ill humor. The Sheriff dug his spurs into Champlain's sides, and the horse jumped, more up than out, and was off running after the robbers.

"Load that d— thing!" Sheriff Hoogkirk yelled as he flew away.

I'd no more rifle balls about my person than were in the rifle barrel.

"Ye got ammunition?" I yelled at Pete. Pete shook his head.

Mr. Tate was a few hundred paces down the road, Casey right behind him. Pete took off after them, fast for being gimpy as he was ever since catching a tree limb in the leg. Everyone was running, everyone was yelling, and the robbers were nearly out of sight on their horses out front.

Even in the early afternoon on a hot day, Main Street is crawling with people. That day, Main Street was stampeding, all the buildings emptied and all the people running westward, moving like they move only when something big is burning.

A cart came hurling up the street, bumping over the ruts behind the jerky gallop of the mule pulling it. The runners on the road parted as it passed, the driver yelling bloody murder for people to get out of the way, out of the road!

The cart kicked up an incredible cloud of dust that became almost muddy mixed with the moisture in the air. People were out of their storefronts, running and waving their arms, everyone yelling at the robbers to stop, but, naturally, the robbers didn't take heed. I was panting like an old dog on a hunt, but I still held Sheriff Hoogkirk's unloaded gun, so I couldn't give up chase. The robbers must've passed the schoolhouse, for our race ran by the schoolhouse, now empty, the poor school ma'am standing resignedly on the stoop, her hands on her hips, a few of the more dutiful girls peeking through the doorway.

That was the edge of town, and then the storefronts gave way to fence lines and cultivated fields. Boys from the field ran out to join the frantic parade, and their dogs came barking with them. Ladies stood in their doorways and waved handkerchiefs and old men trotted along in the rear.

I reckon the robbers were gone long before we quit running after them. I finally caught up with the Sheriff, who had pulled up his horse at the bridge over the Schuylkill. The road continues beyond, but it's flanked by dense wood, and the Sheriff said he couldn't see the robbers anymore. I couldn't see them either, but I couldn't see much, and I couldn't hardly breathe, either.

I stumbled around and gasped for breath, and the crowd in front of the bridge kept growing as more of our procession reached the bridge and accumulated there. They were all grumbling about those darned boys. Then talk grew about Injuns, and ruffians, and the Revolutionary gold and jewels that the robbers had gotten away with.

I stumbled through the crowd to the Sheriff, easily visible above the rest on his big sorrel gelding. I finally reached him, without even any shoving, for they all seemed to give way on account of the rifle I carried at my side.

The Sheriff glanced my way.

"Lordie's drawers! There ye are. With me rifle, moreover."

"Yessir."

"I had 'em in me sights, but I ain't had no gun."

"Yessir, well, ye did gallop off, sir."

The Sheriff grabbed the gun roughly.

"It's still not loaded, though, sir."

"By Jove, all this time an' ye've not even loaded it?"

"I didn't have the munition, sir."

"Well git some and load it fer me, will ye? An' hold me horse." He swung down from the saddle, nearly putting my eye out with his spur as I moved toward the horse to comply with his order. He stalked over the bridge and started peering into the thick undergrowth as I fiddled about with the saddlebags, looking for rifle balls.

'Twasn't hard to find, for the rifle balls were in the antiquated powder horn, affixed to the cantle with brass buckles. I took out a ball, unintentionally dampened it with my sweat, loaded it into the muzzle, and then carried that firearm with the caution due a poised rattler across the bridge to Sheriff Hoogkirk. I had to bring Champlain along with me—he followed sweetly as a dog.

The Sheriff took the rifle with such preoccupation that I'd've preferred to continue holding it myself.

"St—eh. I'll take the horse."

I abandoned the poor horse to the Sheriff and took a speedy retreat.

The Sheriff swung back upon his mount heavily. He is an imposing figure, and I wasn't the only one pleased he'd take the time away from running his own farm to act as the Sheriff. Not all towns had one, which Mrs. Hoogkirk was quick to remind anybody not satisfactorily pleased with his work, or stingy when it came time to support the position.

Sheriff Hoogkirk rode his horse to the center of the bridge so he could address the crowd properly.

"We've got ourselves a couple of robbers. It's lookin' like they fled into the woods."

"What'd they take?" an onlooker asked.

"Well—they robbed the bank."

"Sure, but what from the bank?"

"Is Mr. Tate here?" the Sheriff asked.

"Aye," Mr. Tate yelled. He was dripping, his cravat limp and sticking to his skin, his face red and shining from running and yelling.

"What'd they steal, Mr. Tate?"

"Ye'll have to ask me lousy clerk fer that," Mr. Tate yelled back, rounding on Casey, who'd been hovering at his elbow, still pale, but shining with a sickly sweat. He grabbed the lad by the cravat and pulled him forward. Yet Mr. Tate went on ahead and answered the question himself.

"But I can already tell ye 'twas bank notes. Lousy thieves ran away with bank notes, and a lousy lot let 'em!"

"Now, now, sir," the Sheriff started. It seemed as if he wanted to continue in a conciliatory vein but could come up with naught more to say. "Well, Casey, do'ye've a thing to add 'bout what was robbed?"

"They were armed, sir. 'An they wanted paper notes."

"And ye gave them the paper notes, did ye?" Mr. Tate yelled.

"They were armed, sir."

Mr. Tate dropped Casey's collar in disdain.

"What're'ye do'in here, Sheriff? They're gettin' away."

"As I was saying," Sheriff Hoogkirk continued, "the robbers have fled into the woods. I will lead a party to pursue them."

The crowd began to break up. Everyone had heard as much as anyone knew about what had happened, and there were no more robbers in sight nor flashy pursuits. It hardly even looked like a fight would break out. Farmers needed to get back to their fields, merchants to their shops, boys to their errands, and children to their schooling.

"Who will join the pursuit party?" the Sheriff asked. This begot no answers and only hastened the crowd's breakup.

I made my way back to Mr. Tate and Casey. I was a bit fearful, for Mr. Tate was in a frightful temper, and I was not completely innocent, on account that I'd dawdled on my way back to the bank. Had I not stopped to talk to the Sheriff and Pete, I'd've been back at the bank by the time the robbers walked in. What I'd've done to protect the bank, I reckon was nothing, so upon full review, 'twas lucky for my career that I'd been absent.

Mr. Tate glowered at me. "There ye are. Didn' catch 'em, I see."

"No sir. I could go with the Sheriff, sir. Part of the pursuit party."

"Good grief. Ye will capture the robbers, will ye?"

"We shan't just let them get away."

"Aye, go on, off wid' ye. When ye get back, Casey must tell ye all 'bout what must be done."

There was an ominous ring to it, but I was too pleased at getting out of the rest of the day of insufferably dull paperwork and Mr. Tate's ill humor to wonder at it then. Instead, I handed Casey the signed form from my house call to Mr. Willerson. Mr. Tate snatched it out of Casey's hands.

"I'll handle that," he said. "Now there's work to be done." He was stricken, suddenly, and his eyes bulged from his ruddy face. "Who's watchin' the bank?"

There was no one back at the bank. I remembered Mr. Tate charging out of the bank after Casey, the door slamming shut. It wouldn't be locked. Of course, the gold, jewels, and important documents would be locked up in the safes in the back of the building, but Tate's Banking and Loans had already been robbed once that day.

Mr. Tate stuffed the paperwork back into Casey's hand and sprinted off towards town. Casey looked at me with dismay and ran off after him. I found myself almost alone with the Sheriff as the few remaining in the crowd were drifting away.

"I'll go," I said.

"That's a good lad," the Sheriff said. "Who else?"

No one else volunteered.

"Mr. Moors?"

Mr. Moors's wife was expecting him for supper.

"Mr. Butler?"

Mr. Butler was rather busy.

The crowd disappeared in earnest now, people hurrying away before Sheriff Hoogkirk could call on them by name.

"Right, lad, it appears 'twill be just us," Sheriff Hoogkirk said. "But ye don't have a horse?"

I agreed I did not.

"Ye'll have to borrow a horse, then," the Sheriff said. "Ask of the Dunlaps."

The Dunlaps' farm bordered the road where we stood, and I caught sight of Mr. Dunlap hurrying away. I ran after him.

"Mr. Dunlap. Mr. Dunlap, sir."

"Aye, lad?"

"Might I beg use of a horse, sir? I'm to join the pursuit party, ye see, and I need a horse."

Mr. Dunlap scowled, but I reckon he thought the next request would be for him to join the party, so he nodded and jerked his head for me to follow him.

Sheriff Hoogkirk saw me wandering off with Mr. Dunlap and jogged his horse over to join us.

"Right good of ye, Ty."

Mr. Dunlap brushed it off. "If I don't be getting this horse back right as I send 'er off, I'm a comin' ta ye, Hoogkirk."

"Why don' ye come along with us?"

"Ye'll git the horse an be 'appy, or ye'll git nothin' at'all."

The Sheriff was quiet, and Mr. Dunlap and I walked on to Mr. Dunlap's farm, Sheriff Hoogkirk riding big Champlain lazily beside us.

The Dunlap barn is a weathered old structure, and so covered in dust ye can't see the gray of the aged timber. The horse was tied up to a post just outside the barn, a motley bay roan that blended against the beams behind her, her sagging back and drooping lower lip giving her a doleful appearance. A single twitch of the ear was her only acknowledgement of our approach.

"Saddle's here, bridle there," Mr. Dunlap said, ducking inside the barn and returning with the saddle, which he swung on the horse's back without ceremony. He had the horse bridled in another few seconds.

"All yours," Mr. Dunlap said, handing me the reins.

"Thank ye, sir," I responded. I swung up easily, though I found the stirrups far too long once I was astride the mare.

"What's her name?" I asked.

"Name?"

"The horse's name."

"Oh, that's just the little mare."

Sheriff Hoogkirk was already loping back towards the bridge. I thanked Mr. Dunlap again and loped off after him.

Little Mare had more sprite in her step than you'd've known by looking at her. She caught up with Champlain in a moment and would've raced on ahead had I not held her back. She shortened her stride and trotted along, taking three or four steps for every one of Champlain's. I bounced up and down on her back, not enjoying my trip down jumble-gut lane.

The Sheriff and I pulled our horses up at the bridge. Poor Little Mare was already breathing heavily, and her coat was spiked with sweat. We clopped across the bridge.

"Now here's where they went into the woods," the Sheriff said, pointing down a deer path.

"How do ye figure?" I asked.

"Them there's the prints."

There were some hoof prints leading into the woods, but the path wasn't nearly big enough for horse and rider, anyhow. But Sheriff Hoogkirk steered Champlain into the trail, ducked close to the horse's neck, and they made it into the woods.

Little Mare didn't need me to tell her she was to follow. I pressed myself as close to her neck as I could, gripped the reins loosely with one hand, and beat away the scraggly tree limbs and brambles with the other.

Branches and thorny vines clawed at me, and I kept my head down. The sun was drooping, and under the thick foliage, 'twas already dusk. I trusted the Sheriff was looking out for tracks, for I was not, only allowing Little Mare to follow blindly. It occurred to me that I was as useful to the Sheriff's pursuit party as I was in the bank, which is to say, not at'all useful. But 'twas too late to turn back, and my presence, if only for being another body, had at least been requested.

We continued on for another hour or so, my shirt taking a terrible beating and my hair collecting pounds of twigs and leaves. It became dim and cool in the woods.

The Sheriff stopped his horse and Little Mare had her nose resting on Champlain's rump before she, too, stopped.

"I've lost the trail. Can't hardly see a thing. Ye've got young eyes. What can ye see?"

I responded truthfully that I could see no tracks.

"I reckon we lost it way back by the hill. We'd need to double back and find it again, but 'tis too dark to see a thing."

"Aye, sir."

"They're good and ahead of us by now. Pursuit is useless. We'll have to keep our eyes and ears open, and we'll find 'em some other way."

"Aye, sir."

"Right, well let's get out of these confounded woods. I'm gut foundered an' workin' on fiddler's pay."

Turning the horses round was no small task in the thick undergrowth, but the horses were willing enough to fight the elements and get the job done. I let Little Mare find our way out of the woods, which she did with such grace that we emerged from the trees in the side yard of the Dunlaps' property.

Sheriff Hoogkirk raised his arm in parting, silhouetted against the dim fog of the early evening. "Eyes and ears open. Remember this. Eyes and ears."

"Aye, sir," I said. Sheriff set his spurs to Champlain's sides, and the horse bounded away. Little Mare was now more than happy to let him go. She trotted up to the old barn. I stripped off the saddle and bridle and set it back in the barn, and then I thought of brushing the old horse. I couldn't find a brush in the barn, so I wandered out to the well. I drew some water and gave myself a good drink, for I was parched as could be. Then I drew another pail full and offered it to Little Mare. She slurped up the entire pail and then let a good bit of slobbery, green-tinged water dribble to the ground when she started clapping her lips as if she were trying to talk.

I drew another pail, and Little Mare bumped me with her nose, as if to say she'd like some more. But she was getting no more water, on account that she'd already wasted a good bit in washing out her mouth. Instead, I dumped the water over her back. It slicked the coat on the top of her back to her skin and dribbled down her sides, leaving most of her dry. But you might think I'd doused her with flaming whale oil from her response! She pinned her ears back and sidled around like a yearling who'd never been touched.

"Who goes there?" A voice boomed from the house. I nearly jumped out of my skin.

"Chester. Chester Carter. Just returning your horse, sir," I said.

A light bobbed toward me, and then Mr. Dunlap appeared, carrying a lantern.

"Didn't catch 'em, then?"

"Nay."

"Done gone and gave up, did ye?"

"Well on the pursuit, I suppose. But we're to keep our eyes and ears open."

Mr. Dunlap grunted. "Hah. That right? An' what're'ye doin' to me ol' 'orse, now?"

"Cleaning her up a bit."

"Ye sure did work 'er good."

"'Twas mostly walking, really," I said. I hoped it was too dark to see any of the nicks and scratches Little Mare had sustained from walking through the dense woods. "I reckon I'll get some more water to wash her off."

"Nay, don' waste any more of me water. Ye done gone an' dumped it all on the ground, it seems."

I refrained from fetching more water, and Mr. Dunlap tied his horse back to the post and dumped a healthy serving of oats in the trough within her reach. Little Mare ate with relish.

"Are ye staying fer supper?" Mr. Dunlap asked me. It caught me off guard, for I'd never received more than a greeting, much less a supper invitation, from Mr. Dunlap before that day.

"Nay, thank ye," I said. "I've got to appear back at the bank."

Mr. Dunlap tipped his cap at me and sauntered back to his house without another word. I started back to the road, on the way back into the town center, feeling suddenly very hungry.

Chapter Two

I arrived back at the bank as the last of the dusk was leaking from the sky. I was itching in my clothes, wet from sweat, and still covered in burs, twigs, and leaves. I walked up the front steps and pulled open the wooden door. The bell tinkled gayly, and I cringed at the sound and wished it were quiet. I immediately felt the ill humors inside the building sink into my skin and settle on my shoulders. A few candles flickered, but it wasn't much brighter than the street outside.

Mr. Tate emerged from the shadows brusquely. "Any luck?"

"No sir," I said.

"Did ye let that good fer nothin' Sheriff just give up?"

"No, sir, we're to keep our eyes and ears open."

Mr. Tate laughed bitterly. "Casey will explain the situation. Goodnight." He brushed by me and exited the door I'd just come through.

Casey sat slumped by the back-room door. I took a stool across the teller's counter from him, close enough for conversation but far enough to mollify my self-consciousness about my smell.

Casey waited for the door to slam and Mr. Tate's angry footsteps to fade.

"Well, they stole the broken bank notes."

He was referring to the paper promissory notes Tate's Bank and Loans issued. They were redeemable in gold at Tate's, or any other bank with an agreement with Tate's, and they were commonly transferred among lay people as a sort of paper currency.

"Then we can just cancel them." I was relieved the robbers made off with a bunch of paper rather than gold or silver mint.

"Well, ye see, they were just freshly printed. And I was in the process of accounting for all of them when the robbers came in. I reckon that's why they went for the notes rather than the vaults."

Casey paused.

"Oh?" I asked, "lucky you were doin' that, I reckon."

"No, no, no! Don't ye see, they weren't accounted for, and our accounting on the earlier notes is scanty, and this print was exactly the same as last round."

"Oh."

"They might've well stolen gold for what they got. We've no way of knowing which notes were stolen and which were rightful."

"Oh."

Casey laid his head in his hands on the teller's counter. "Ye can leave. Mr. Tate only wanted ye to know the situation and then go on home."

I rose. "I'll see ye on the morrow, then."

"I don't know if you shall or shalln't. Ye might be the only apprentice here by the morrow."

"Surely not!"

"Surely so," he moaned.

"But 'twasn't your fault the accounting's spotty. Or that ye hadn't finished."

"I let 'em have it, all the same."

"What would Mr. Tate expect? Ye to get shot over a few notes? For shame!"

"Aye, well, mention it to Mr. Tate if ye get the chance."

This made me quiet, for I didn't ever expect to have such a forthright conversation with Mr. Tate. I meekly bid Casey adieu and walked out of the bank.

I walked straight back to my boarding house, tidied myself as much as I could, ate, slept, woke, and returned to work the next day.

Both Casey and Mr. Tate were already in the bank when I returned the next morning, and both seemed in diligent spirits.

"Chester, lad, you're needed by the Sheriff, though he doesn't know it yet!" Mr. Tate said.

"Yessir."

"You're to find the Sheriff and go with him to the races in the pleasure gardens. Lots of nefarious folk gamblin' there, loose bills galore. See if ye can't track down some of ours there."

"The races, sir?"

"The Sheriff ought'a know. Just make sure you speak with the bookkeeper and get her to be on the lookout for Tate's Bank and Loans notes. Make sure everyone who brings 'em in can answer to where they come from. Get a handle on the accounts, too, if ye can."

"Yessir."

"Do ye understand what yer doing, lad?"

"Yessir," I said, though I wasn't sure I did.

"Off with ye, then."

I could hardly believe my luck at being sent out of the bank for a second day in a row. I nearly skipped onto the street.

'Twas a nice morning, sunny, and not yet too hot. I wasn't sure where I'd find Sheriff Hoogkirk, but I figured I'd best try his house first. 'Twas a good mile of a walk, but I didn't mind. I felt happy and useful enough, even if it were to take all morning to find the Sheriff.

He was at home, though. Mrs. Hoogkirk came to the door when I rang, and she sent me out to the barn where her husband was fiddling with the old iron plow.

"How do ye do, Sheriff Hoogkirk?" I said, upon entering the barn.

The Sheriff visibly started. "Heavens. Announce yerself, do!"

"'Tis Chester Carter, here, on an errand from Tate's Bank and Loans."

"Right sure 'tis. Now what does the bank want, pray tell?"

"Mr. Tate requests that you accompany me to the races at the pleasure gardens. He says you'll know where that is."

"Well sure I do, but I stay away from there if I can help it."

"Mr. Tate thinks folks might be dealing with our notes there."

"Mayhaps."

"Well, will you go with me?"

"I suppose a sheriff must rise to the occasion when duty calls, such as this. I'll go with ye, lad."

"Thank ye, sir."

"It's four or five miles off. We'll take horses. You can take Orleans."

I followed the Sheriff like a shadow as he bustled around, filling saddle bags, taking down leathers and irons, finding ropes, setting them down, and wondering where he'd set them.

"Get those horses, will ye?"

There were but two horses in the run. One was Champlain, the Sheriff's sorrel gelding, and the other must be Orleans, a sturdy bay that looked more suited for the plow than a saddle. They came to me like dogs and insisted on their oats first.

With some more bustling, the horses were saddled. Sheriff Hoogkirk found a dust-covered saddle beneath empty seed bags. The leather groaned as I swung up, and it creaked as we rode away at a walk, Sheriff Hoogkirk yelling "Farewell!" until Mrs. Hoogkirk was good enough to come out onto the front porch and wave us off.

"'Tis some five miles north," Sheriff told me. "Mostly north. Almost due north. We might as well pick up a trot."

This we did. Orleans was almost as bouncy as Little Mare, which made speech difficult, but I prevailed.

"What kind of races?" I asked.

"Horse, of course."

I reckon if I'd had to guess, it would've been horses, though I'd seen naught more than the informal race down a country road and couldn't imagine anyone racing horses in a garden. I recovered my breath and posed another question.

"Why don't you like to go to the pleasure gardens?"

"Brings out the gamblers, the drinkers, the slovenly, poor trashy folk, an' horses ain' nobody got no business ridin'. Makes fer all sorts of brawls, cheatin', duelin', and other such breakin' the laws. Best to stay away."

"Even as the sheriff?"

"'Specially as the sheriff."

We were quiet for a while, and then Sheriff amended. "'Tis a bit far from the ol' farm to be convenient, anyhow."

At a comfortable (for the horse, not I) trot, we arrived at the pleasure gardens within the hour of beginning our journey.

We came upon a lane that wound off the principal thoroughfare and passed into some manicured greens. It took us through a wrought-iron gate with an iron fence extending from both sides, the tops twirled fancily. A sign advertised the theater, a huge white stone building that stood behind a grove of well-spaced trees. 'Twas remarkable simply for being made of stone, and all the more so for its columns, curved facade, and green roof.

Sheriff steered us down another path, though, away from these attractions, and when we crested a hill, we came upon what almost looked like a miniature city laid out below us. Long, skinny, green-roofed barns lay haphazardly about, all more or less surrounding an oval track with a white picket fence around the border and a pond inside, reflecting the blue sky and wispy clouds. It looked to me like an idyllic mirage.

But as we drew closer, the wooden barns turned a dusty tan, the weathered slats sagged and cracked. The path became rutted with hoofprints in mud now dried, and the grass became cropped close, with large patches of bare dirt. Still, 'twas beautiful to me.

Horses stuck their heads from the barn windows, whinnying at Champlain and Orleans or chewing the receding window frames. Champlain pranced and tossed his head to see the others. He sidestepped into Orleans, who pinned his ears, until Sheriff Hoogkirk clapped Champlain's sides with his spurs and sent the horse spurting forward. Then the Sheriff hauled on the reins, and Champlain put his nose to the sky and swished his tail angrily, still prancing like an officer's dancing horse.

A procession of tired-looking old men and young wrangler-types, most with bare arms, led sweat-lathered horses past us, back to the barns. Racing horses, I presumed. A few jumped and tap-danced to see Champlain, and Champlain did the same, to the Sheriff's chagrin.

A crowd of people stood gathered against the near edge of the dirt track, leaning on the picket fence, which looked more gray than white the nearer we drew. There were ladies with garish feathers in their hats, men with their shirt sleeves rolled up and their cravats askew, and barefoot children, all ambling, bumping, and jostling about.

We neared the crowd, Champlain still acting fresh for having jogged the five miles from town to the gardens. Sheriff pulled his horse to an almost stop and swung down heavily. He pulled the reins over his horse's ears and handed them to me.

"Hold this horse. I'll find the moneychangers."

I took the second set of reins and watched Sheriff Hoogkirk stalk away. Champlain tried to follow, but then he settled down and we both turned to watch the crowd with undisguised interest.

A little old fellow in a stained shirt and knickers, no coat nor cravat, sauntered up to my side. He would've caught me completely unawares had Orleans not looked quizzically at the arriver. The man looked up at me with pale blue eyes and a sideways smile from his stubbly chin.

"Ye got a 'orse in the race?" he asked, his voice tobacco stained as his teeth.

"Nosirie," I said.

"Then ye best git yer 'orses outta the way. Ye'll be causin' trouble with the runners."

"Really?" I asked, glancing around for an appropriate place to retreat.

"No," the old man said. "Jus messin' with ye. If these folk cain't handle their horses, they got no right enterin. Break yer 'orses, that's what I's tell 'em. If they don' listen, that's their problem an they ken keep their 'orses off this here track."

I nodded, pretending to commiserate.

The little old man stuck his hand up to me to shake. "Name's Hendry Drink."

"Chester Carter," I said. "Pleased to be acquainted."

A line of fresh horses led by the tired old men and ruddy boys marched past us, on their way to the track. Champlain was suddenly fresh and interested again.

"Heavens ta' Betsy. Break yer 'orses 'fore bringin' 'em here. Let me hold 'im," Hendry Drink said.

I surrendered Champlain's reins. Hendry jerked them once and slapped Champlain's chest with the loose ends of the reins, and the horse decreased his fidgeting considerably.

"They're not my horses," I said. "They're the Sheriff's."

"That so? 'Bout time we had a sheriff in these parts."

"Why's that?"

"I shan't talk ill of a body, but I know plenty 'round these parts who could use a little law. Some people cain't git ta gamblin' without gittin' ta cheatin' jus a wee bit."

"We're only here looking for the folks who robbed Tate's Bank and Loans yesterday," I said.

"Pity. Ye could stick around."

The racing horses were in a round pen off the side of the track now, being walked around in circles as the onlookers pointed and spoke among themselves.

"Do ye have a horse in this race?" I asked.

"Aye. Chestnut filly. She's a fast bundle o' bones."

We looked after the chestnut. Her coat gleamed in the sun. Really, the horses alone looked well-kept in this corner of the gardens.

"Well, I've got ta go an saddle 'er up, now," Hendry said. "Course my folk cain't handle it on their own. An' me, an ol' man, saddlin' me own 'orse." He shook his head and gave me Champlain's reins before walking off, barking at the lad who held his horse, "where's that good fer nothin' saddle boy? 'Cain't he be on time fer anythin'?"

Boys finally ran out with the saddles, which looked small even in the arms of the young lads. The saddles went easily onto the horses' backs, with a man on each side ready to tighten the girths and a man in front holding the horse by the head. It seemed always to be a three-person job. Some horses kicked and jumped, and the men responded by folding back the horses' ears, twitching their lips, or twisting handfuls of skin from their gleaming coats. I couldn't hardly tell that anyone, Hendry included, had a fully-broken horse in the race.

The riders came out next, light men and boys with bright shirts, and they were thrown onto the horses' backs easier than bales of hay were thrown into wagons. A bugler sounded first call, and the horses were dragged or prodded to the starting line.

The horses were lined up enough, dancing and prancing, handlers enough out of the way, people crowding the rail. A man raised a white flag, and then it dropped, and the horses were off. The crowd cheered as the horses galloped down the far end of the track. They strung off into a line and rounded the far turn, the sound of hooves growing louder as they neared. They rounded the near turn, sending up a cloud of dust that hung in the air long after they passed. The ground shook as they passed, heading for the backstretch, riders crouched low over the horses' necks, waiving their crops, whistling, and yelling.

They passed the finish line and rounded another turn before the horses slowed. One by one, the horses stopped, turned, and plodded back to the crowd. I couldn't tell who won, but everyone else seemed to know, and ladies jumped or shook their fists while the men cussed unabashedly as if unaware of the ladies.

A string of tired, sweat-drenched horses was again led by, back to the barns. I caught Hendry yelling to another man that he'd best tell his rider to keep his own line or take him off the horse if he knew what was good for him.

With the horses gone, the crowd settled and thinned. Hendry returned to my side, this time with a young man covered head to toe in mud and dust. Only the space near his eyes appeared to have been splashed with some water, which left streaks of mud through the dust as it had dribbled down his cheeks and dried. He looked like Pa after a full day of plowing, except, Pa would say, Pa would have an honest day's work to show for his appearance.

"This is me boy," Hendry said.

The young man extended a muddy hand. "Berton Drink."

"Chester," I said, shaking his hand and then resisting the urge to wipe the dirt off on my breeches.

"Youse said you was lookin' fer some bank robbers?" Hendry asked.

"Aye. We figure they might try to exchange the notes they stole here so they can't be traced back to the robbery."

"Berton 'ere says e's 'eard of that robbery."

"Is that so?" I asked. "Do ye know who did it?"

Berton frowned. "What I heard is that 'twas a couple of Injuns."

I shook my head. "No. 'Twas only a couple of men dressed as Injuns. Poorly so, at that. They weren't real Injuns, I'm quite sure of it."

"What if they were real Injuns poorly dressed as white men?" Berton asked.

I shook my head. "They didn't look like Injuns."

"Well sounds like ye know yerself who done it," Hendry said.

"Nay, I only saw it happen, but I don't know who 'twas."

"Ye saw it happen? Why didn't ye stop 'em?"

"I tried. The whole town was after them, but they got away."

"Got away?" The Drinks were still bristling with incredulity when Sheriff Hoogkirk returned.

Sheriff nodded at the Drinks. "Sheriff Hoogkirk."

"We heard tell 'bout yer bank robbery," Hendry said.

"Be most obliged if ye keep yer eyes and ears open. Be on the lookout fer people tryin' ta exchange notes from Tate's Bank and Loans."

"Right. And don't let 'em git away next time."

Sheriff Hoogkirk put his left foot in the stirrup, swung his right over Champlain's back, and settled into the saddle without another glance at the Drinks. He wheeled Champlain around and set him looking up the hill we'd come down an hour or so earlier.

"We're done here," he said.

I waved at the Drinks and followed suit.

"Come back any time," Hendry Drink said.

I'd let the Sheriff investigate entirely unsupervised, I realized as we rode away. 'Twas only concerning to me on account that Mr. Tate had tasked me with much more that morning, and it didn't do to disappoint Mr. Tate.

"Did ye find the moneychangers?" I asked.

"They're all round," Sheriff responded. "Folks bettin, folks askin fer change. But I found the bookkeeper, and she keeps her some records of the major wins. So anyone claiming to come into a good bit of gold bettin' on horses can be taken to account."

"Did ye ask her 'bout the bank notes we're looking for?"

"Aye. She promises she's seen nothin' out o' the ordinary."

That was enough to satisfy my understanding of due diligence.

Chapter Three

We arrived back at Sheriff Hoogkirk's property by early afternoon. We splashed some water over the horses and let them loose in the run, and Sheriff invited me inside for dinner. I gratefully accepted.

Mrs. Hoogkirk made us corn cakes, which struck me as odd for midsummer, until she explained her need to empty her barrels of last year's dried corn before it became autumn again. Mr. Hoogkirk was notably good at cultivating corn and little else, so corn is all the little homestead cultivates, save Mrs. Hoogkirk's garden.

After dinner, I returned to the bank and my proper duties therewith. Of course, I dragged my feet just a tad on the way back down the road. 'Twas warm, and I was (rightfully, I think) tired. Mostly, I was uninterested in returning to the bank and whatever menial labor awaited me there.

Casey sat at the teller's counter, alone in the front of the bank, when I arrived. The bell tinkled and the open door spilled a shaft of bright light over his narrow shoulders, which caused him to blink and look up. The door swung shut and all was dim. The bank was especially drab compared to the out of doors, everything appearing only shades of brown in the muted light, from the walls to the floors, and even Casey's curly hair and tidy waistcoat.

"Good heavens, finally back, are ye? I trust you at least found the Sheriff."

"Of course I found the Sheriff, and I've been to the pleasure gardens and back already today," I retorted.

Mr. Tate emerged from the back room. "I believe ye were to send 'em to me when he returned, not question 'im yerself," Mr. Tate told Casey.

"Aye sir, he's only just now returned," Casey responded.

"Well, come along, then, Chester."

I wound around the counter and glimpsed a pistol laying on the teller's counter, out of view from the front. I looked again, found that it really was a pistol, and followed Mr. Tate into the back room. We did our accounting and Mr. Tate held meetings in the back room. 'Twas even dimmer than the front of the bank, and just as brown, though there was a beige carpet with some indecipherable design, which may've claimed some color for itself in the distant past.

"First off, did ye find anything?" Mr. Tate asked, sitting behind his wooden desk which was scuffed on top.

"The Sheriff found the bookkeeper and has her on the lookout for your notes," I said.

"Right, I'll have a word with this Hoogkirk about this later. Now, I want ye behind the counter and Casey back here accounting, where I can keep my eye on 'im."

"Yessir," I started to rise, but Mr. Tate stopped me.

"Hold up, I've got to instruct ye. You're to start taking down details and asking questions when anyone exchanges notes here, or does any other business with us, for that matter. I want ye asking why, what for, where they got their money, all of it."

I gaped at Mr. Tate. It would be tactless to ask such a question in polite society and even less acceptable to ask such questions outside of the gentlemen's circles, where a man's business was understood to be entirely his own.

"Surely no one will stand fer that," I said. "Moreover, they'll flay me alive fer that."

"Have ye no more courage than Casey, lad?" Mr. Tate asked. Is there a decent way to answer a question like that? If there is, I still haven't learnt it. I fidgeted and said nothing.

"Believe me, son, these are queries that every banker worth his salt compiles. I've got lists and lists of the sort in my files."

"I've never asked these questions before, sir," I said.

"You haven't yet learned the art. Course I know the ways to gather such information. Discreetly. Mostly I'll ask one farmer what the other's doing, or the wife about the neighbor. Most of 'em like talking about their own projects, too, as long as they think they've brought it up themselves."

I nodded, though I doubted Mr. Tate took stacks of notes on idle prattle. "But what if we know him?"

"What if we know him?"

"And we know he's honest? Not a robber, that is."

"Ye still must ask. Fer what if he honestly sold something to the robber for the notes? We'd need to know who 'twas to follow the trail. The most honest among us are most easily hoodwinked."

It may be true, but it'd be just as true that folk would take such questions as a personal affront, and I wanted no part in being the affronting party.

"Now Chester, I've always felt a sort of kinship with you. We both come from farming stock, looking to make a way in the professional world. You, I know, are particularly looking to enter polite society in town," he looked pointedly at me, and I blushed, thinking of Miss Alida TenEyke. "I fancy meself as taking ye under me wing, helping ye along to understand what goes on in business. The Sheriff may pretend to investigate, but 'tis really up to us to mind our own. That is the strategy, the reasoning behind it. The understanding is the most valuable part of any apprenticeship, I've always said. And I do intend to impart it unto you."

I remained silent, not quite in the mood to be properly grateful. I hadn't realized Mr. Tate considered me a charity case. Though my tasks were trivial, I'd thought they rendered value enough to make my apprenticeship mutually beneficial to Mr. Tate and me.

"Alright, back to the counter with ye."

I began my exit.

"The pistol's loaded. Don't cause any trouble, but we shan't have another robbery."

"Yessir."

"Casey! Come back for this accounting."

Casey and I brushed shoulders though the doorway, and I offered him a small smile which felt traitorous, after my conversation with Mr. Tate.

I remained behind the counter, in a lonely stupor, until the bell finally tinkled, and Mr. TenEyke walked in. I straightened instantly.

"Hallu, Mr. TenEyke."

"Good day to ye, Chester."

I had no mind to question Mr. TenEyke about the source of his funds, even if he had walked in carrying a stack of Tate Bank and Loans notes and asked for them all redeemed in gold. Mr. TenEyke was as honest as the day was long, everyone knew that, and folks as well-to-do as Mr. TenEyke never had any business robbing banks. These were all good reasons not to harass Mr. TenEyke with questions, above the general respect for the personal dignity and privacy of any valued customer. But the real reason was Mr. TenEyke's daughter. I'd won Mr. TenEyke's permission to court her only after securing my banking apprenticeship and suffering Mr. TenEyke to visit the bank and question Mr. Tate about my character. Mr. Tate had been most generous in his answers, insisting he only took on the top of the line, and he hadn't seemed put out at all by such an interesting call. But I'd never outlive the favor. Mr. Tate chortled over it often and seldom let a week go by without reminding me to present my best for the lovely Miss TenEyke and her esteemed father. I simply could not risk offending Mr. TenEyke with an interrogation. Unfortunately, I couldn't risk losing my good graces at the bank for the same reason.

"What can I do for ye, Mr. TenEyke?"

"I would like to withdraw some of the gold I have on deposit."

Mr. Tate appeared from the back room.

"Ah, Mr. TenEyke. What a pleasant surprise," he said.

Mr. TenEyke smiled, and I think he knew Mr. Tate had not been surprised, for he'd been listening to the exchange from the back room. "The pleasure is mine."

"What brings you here today?"

"I was just telling Chester that I'd like to withdraw some gold I have on deposit."

"Of course, of course, it can be done," Mr. Tate said. "We certainly have it here. But may I ask what occasions this? Not of course, inquiring into your personal matters, only wondering, sir, if this has anything to do with our recent bit of excitement."

"To be most frank, sir, it does."

"Of course ye will do as ye will, but, dear sir, do know that no gold was stolen. Your gold is most safe here. Safer here than anywhere, I daresay. They only made away with paper bills, which are much less securely guarded, of course. And I will see to it that no other such robbery shall happen here."

"Oh, I do believe your establishment to be as good as any. I will not withdraw all of my funds. I only wish to avoid having all my eggs in one basket, as they say."

"Yessir, most astute of ye. Well, then, how much will ye be withdrawing?"

I slid the slip of paper across the counter to Mr. TenEyke, who made his marks and tallied his sums, and then handed the paper directly to Mr. Tate. Mr. Tate looked begrudgingly at the paper and disappeared into the safe room.

"How are you and your family, sir?" I asked.

"We are all well. And you and your family?"

"We are also well, thank ye."

Mr. Tate returned with a black velvet bag, which he handed to Mr. TenEyke.

"Thank you, sir," Mr. TenEyke said. "As always, 'tis a pleasure doing business with you."

Mr. Tate bowed. "The pleasure is mine, sir."

Mr. TenEyke left the bank to a tinkling of bells and Mr. Tate rounded on me. "Ye can't be letting' folk withdraw half their savings so casually, without a word."

"But he didn't want anything to do with notes," I said.

"Mr. TenEyke is one of our biggest depositors. He takes his money out, there go the loans, there goes our livelihood. Not to mention what happens if he goes and tells of what he did. There could be a regular bank run, and then we won't have the funds to cover them all. Disaster!"

"I couldn't tell him no, though. 'Tis his money."

"Nay, but ye must do more to counsel against such things. 'Tis good fer a man to have his money in the bank, and ye must be the one to tell 'em so. Good fer the man and good fer the bank, and what's good fer them is good fer the town, and good fer America. 'Tis dissocial to bury yer gold in yer yard where it can't be invested."

"Yessir."

"That's a good project fer ye. Make a list of all the reasons to keep your money in the bank, do. Whilst ye sit here."

"Yessir," I said, as Mr. Tate disappeared to the back room again. I took a sheaf of paper, inked a quill, and started my list with "patriotism."

We had no more clients appear the rest of the day, so I was a good deal alone, working on my list, my eyes often drawn to the pistol sitting coolly on the counter. Finally, the clock struck closing hour. Mr. Tate locked up, and we three went our separate ways into the warm evening.

The next day being Saturday, I had to attend to but a half day at work. Mr. Tate put me in the teller's stool, again, but every time he heard the tinkling of bells, he was in the front room with me, supplanting my role as teller. I wouldn't've minded in the least had I had anything else to do in the teller's stool, or if I could simply be dismissed from my post for the day. It does wear on a body to feel perfectly useless. But all Mr. Tate would say of the matter was:

"Watch and learn, m'boy. Ye'll get where ye need to be."

The half day dragged on just as long as any of the regular days, but, finally, I was a free man. 'Twas a cloudy day, but my heart soared as I stepped outside to a day and a half of leisure.

Firstly, I made straight for the TenEyke house. I was invited to the TenEyke's for dinner on Saturdays, and then I was given leave to walk with Alida in the gardens surrounding their home.

I left Main Street and turned down a side road, packed dirt like every other road in town, save Main Street. 'Twas better for walking, for fewer carts and carriages demanded your attention or your life, and the inns and houses began popping up in place of the businesses. The wooden buildings were all most cheerfully done, with paint not too poorly peeling and with bright shutters. Most had little gardens in the front or the sides, and they had rocking chairs and benches on the porches and in the walks. The farther from Main Street I drew, the larger the houses, yards, and trees grew. Here, ancient trees could shade the width of the street when the sun shone.

I came upon the TenEyke house with a grin on my face. 'Twas a grand old house, bright white, all of its many windows cheerily framed with blue shutters. The pitched roof rose from the second story, which had its own porch, and I was only a little nervous when I stepped upon the walkway.

Low shrubbery lined the brick walk from the street to the front steps, and more shrubs hugged the foot of the house. I walked onto the porch and rang the bell.

Rosie answered, as she always did. She was a matronly woman, stout and red in the face, who thought 'twas part of her job to scare lads like me straight but had left off her best efforts at such years ago.

"Mr. Chester. Good afternoon."

"Good afternoon, Miss Rosie," I responded.

"Now let me see here." Rosie studied me closely. "Haven't ye a handkerchief? Wipe that face, do, 'tis shining and grimy as though ye've been working the fields."

Rosie thought it a terrible thing to appear as though you'd been working the fields, though it is honest and noble work, to be sure, my family work. But Alida was not inclined to marry a field hand. She'd been born and raised in town, the daughter of a professional man. Thus, I agreed 'twould be dreadful to look like a field laborer in her presence.

Alas, I couldn't find my handkerchief. I had but two pockets, and I checked each twice, but no handkerchief presented.

Rosie sighed. "Such is the way with men. One day it's the handkerchief, the next the shirt, the next they're walking about without a head on their shoulders." She handed me a handkerchief, but she was so displeased by my method of dabbing at my face that she took it back and scrubbed my face and neck herself. I felt rather raw about the face after that, and I hoped I didn't look it, but Rosie was finally satisfied and let me inside.

"For heaven's sake, do take your hat off," she said as I stepped past her.

I took my hat off and gave it to Rosie.

"To the parlor. Dinner in a quarter hour."

"Yes ma'am," I said.

The parlor walls were adorned with molding and wainscot, all an even shade of white. Windows looked onto the small garden outside, framed with burgundy drapes. A carpet covered every inch of the floor. Simeon, Alida's older brother, lounged in one of the stiff-backed chairs that lined the walls. He nodded at me as I entered, but he did not rise.

"Good day, Simeon," I said. I chose a chair near the door, which I realized, too late, was uncomfortably close to being opposite Simeon.

"How'de'ye'do," Simeon responded. He was a seed merchant by day, but he used his storefront as a tavern in the evenings. I never spoke of the tavern to the TenEykes, for 'twas the sort of thing that people whispered about—how did a TenEyke come to run a tavern? Especially when trading in seeds was straight as a poplar and plenty profitable for a single man of some twenty-odd years.

"Alida ought to be here shortly," Simeon said, and no sooner was Alida in the doorway.

I rose and bowed. She smiled and offered me a dainty hand, which I took and kissed. Then she walked to a chair, her pale, lace-fringed dress swaying gently over the carpet, and immediately picked up her embroidery.

Soft, blonde ringlets fell about her face, and she wore a tight bun atop her head. She was fair as her dress, just slightly pink. She looked at her embroidery and addressed me.

"Mr. Carter, I hope you have been well this week."

"I have, thank you, Miss TenEyke."

"I hear there was terrible excitement at the bank."

"Yes, indeed, 'twas a robbery, and half the town turned out to chase the men. But they got away."

"My, how dreadful."

"Yes," I agreed, though I couldn't stop myself from thinking that I hadn't minded the excitement for a change.

Rosie tinkled a bell somewhere and we walked into the dining room. Mr. and Mrs. TenEyke were already present. The sir greeted me with a bow and the ma'am a gentle curtsy. We sat as usual, I in my cherished spot next to Alida.

There was good food, and plenty of it. Chicken and pork, stewed vegetables, creamed corn and sliced potatoes, and bread rolls that made my dear ma jealous whenever I mentioned how soft and light they were. The pinnacle of my week was dining at the TenEyke's house, and not only because of Alida.

Mr. TenEyke kept the conversation on pleasantries. The seed business was going well, he elicited from his son. I mentioned I thought my pa and elder brother, Duncan, ought to be by next week for their order, and Simeon informed me they'd already placed their order. This pleased me, for I liked our families to associate whenever they may, but I was a tad sore they'd come to town without calling on me at the bank.

"Now that I'm thinking on it, your pa did mention that he didn't find ye at the bank. I reckon he called there first," Simeon said.

"My! I wonder how I missed him. Do ye recall which day it 'twas?"

"'Twas only but yesterday."

"Oh! Yesterday I was out the entire morn', running an errand for Mr. Tate. I went with Sheriff Hoogkirk to the pleasure gardens and racetrack, some few miles hence, to investigate the robbery."

I glanced at Alida. I'd been hoping not to mention the robbery again, for it didn't cast my profession in the most stable of lights, but I'd hoped Alida would be impressed at my being sent to track the criminals down. She looked more concerned than impressed, though, dear girl. I supposed I didn't mind having her worried for me.

"Were ye, now?" Mr. TenEkye asked. He glanced pointedly at Mrs. TenEyke, who frowned. I cursed my tongue.

"Aye, sir."

"Well, sure sounds a good place to look out for robbers and the like. Did ye find your men?"

"Nay, sir. But we made some inquiries and asked for future updates, so I reckon 'twasn't all for naught."

"Fine, fine."

This line of conversation fell quiet, and Mr. TenEyke picked up on the weather. Fine and fair all week, and he could only expect more of the same. A touch warm and damp for comfort, but nothing unexpected in the summer months. I heartily agreed with this, and everything else Mr. TenEyke said over dinner, until the plates were cleared away and Alida and I were free to take our stroll in the garden.

'Twas a small garden, with only one cobbled path making an irregular, oblong loop along the side of the house. There were the shrubs, the bushes, the flowers, and two flowering trees, which were now uniformly green and surrounded by rings of decaying petals upon the soil. One bench stood in the shade of one such tree, and occasionally Alida and I took a seat, but more often, we walked laps and laps around the little garden. I was all too aware of Mrs. TenEyke perched in the parlor with her mending in hand and an eye out the parlor windows, which offered an unobstructed view of the garden.

"'Tis always such a pleasure passing an afternoon with you and your family," I said, offering Alida my arm. She slipped a gloved hand into the crook of my elbow, and we started our first pass around the garden.

"I do appreciate you calling," Alida said.

"Beautiful day."

"How goes your work at the bank?"

"Oh, quite well," I said. "Mr. Tate has given me the most interesting responsibilities when it comes to investigating—"

"I do hate that you had to go to the races."

I peered, surprised, into her face, having to bend a trifle to see under the bill of her bonnet. "Whatever for?"

"A most unseemly place, that."

I was most taken aback, for I thought it a most marvelous place.

"Why do you say that? You have not been, have ye?"

"Good heavens, no!"

"Well, perhaps it is not as bad as you think. Plenty of well-bred horses. Shiny and healthy and fast."

Alida shook her head. "Do be pleased to stay away from the gambling. 'Tis a terrible, nasty, vulgar habit among too many gentlemen," Alida said.

"Certainly, certainly," I said. "I wouldn't gamble even had I money to lose." At this, I wished I hadn't called attention to my less-than-stately financial situation, even more than I wished I had spared this lady the impropriety of discussing money matters.

Alida only nodded, and I hurried to change the subject. "Have you painted much this week?"

She had done a little watercolor study. We took our usual laps and laps, discussing nothing more interesting, until Rosie appeared and remonstrated that Alida ought be out of the sun by this time on such a warm day, and I regretfully walked with her back to the entryway. Rosie handed me my hat, and I bowed to Alida, kissed her hand, bid her a pleasant week, and took my leave.

Chapter Four

I headed now to my parents' house, where I'd spent Saturday evenings and Sundays ever since I'd moved to town. 'Twas an hour and a half of a walk at a brisk pace, but a pleasant enough walk after a week of being cooped inside. The road was dry and packed, the hills gentle, and woods lined the streets in many areas, shading my progress.

Still, I was slick with sweat by the time I saw the winding way which forked from the main road towards the farm I still considered my home. Chestnut trees shaded the way, already adorned with their spikey green clusters. I remembered fondly when my pa planted those trees, when I was too young to do more than run along with pails half-filled with water to give the saplings a drink. I turned onto the way. 'Twas only a little rutted, I was pleased to observe. How many hot days had I spent alongside Duncan, Garret, and Tim, digging deluge ditches parallel to the road and filling in the ruts? To my right, a graying split-rail fence created a run for the few goats, horses, pigs, and cows my pa kept, and to my left spread the rolling acres of wheat, just beginning to turn from bright green to golden. Oat and barley fields lay behind the house, which was small and low and shaded by aged oaks.

The two hounds galloped at me on twig legs, barking enough for fifty dogs. They were still barking when they reached me, wagging their tails and clambering over each other for a pat on the head. I patted each, and they wound around my legs, tripping me up until I could hardly walk forward. I shooed them out of the way and started running towards the house. The dogs bounded along beside me, still barking.

Suzanna was the next to come running at me, grinning merrily. She met me in a hug but pulled away quickly.

"My, you're rather warm."

"'Tis a warm day, and I've been walking some six miles."

"Well, Ma and I baked a rhubarb pie for tonight, and Garret wrote to say he's coming home, too. He should be here any moment, I reckon. I almost thought ye were him."

"Is that why ye came out running to meet me? Why, I felt rather good 'bout meself."

"Oh, bully, Chester, I see thee every week. And glad of it, I am, too, for Duncan is far too serious and always figuring, and Timmy does vex me so."

"And what do ye tell them 'bout me?"

"Oh, I mostly wonder about your dear Alida. How is she? You saw her today?"

"Aye, she's well."

"Very beautiful?"

"Aye."

"And accomplished?"

"Aye. She sings and paints and plays the pianoforte and speaks French."

"My, hurry and marry her, do. I can't hardly wait for a sister, and Duncan's hopeless until he can find a heart for something other than his farm, and Garret doesn't have any prospects I can tell of, and Timmy's too young to be taken seriously."

"I'm too young to be taken seriously," I said. "I should surely need a proper position to satisfy Alida's father, not just some apprenticeship."

"Well do hurry with that, too. Say, Pa said there were some Injuns robbin' the bank."

By this time, we had reached the stoop, and I was saved from answering by Ma opening wide the door and giving me a great hug before pulling away and looking me in the eyes.

"My, dear, you'll have to wash up before supper. Why don't ye go on and do that. Suzie, ring the supper bell and then come along and help me. Oh, Chester, dear, I'm so glad you're safe."

I meandered to the side yard and doused my face and neck with water from the barrel. I dried myself with a rag. The dogs ran barking down the road. Suzie ran off after them. I made my way, much more slowly, down the road to meet Garret.

"Have ye met any ladies?" Suzie was asking Garret when we met on the road.

"Nay. We've been over this before. The ladies don't attend the university."

"Garret! Good to see ye," I said. I shook his hand warmly. It'd been months since I'd seen the older of my younger brothers. He pulled me into a hug. He was just a hair taller than me, but significantly broader.

"I'm that glad to see thee," he said.

"But surely ye can socialize when you're not studying. 'Tis Philadelphia, after all. So many fine ladies live in Philadelphia."

"Is that so?" Garret asked. "Might you make me an introduction?"

"Oh Garret, don't tease me so. Whatever do you do there in the evenings?"

"Why, I study, and I apprentice."

"You're as bad as Duncan," Suzie said.

Ma came out the door again as we neared the stoop.

"Garret, dear boy!" she said, hugging Garret. "What a blessing 'tis to have ye home. What a blessing to have all my children under one roof tonight, Garret and Chester home from the big cities."

It was nice of Ma to include me in the statement. 'Twas Garret who had moved off to the big city to study law at the University of Pennsylvania. I had only moved into town to apprentice at Mr. Tate's bank.

Pa, Duncan, and Tim came in from the fields, rinsed themselves at the pump, and joined us inside. Eventually, we were all seated at the dining table, with no thanks to Suzie, who was precious little help to Ma with all the excitement happening outside the kitchen.

At supper, Ma and Suzie had an unending stream of questions about Philadelphia and the University and the like. Garret was already in his second year, but he visited infrequently enough that his living situation remained a novelty.

"How do ye like the studies?" I asked.

"Like it? Oh, just fine. I reckon it'll be better to practice law than study it, though."

I wished I could feel that hopeful about the prospects of banking over apprenticing.

"Won't ye come back to town to practice?" Ma asked.

"Sure, I may. Although my clerking in Philadelphia might lead to something there."

"It would be nice to have two family professionals in town," Pa said.

"What about me?" Tim asked.

"Are ye to be a professional in town as well?" Pa asked.

"I reckon I might be."

"That'd be right fine. We can have three professionals in town."

"And you all can visit every week," Ma said.

Duncan was not going to town. His place was in the countryside, growing wheat like Pa, and he knew it and loved it.

***

Sunday passed in a sweet haze of church songs and sweat from helping Ma in the garden and helping Pa in the shed. Suzie was ever present, chattering merrily, and my brothers were in flux, a different group of two or three of us always around, boisterous and merry. Ma had a hundred hugs for me and a thousand for Garret and indefatigable patience for everyone else.

On Monday morning, I arose with the dawn in a dismal way, for I had to return to town and my work there. Pa was awake, sipping coffee and figuring the numbers, and Ma had breakfast warming for Garret and me. It didn't taste half as good as our supper the night before.

I might've cried as I hugged Ma and Pa goodbye. Never mind that I'd be back in but a week, and that I'd been living off in town for nye on a year.

Nay, neither the bustling town nor its bank nor even proximity to Alida could lighten the prospect of another week at Tate's Bank and Loans in town.

The sky was still dim as Garret and I walked the lane together. We were quiet, still in the throes of sleep and contemplating our coming weeks. Garret would accompany me the entire way into town and simply continue onward to Philadelphia afterwards. We traveled east, the sun rising directly in our faces, already uncomfortably warm.

'Twas still early when Garret left me at Tate's Bank and Loans. I hugged him and watched him continue southward with his purposeful step. He walked quickly: he said because he always had more things to do than time to do them. And he did have a long walk ahead of him that morning, the poor soul.

I meandered around for a spell longer until I caught sight of Mr. Tate walking to his bank. I caught up with him at the stoop as he unlocked the door.

"Mornin,' Mr. Tate."

"Good mornin,' Chester."

We walked inside. It was dark as night inside, and I listened to scuffing and footsteps as Mr. Tate lit the lamps and drew aside the curtains to the early morning outside.

"Chester," Mr. Tate said. "Exciting prospects for ye. I've a mind to travel to some of the other banks in the surrounding area, to track down these bills, ye see, and thee shall accompany me."

"Oh. Aye, sir," I said. I wasn't sure that this really was an exciting prospect, for Mr. Tate's assignments so rarely were, but it sounded superior to sitting at the clerk's counter.

"Ye drive a cart, don't ye?"

"Aye sir."

"Go on and order a cart and a horse from the livery, do. Tell 'em we're heading to Philadelphia and every bank along the way, do. Have him write up a bill."

"Yessir," I said. I left the bank and walked down the road.

The stable doors were open, and I entered cautiously. Mr. Dover was flinging manure from the stalls to the wheelbarrow standing in the aisle.

"Good morning, sir," I said. Mr. Dover emerged from the stall, his coveralls hanging from his lanky form, his greasy hair tied back, but not neatly.

"Good morning."

"Mr. Tate would like to rent a horse and a cart, please sir."

"Where to?"

"Philadelphia and the banks surrounding."

"He tryin' ta warn the others 'bout robbery?"

"Nay, he's looking for the stolen notes."

Mr. Dover shrugged. "Who's driving?"

"I am, sir."

"Ye know how?"

"Yessir."

"Be sure ta use the brake. I don't want me horse coming back with lines on 'is rump. An' light on the whip, mind. They know their job. An' plenty of water an' time fer walkin'. 'Tis blasted hot."

"Aye, sir."

"Have you got any money?"

"He asked for a bill, sir."

"Course he did. An' he's the one supposed to be givin' out loans. I ain' in the business of loans."

"I'm sure I can bring the payment before we head out if that's an issue, sir," I said.

"Nay, I'd wager he's good fer it. Jus a moment, here, I'll get ye set up."

He picked a big chestnut from the pasture and ran a brush over the horse's flanks. The horse ducked politely to make it easier for Mr. Dover to throw the heavy leather and iron collar over his head, and then he practically backed into the shafts of his own accord. Mr. Dover had him hitched in another moment.

"Right," Mr. Dover said. "Whip's on the seat, but easy with it. Use the brake. Avoid the ruts, stay away from mud, and keep to the center of the bridges."

"Yessir," I said. "Thank ye, sir."

"Go on, then."

I climbed into the driver's seat and took up the reins and the whip. It had been a while since I'd last driven Pa's harvest cart, but I knew how. Still, I shrank under Mr. Dover's disapproving gaze.

I clucked to the horse. "Walk on." He stepped out at a jaunty walk, and I took him around the side of the livery and back down the street towards the bank as Mr. Dover watched us go.

We reached the bank, and I pulled the horse up at the curb in front. I didn't dare leave the cart unattended to run inside, though I'm sure the red horse knew to wait, so I hoped Mr. Tate would look out the window.

Casey walked up the street towards us. "What're ye doin' with a cart?" he asked.

"Mr. Tate is traveling 'round to other banks to look for his stolen notes," I said.

"And you're a cart driver, now?"

"I reckon."

Casey raised his eyebrows. "I'll tell 'em his cart's ready."

Casey disappeared inside, and a few minutes later Mr. Tate appeared with his leather satchel. "Nice lookin' horse," Mr. Tate grunted as he climbed inside. "But that Bill character can't keep his carts clean to save his life." He swatted at the bench seat with his handkerchief before sitting with a sigh.

"Well, let's get to Melly's."

Mr. Tate called Morgan's Bank "Melly's." Perhaps Mr. Tate meant to demean, but I'd heard it so often, though only from Mr. Tate, that it seemed normal and natural and not at all offensive to call Morgan's Bank Melly's.

Melly's was at the edge of town, and we arrived in short order, even though I asked the horse to swerve to avoid the ruts and potholes. Mr. Tate cursed every time his briefcase was upset.

We pulled up in front of the humble storefront, and Mr. Tate climbed down and strode inside.

"Back in a minute," he called over his shoulder. I was left with the cart and the horse, who put his head down and cocked a back leg, patient as a platitude.

Mr. Tate was back within a quarter hour. I'd climbed down from the cart to stand in the shade while keeping the reins in hand. The sun was earnest, and 'twas already a hot day.

"All aboard, let's get'er goin,'" Mr. Tate said, nearly beating me back into the cart. We were off, back down the road before I asked Mr. Tate where to.

"Head south. We'll see how many banks in Philly we can call upon today."

I clucked to the horse, who obliged with a trot and didn't suffer me to wave the whip, which I appreciated for Mr. Dover's sake. We left the town and trotted in merry silence onward. It'd been mayhaps half an hour when we came upon a figure walking our way down the road.

"Oh! That's me brother, Garret!" I said, giddy at recognizing the back of his head as we neared, though I'd have known if I'd stopped to consider that he'd be on the same road as us, heading towards Philadelphia. "He's on his way back to Philadelphia for his schooling."

"Well pull up the cart, do."

I slowed the horse to a walk. "Oye! Garret!" I called.

Garret turned, surprised, and his face broke into a grin. "Fancy seeing you here, Chester! Hullo, Mr. Tate."

"Are ye wanting a lift to Philadelphia?" Mr. Tate asked.

"Are you going to Philadelphia?" Garret asked.

"Aye. Or I'd not've offered, lad, but we haven't all day."

"Aye, sir, I'd be much obliged."

Mr. Tate jerked his thumb at the cart. "We got some space."

Garret climbed into the cart by way of the wheel, and we started onward again. The horse's sweat lathered where the harness rubbed against his skin and caused it to foam. I would've liked to water the horse, though we hadn't been at a long pull, yet.

"What're we on a pleasure cruise?" Mr. Tate asked.

"No, sir, I was only giving the horse a rest."

"The horse just got a rest. An' 'tis his job, fer crying out loud. If he can't handle it—"

I clucked to the horse, and the horse picked up a trot once more, though not so quickly as before.

"What brings you two to the city of brotherly love?" Garret asked. "Chester failed to mention ye'd be visiting."

"Oh, I've got to secure my connections with these other banks. I wrote 'em already, but I ain't sure they're impressed by the importance of the issue. Got to see 'em and be sure they'll be on the lookout fer those stolt' notes," Mr. Tate said.

"Setting aside competition?" Garret asked.

"Nay, I hardly compete with the Philadelphia banks. Different clients, we have. But we're close enough, so I accept notes issued by their bank and vice versa, and then our notes are worth more, see?"

"Ah. Aye," Garret said.

We were nearing the outlying buildings of Philadelphia.

"It'll be up here, amongst this rubble somewhere," Mr. Tate said slowly, leaning out of the cart and scrutinizing the buildings. "Mulligrubbin's sommin.'"

'Twas Mulligan's, and Mr. Tate alighted and strode into the building in a hurry.

"What're'ye, a common groom?" Garret asked.

"Well for today, mayhaps," I said. "Sure does beat being a clerk, though."

"You hardly moved to town to apprentice as a groom."

"Sure. 'Tis only what needs to be done today. I don't drive carts every day."

"Come, now, there's no reason Mr. Tate can take his apprentice all the way to Philadelphia yet can't let said apprentice sit in on the business meetings therein."

I agreed hesitantly.

"Well then, ask to attend the next meeting. Does ye no good to be sitting out here with a horse."

"Alright," I said.

"Right. Well, anyway, I best be on my way. Tell ol' Tate thanks for the ride, will ye?"

I promised to do so and shook my brother's hand. He jumped down from the coach and fell into the lines of people hurrying down the street.

I climbed to the street next, the ground hard beneath my stiff legs, and led the horse around, hunting for some water. The cisterns beneath the portico eves were dry. I reckon it'd been a fair few days since we'd had a rain. I wasn't keen on hunting around for water too far from Mulligan's and leaving Mr. Tate stranded, so I patted the sweaty horse, then dried off my hand on my breaches, and told him, without looking him in the eye, that I'd find him some water before too long.

Mr. Tate was longer in Mulligan's office than Melly's, but he was back on the street presently and the two of us boarded the cart.

"Where's the brother?"

"Oh! Yes, Garret would be off to school. He did wish me to relay his thanks for the ride."

"Humph."

"And, sir, if I may, I was wondering if I might accompany you in your next meeting. To see what you're doing, and such."

"Humph," Mr. Tate said. "Can't say I'm not glad to see something of ambition in ye. If ye can find someone to hold the horse, come along in."

"Yessir."

"Here! Here 'tis. Stop. Nay ye passed it."

I got the chestnut stopped and Mr. Tate jumped down. "Meet me in there," he said, and walked off.

The streets were crawling. There were no hitching posts, not that I thought that would settle with Mr. Tate, who was newly afeard of being robbed. "Ahoy!" I called to a lad wandering the street. He looked up. "How would ye like to hold this horse for me for a penny?"

He grinned. "Sure would."

I jumped down from the cart, bringing the reins with me. "Ye think ye might get 'em to some water, too?"

"Sure, I knows where they water the horses."

"Good lad." I handed the reins to this lad, feeling a twinge of foreboding and wondering if further interrogation would improve the chances of this actually being a good lad. He looked well enough like a good lad, so I left it at that.

"Don't stray. I'll be 'bout a quarter hour. Ye can have your penny when I return."

The lad nodded and held the reins, standing by the driver's bench. I hurried to the bank.

It looked much the same as Mr. Tate's bank. A clerk nodded to me from behind a counter as I entered.

"How can I help you, sir?" he asked.

"I am Mr. Tate's apprentice, sir," I said. "I'm to join him as he discusses business with..." I cast around for the name of the bank, couldn't find it, and rephrased the sentence. "I'm to join Mr. Tate in his business discussions."

"He didn't mention any such thing," the teller said. "Perhaps ye can wait here."

"Nay, sir, could you direct me to where this meeting is occurring?"

"'Tis already begun, and the bankers hardly take kindly to such business being interrupted."

"Aye, sir, but I was expressly ordered to join Mr. Tate after situating the horse and cart, which I have just done. He is expecting me, sir, and surely will not be disturbed at the interruption."

The teller frowned at me smugly. "Perhaps ye will like to take a seat in the parlor?" He nodded to the chairs on the wall behind me.

I was exasperated. I would *not* like to take a seat. That was no better than sitting outside with the horse—worse, perhaps—and now I would be called upon for a penny for my troubles. But I had argued all I thought I might with this teller. I looked hard at him and began my retreat to the back wall when I heard a door open from behind the teller's counter.

"What's all the fuss?" a voice asked.

"Chester, is that ye?" Mr. Tate called.

"Aye, sir."

"Well hurry on and get in here," Mr. Tate said.

"Yessir," I said. I looked pointedly at the teller, who grudgingly opened the half door in the counter to let me into the back of the bank. Then I wound my way to the open door and ducked inside, closing it quietly to the swell-headed teller out front.

Mr. Tate sat across an imposing oak table from a man dressed in a neat tan suit with polished bronze buttons. His white hair lay over his jacket collar, tied back with a ribbon. He looked bemusedly over little round spectacles.

"Well, Mr. Tate," he said. "I believe when we left off I was telling you I will not share the records of transactions I handle for clients here."

"Then I'll ask ye to reconsider, good sir," Mr. Tate said. "We've got robbers loose on the road. If they get away with this, they'll strike again, and then it'll be open season on the banks. No bank is safe. We must band together, or no one will have a bank to bank with."

"Even if I believed in this apocalyptic prediction, I am in no position to betray the trust of my clients by sharing the details of their financial transactions and situations."

"I'm not asking ye to shout it from the rooftops," Mr. Tate said. "I meself am another banker. It shan't hurt your clients to share their information with another banker. I daresay they expect their information to be common among banks."

"Perhaps that is what your clients have come to expect at your establishment, but mine place a great deal of trust in the bank and expect confidence." Mr. Tate bristled, but before he could speak, the white-haired man continued. "I would, however, be willing to pause my exchange of Tate banknotes at my establishment. If all the banks did this, it would funnel your stolen notes back to you."

"Nay. Bad for the value of me notes. I can't have 'em only accepted at one institution."

"Bad for *your* business, perhaps. While sharing confidential customer information would be bad for *my* business. Perhaps you can understand my point?"

I was both utterly enthralled and utterly uncomfortable as I stood in the corner, observing this debate, thoroughly ignored by the bankers.

"How's this," Mr. Tate began, leaning forward in his chair. "Ye know what I'm looking for: me notes getting exchanged by someone who has no business owning me notes. If ye could keep a lookout for 'em, and alert me if ye find anything, I'd reckon we could get this thing solved."

The elder banker nodded slowly. "Alert you to nefarious transactions. I suppose I can do this."

"Suspicious, if ye please," Mr. Tate corrected. "Ye needn't sell the jury on it before ye send word to me."

"I'll make that determination if the situation arises. For I cannot abandon my clients, and falsely accusing them of robbery won't do."

Mr. Tate stood. "Of course, of course. Ye will use your esteemed judgment. Surely no one is asking you to accuse anyone. I can surely be discreet. I see we have reached an agreement, dear sir, and I thank ye kindly for your time and your willingness to help in this matter."

The other banker followed suit and shook hands with Mr. Tate. "Good day to you, sir." He bowed to me. "And you, sir."

I returned the bow. Mr. Tate let himself out of the office and motioned for me to come along. I followed him meekly back through the counter, which he let us through without regard for the clerk there, and then back out into the street.

Chapter Five

The horse and the cart were waiting for us, the young boy sitting proudly in the driver's seat.

"I offered him a penny, sir," I said. Mr. Tate harrumphed and fished a penny out of his pocket.

"Here ye are, lad," he said, and dropped it into the boy's hand, before climbing up onto the bench seat of the cart. I hurried around the horse as the boy jumped down from the driver's side.

"Did ye take him to water?" I asked.

"Aye."

"Did he drink?"

"Aye."

"Thank ye," I said, climbing up into the cart. I hoped I could trust the boy, who now scampered off. At least he'd been good enough to keep the horse for us.

"Come along, let's get on," Mr. Tate said. I clucked and the horse moved away from the curb.

"Exactly what I wanted, that," Mr. Tate continued. "Let this be a lesson to ye in negotiations, Chester."

"Really, sir?" I asked.

"Aye. I knew the ol' man 'twasn't 'bout to let me peek into his books. The ol' fox is probably ashamed by all the notes he takes. Nay, I don't hardly want to see those, anyhow. I wouldn't be opposed, don't get me wrong, but

I've got more pressing matters, anyhow. What I prefer is exactly what we got—the ol' man does the work and lets me know if he finds anything. Ask for what you want and ye might get what you need."

I nodded along. Mr. Tate had played it well in the office if he really were happy now, for he'd seemed most flustered then. Or he was playing it well now, and mayhaps he was now truly disappointed.

"Watch and learn to a few more," Mr. Tate said. "Then mayhaps I'll let ye handle one of yer own."

"Aye, sir," I said, though I wasn't sure I wanted to handle one of my own. The good news was that I knew enough of Mr. Tate's style of business to know I'd never be acting on my own in Mr. Tate's presence.

Mr. Tate directed me down a side road and then yelled for a stop so suddenly that I was surprised to find there was no small child running across the street.

"Get the horse and come along," he said, hurrying inside. I found another loitering boy to watch the horse and hurried after Mr. Tate. I caught up whilst Mr. Tate was still conversing with the clerk, insisting that he ought to have a meeting with the owner now, thank ye.

Mr. Tate got his meeting, and it went much the same as the last one, with Mr. Tate purporting, as we drove away, to have gotten everything he wanted. We continued on like that all day, until the storefronts put up "closed" signs and Mr. Tate begrudged us to make the journey back to town.

The poor horse must've been good and tired, and plenty hungry, but when I set him on the path out of the city, he perked up and trotted towards home with enthusiasm.

We returned to the livery, which was dark and quiet. Our only greeting was from horses putting their heads over the stall doors. Mr. Tate sent me to the house to "bang" on the door, so I knocked politely for a few minutes with progressively more force until I was nearly pounding the door.

Finally, Mr. Dover came to the door, still clad in his coveralls but wearing a nightcap.

"What's this? Back at this hour? I had a min' ye'd made off wid me horse."

"No sir, we're back from Philadelphia."

"Philadelphia! Well I'll be. I ought ta charge ye extra fer such a trip with me horse."

"Perhaps you can take that up with Mr. Tate," I said.

"Come along." He led the way back to the stables, mumbling about being dragged out of bed.

Mr. Tate climbed stiffly down from the cart, and Mr. Dover maneuvered the cart into its spot and unharnessed the horse.

"How much do I owe you?" Mr. Tate asked.

"One dollar."

"A dollar? That's absurd!"

"'Tain't, either. Ye had me horse an cart all day an into the night, took 'em nigh all over creation, and brought back me horse so dog tired that I'll have to rest 'im tomorrow."

"I know you only charge three quarters of a dollar for a day with the horse and cart."

"It'all depends on the miles and the work and the time. Ye've done gone and tuckered me horse out an put plenty o' miles on this here cart, an not over good roads, neither."

"Eighty cents sounds more than reasonable."

"If ye'd wanted to bargain on the price, ye oughta do that before ye go on and take me horse for a full day and into the night and then drag me outta me bed. Ye owe me one dollar, and you're getting a pretty bargain."

Mr. Tate grimaced and handed out the money. "We'll need a horse and cart again tomorrow. How's about three quarters of a dollar for the day?"

"I'll give ye a discount. Eighty five cents for tomorrow."

Mr. Tate handed him the two days' payment, and then we walked away, letting Mr. Dover tend to his sweaty horse.

"Folks these days think bankers are made of money. They think we print it," Mr. Tate grumbled to me. "Well. Pick up the horse tomorrow and have it at the bank by nine. And don't let him try to give us the same horse."

"Yessir," I said. I turned east, heading back to my boarding house where I hoped I could still find some sandwiches left out for me, for I was gut-foundered. Mr. Tate kept the path north. I wondered if he was headed to the bank or to his own home. I wondered if he slept or socialized. I wondered if I'd ever have occasion to ask.

***

Mr. Dover did try to give us the chestnut horse the next morning, but I reminded him that his horse was tired and needed a rest. Instead, I drove to the bank with a bay.

We spent another long day traversing what felt like all of Pennsylvania. We spoke to many bankers. The conversations were all quick, and they all blurred together. We returned to town very tired, with a very tired horse, and dragged poor Mr. Dover out of bed again.

"That's all for that kinda work," Mr. Tate told me as we left the livery. "We've visited all the banks I wanted to visit. Tomorrow we'll write letters to all the rest."

Though the cart driving was exhausting, I was disappointed to hear I'd be back in the dim bank, doing dull clerical work the next day. The most welcome respites never last long.

***

The bank seemed more drab than ever when I walked inside the next morning. Casey was already inside, manning the clerking counter. Mr. Tate was in the back room.

"That Chester?" he called through the closed door.

"Aye, sir," Casey and I responded.

"Send 'im back."

I walked to the back room.

Mr. Tate slid a sheaf of paper filled with cramped writing across the desk. "The first letter's done. I'll need about thirty more of these, just changing the name of the addressee, of course. And you'll have to address the envelopes. I've got a list of the banks somewhere—"

He rifled around in his desk and pulled out a binder. "They should all be in here. Not too organized. If we visited a bank in person, write 'em a letter confirming our agreement. Start a list so ye know who ye've written."

"Yessir," I said. I took the original letter and the binder to the little desk in the corner. I set the things down and opened the binder. 'Twas a mess of old letters and addressed envelopes from various banks, some addressed decades back. Some were bound with twine, others were simply pressed between blank sheets. The ink was smudged in some and fading in others. My stomach fell as I contemplated the project.

"It'd be fine if ye could get it done today," Mr. Tate said. "But at the least, be sure to post what ye finish before the post goes out today."

"Aye, sir," I said. "I'll do me best."

I settled down, looked at the first envelope in the box, copied the name and address onto a spare sheaf of paper, and then began copying down Mr. Tate's original letter.

'Twas insufferably dull work. And slow work, and the dullness made it slower. Mr. Tate wrote in long, convoluted sentences, and I was continually referring to the original to get the words in the right order, and then the letters, too, for spelling has naught been my strong suit. Mr. Tate's longhand didn't always give me the best idea of what the letters were, though, so in many of my words, I simply squiggled lines in for letters to give the impression of the word without having to choose the letters for fear I'd choose wrong.

I finally finished the first letter and laid it on Mr. Tate's desk for signature.

"What's this? I don't want it. Put it in an envelope and mail 'em together."

"Simply for your signature, sir," I said.

"Nay, nay, ye can sign for me."

So then I signed for Mr. Tate, too, first practicing on my scratch sheet to get the flourish of the T correct.

I was not near finishing by 2 pm, when I needed to post the mail, but I'd almost convinced myself I was Ashley Tate, and I was begging my most esteemed partners in business for their help in bringing criminals to justice and making the world a safer place for the good work of financial institutions to continue to benefit society. My hand was smudged with ink and disobeying my mind, my neck had a crick, my eyes were bleary, and my head ached. I was relieved to step out into the daylight and take a trip to the post office.

The trip across town was too short, though I drew it out as long as my conscience would allow. Then I was back in the bank, copying down more letters for the rest of the afternoon. The next day I continued with the letters, and the day after. I now had a personal vendetta against those rascal robbers who caused me to be given such a task.

My mood only soured further when I received word from Ma that Tim and Suzie had fallen ill with some communicable disease and Ma forbade me from returning home that weekend. Forget the fact that I'd lived with Tim and Suzie as they suffered various communicable diseases before. Now, I was hardly more than a frequent visitor to be shunned during sicknesses. That Ma was only looking out for my health didn't make me feel any better about it.

When Saturday afternoon rolled around, blessedly, though it had surely taken long enough to get there, I called upon Alida. Dinner was pleasant, and walking with Alida was pleasant, though the weather was so dreadfully hot that Rosie bade Alida to come back inside after only a few turns around the garden. Then Rosie bade me goodbye, and I was forced to return the gesture and walk away, though I had nowhere to go and felt swindled of the time I ought've been spending with Alida.

***

I rambled around the streets, sweating in the hazy afternoon, thinking I'd just bide my time until supper at my boarding house. Then my thoughts somehow turned to the pleasure gardens. Never mind that I'd been admonished to stay away from such a place, 'twas the only place that seemed to welcome me, and my feet turned in that direction.

'Twas a fair walk, but I had time and nothing else to do, nowhere else to go. So I walked to the pleasure gardens and arrived at their gates drenched in sweat and hungry again. I might've explored the theater or the footpaths that wound through flowers and around ornamental trees and tiny fishponds, but I went looking for the horses. I crested the hill and looked down upon the racetrack at the right moment to see a line of horses lunge forth and gallop around the track. The rumbling of hooves floated up to me as they rounded the near turn. One horse pulled away from the rest and won handedly. I started down the hill, towards the commotion.

"Ye gallop, boy?"

A small, stooped man stood beside me.

"Pardon me, sir?"

"Ye gallop?"

"I s'pose I have before."

"Ye don' gallop here, then?"

"No sir."

"Would ye like to?"

"Sure I would," I said.

"I need me a new gallop boy. I used to do it meself, but now I don' on account o' me ol' knees."

"Oh."

"'Tis near impossible to keep a gallop boy these days. They're always runnin' off o' not showin' up o' finding another trainer. Can't hardly keep the horses in shape without some more folk willing ta gallop in the mornings."

"Well, sir, I fear neither am I fit for a gallop boy. You see, I have another job in town."

"What time do ye start fer the day?"

"9 am."

"Ye got plenty o' time ta gallop in the mornin's. We start right at sunup. Coolest time an' best fer the horses."

"But it takes me an hour and a half to walk back to town."

"I got me an' ol' pony ye can take back and forth. Good ol' pony, he is. Used to be a racer and won me a lot o' money back in the day."

"Truly?" I asked, feeling myself get carried away. "Well, then, I reckon I could gallop for ye."

"Let's try it out tomorrow morn', eh? Ye want ta sleep in the barn so ye don' have to get up so early?"

I professed I'd love to sleep in the barn, and the old man motioned me to follow him. "I'm Georgie Bean, by the by," he said, offering me a weathered and calloused hand. I took it and shook it.

"Pleased to meet you. I'm Chester."

Mr. Bean led me back to the barns. A brown film of dust covered every board, nail, post, and sheet, but 'twas still bright from the sun with all the stall windows thrown open and the sliding doors at the front and end of the aisles standing open.

We walked inside.

"Mine's the K barn," Mr. Bean said, motioning to the letter "K" painted on the wall above the doors. "All the horses near side of center are mine."

Horses popped their heads over the stall doors to watch as we walked past. Hay bales stood stacked in odd corners, wheelbarrows and pitchforks were tipped here and there, and mud, dirt, and loose straw carpeted the aisles. We picked our way along as men crossed paths ahead of us with shovels and buckets, leading horses, or carrying saddles.

"Here ye are," Mr. Bean said, motioning to a stall to our left. It really was just another horse stall, except the straw, hay, and wood shavings were gone, replaced with wooden floorboards. Rickety wooden bunked beds stood on both sides, each with a ratty blanket. The window was open, which made it light and cheerful enough, but 'twas still unmistakably a horse stall.

But I'd be loath to prove myself faint of heart or ungrateful for the bed Mr. Bean offered.

"Thank ye," I said. "Is one of these beds not spoken for?"

"Last I checked there were only two men staying here," Mr. Bean said. "So ye can choose betwixt two beds. Which two, I couldn't tell ye."

I nodded.

"No lights unless it's absolutely necessary, and even then, ye best be dousing yer lantern with water when ye put it out. Barn fires only too common. I'll be back 'round sunup and we'll get ye on a few horses."

I thanked Mr. Bean again, and he nodded to me and then left. I heard his gruff voice speaking with someone across the barn about the state of the aisles.

The afternoon was still bright, so I wandered out of the barn and traversed a good part of the gardens over the hill. I found a man selling corn mash and meat on a stick out of a cart, and I bought myself a handsome dinner that I ate sitting on the grass with my back against a tree. I made my way back to the K barn as the evening drew near. The sleeping stall was empty. I didn't relish sleeping in someone else's bed, so I sat on one of the bottom bunks to wait for my roommates to join me.

I waited and waited as the night fell, and still no one entered. I was sleepy from my long day of wandering. Eventually, my resolve left me. I lay on my back and closed my eyes.

Chapter Six

I awoke to Mr. Bean yelling "up and at 'em!" and a dim dawn light shining through the open window. There were two others in the stall, both stirring but looking like they preferred not to rise, and both sleeping in the other set of bunks. I threw off the covers and tidied myself as best I could with what little I had with me and the few conveniences of the stall. I wandered out to the aisle, found a bucket with water that looked clean enough, and washed my face.

"Ye want water, ye ken go an' fill yer own bucket," a man said.

I apologized, and he smiled.

"'Tis better to get yer own water anyhow, fer you can't trust a pail 'round here to be clean."

"Is that Chestnut?" Mr. Bean asked.

"Chester, sir," I responded.

"Ye'll ride that bay first," he said, motioning to a horse across the way. "Getter brushed an' tacked an' then we'll send ye out."

He began handing me miscellaneous pieces. A brush picked off the ground, a bridle that'd been hanging by the wash rack, an old saddle of chapped leather which had been resting on a stool. I took the items and put them by the bay's stall, but the brush had disappeared by the time I was ready to use it. I hunted for another one, found one in a bucket hanging over a door, and brushed the bay. Her coat shone even in the dim morning light, and even as my brushing caused dust to rise from it and dance in the air.

I threw a sheet over the horse's back and then the saddle over this, and I tightened the girth as the horse squirmed around in her stall. Then I got the bit in her mouth and the bridle over her head—no small task as she was rather tall and insisted on putting her nose towards the ceiling when I did so—and then we walked into the aisle.

Mr. Bean was there in a moment.

"Ready?" he asked.

"Aye," I said, though now I felt all sorts of nervous. The saddle had been incredibly light, the bridle only a few strips of canvas, and the horse was rippling muscles that looked poised to explode as she pranced beside me, not content to walk or stand quietly.

"I'll throw ye up there, then, and I'll walk ye to the track fer the first time so ye know what to do."

I put the reins over the horse's neck and my hands on the saddle, and I bent my leg so Mr. Bean could give me a leg up. And he did throw me up onto the horse, so high that I nearly fell over the other side. I held on uncomfortably, wrapping my legs around her sides and clinging to the horse's mane as she shifted and wiggled beneath me.

Before I felt anything but affeared, Mr. Bean led the horse out of the barn. She pranced along behind Mr. Bean, but she always kept a foot on the ground. I found my stirrups, which were rather short for my liking, and I gathered up the reins.

"Give the lad a cap. He's not that heavy." I heard from the ground.

"Oh bother. Ye haven't a cap?"

"Nay," I said.

"Lend 'im yer cap, will ye?" Mr. Bean said to a boy riding a sweating horse towards us, back to the barn. "I got another in the office ye can take."

The lad on the horse removed his cap with one hand and placed it on my head as we passed each other. I managed to reposition it without unseating myself.

"Thank ye," I said, and then I saw 'twas the Drink lad, Berton.

"Ah, 'tis the Sheriff's boy. O' the Banker's boy. An' with a fast enough horse to catch a pair o' robbers, now," he said as he continued riding away. I chortled nervously.

We reached the track shortly.

"Jog her to the starting line, then gallop her a mile, that's one lap, and then jog her back here and walk back to the barn. Hug the outside rail when yer jogging and the inside rail when yer galloping, and don' run into anyone an' don' let 'er get away from ye."

"Yessir," I said, the jumping in my stomach reaching such commotion that I was very glad to have had no time for breakfast.

"Off wid ye, then." Mr. Bean let go of the bridle and we had a loose horse on the track. Well, not quite loose, on account that I was hanging onto the reins, but the horse seemed intent on testing the strength of my hold.

She knew where she was going, only she wanted to get there quicker. I held her back as best I could, keeping her prancing and sidestepping until we reached the start. Then the horse knew she'd be held back no longer, and there was nothing I could've done to prevent her galloping off had I wanted to. She sprang forward and galloped down the track, and I more or less forgot the reins and clung to her mane for dear life.

I don't know if the horse slowed around the turn or if my sensibilities quickened, but I became conscious of where we were on the track, and I could even see Mr. Bean leaning against the rail out of the corner of my eye. I pulled the horse up as we crossed the finish line, which was a wire strung between two posts twelve or so feet in the air, and she grudgingly slowed and slowed until she was finally prancing again, which is how we made our way back to Mr. Bean.

"What's that fer pace regulation?" Mr. Bean asked as we neared him.

"Sorry, sir?" I was breathing as hard as the horse, and Mr. Bean grabbed the reins and started leading us back to the barn.

"Yer out like a cannon an' then nigh loping 'round the near turn."

"She was raring to go, first, and then I 'spose she settled down."

"Well course she did go on and get tir'd. Wha'd ye expect? Up to you to pick a good pace for a mornin' gallop."

"And what is a good pace for a morning gallop?" I asked.

"Sommin' betwixt the two paces, but even all the way round. Good habit to get yer horse in fer savin' sommin' in the beginnin' an not running outta oats, like."

We had reached the barn, and Mr. Bean ordered me to jump down. 'Twas farther up than I remembered, and my legs had gone sleepy from being bent into the short stirrups, and the jump down jolted my knees. I also found I was all shaky from the excitement of it' all.

Mr. Bean stripped the horse of saddle and bridle in under a minute and handed the horse off to some other lad who took it to the wash stall.

"Right, this one next," Mr. Bean said, pointing to a gray next door. "Same thing. One mile."

I took the sweaty tack and threw it over the horse's back after the cursory brushing, and then I led the horse out to the aisle. Some old man walking by with a bucket full of sudsy water stopped, grabbed the reins, and gave me a leg up without a word, almost before I knew what was happening.

This horse was a bit quieter. He walked nicely out to the track before he took up prancing. Then we pranced around to the starting line, and he took off like a bullet. I reeled him back as best I could and then let up around the turn and urged him forward as we came around the backstretch. It surely all felt good and fast to me.

I brought the horse back and some lads descended on it, unsaddling in an instant and leading the horse away. Lads were walking horses in circles and up and down the barn aisles, and the dust was sparkling merrily in the air, illuminated by sunshine streaming through the windows and open doors.

The Berton Drink lad walked up behind me and took his cap back from my head without a word, taking me by surprise. He continued down the barn aisle, fitting the cap back onto his head without a backward glance.

Mr. Bean was next to startle me by clapping a hand on my shoulder.

"What'd ye' say, lad?" he asked. "Ye comin' back to ride tomorrow mornin'?"

I hadn't thought that far in advance, but I answered affirmatively out of instinct.

"Good. Ye can always have a spot in the barn if ye want it."

"Thank you, sir. And the pony?"

"Ah, yes. Let me show ye." He led me to a stall where an old sorrel with a white blaze covering half his face poked his head over the door. "Here he is. Take one of the older saddles, mind, and if ye bring 'em back by sundown, he can get fed wid the rest."

"Thank ye very much."

"Aye. An here ye are fer the morn. Two horses, eh?" He dropped a few coins into my hand. "There ye are. See ye tomorrow mornin,' same time."

"Yessir," I said. "Thank ye sir."

Mr. Bean was done talking to me, and he walked away without ceremony. I had a full Sunday ahead of me, and I knew I ought to attend church, so I saddled up the pony for a ride back to town.

The poor pony must've never gotten out for exercise, for he acted as if he were still a racehorse, though he looked like an old nag. He was happy to charge up the hill, though he puffed like a pipe at the top of it, so I pulled him up and we walked a spell before trotting most of the rest of the way to town.

I attended the service, arriving late, and a little dirty from my riding.

'Twas coming upon the new week, when I'd pay the boarding house mistress for my stay for the coming week, and I thought, happily, that I no longer needed a place in town. I had a free bed whenever I needed it out of town, and a ride betwixt the two places, and my cheeseparing-self wondered why I should ever pay for a bed if it weren't absolutely necessary. So, without really considering the matter, I approached Mrs. Miller and informed her I would not be staying with her for the coming weeks.

"No? Why on earth not?" Mrs. Miller asked, more than a little offended.

"Ye see, I have a job out of town, now, so I needn't have a bed in town."

"Have ye been fired from the bank?"

"Nay ma'am," I said, chagrined at her first assumption. "I will still work at the bank, only I will commute into town."

"Well then what on earth is this new job?"

"Riding horses, ma'am."

I was excited enough that her presumptuous questioning didn't bother me. I was rather glad that she'd asked so I could tell her without appearing to boast.

"Riding horses? Whoever heard of such a job?"

"Well ma'am, they need to be exercised, ye se."

"Well give 'em a job, eh?"

"They do have a job. They're racing horses."

"Racing horses! What on earth are ye doing mixed up with racing horses?" Mrs. Miller looked positively scandalized.

"Riding them," I said again.

"Oh dear. Dear me. 'Tis really best ye don't get in with the racing horses. Terribly dangerous, and not just because of the horses. That's how good men turn bad, getting into gambling and dueling and fighting. Oh dear, I must write your parents about this."

"Nay, ma'am, I can handle writing my own parents, thank ye please."

"Oh, surely they'll want to hear from me. They did entrust me with your care. And what have I done for ye to be runnin' off down the road with the speculators and gamblers and such?"

"Please ma'am, I believe they entrusted my care to my own self, but I will surely tell them you advised me against this move, if you wish. Please excuse me."

I took my leave as hurriedly as I could without running, and I sincerely hoped that Mrs. Miller would not write my parents. I didn't plan to write to my parents myself, I only thought I'd tell them casually the next Saturday evening when I returned to their house.

I had naught more to do than wander back to the pleasure gardens. I mounted the pony, and we trotted merrily on home.

Chapter Seven

At the first sight of the barns, the pony perked up. My reaction was much more reserved. My stomach turned just a tad as I looked upon the horse stalls, where I, too, would sleep, and I wondered if I hadn't made a mistake. What would Alida think of me sleeping in a horse stall, I wondered, especially when she had voiced her wish that I not associate with the people of the track. I steeled myself, for I'd made my decision and forfeited my spot at Miss Miller's boarding house, and Alida oughtn't be concerned 'bout where I laid my head at night. I'd never bring my wife home to a barn, but until then, I might economize and sleep where I liked.

I washed the pony and returned him to his stall. Then I washed myself in the same wash rack with the same soap and a freshly pumped bucket of water as best I could. There was still light in the sky, but I was well and truly tired. Yet I didn't relish the thought of sleep, not at such an early hour, and not with people milling around the barn, though 'twas decidedly quieter than the early hours. But I had nowhere else to go, so I went to the stall and sat on what I'd claimed as my bed.

I tried to clean the dirt from under my nails, with scanty success, until a head popped over the stall door. 'Twas the Berton Drink character, still wearing the cap he'd lent me that morning and his face still muddy.

"Hullu," I said.

"Ye live here, now?" he asked, skipping the pleasantries.

"Aye. I s'pose I do. Still work in town, too, though."

"Say, ye look familiar."

"I rode here this morning. I borrowed your cap. And I met you and your father a week or so before that."

"Nay nay, I mean familiar from before all that."

"Hmm."

"Where'd ye go to grammar school?"

"'Round Mill Creek."

"The little red building? With Miss Irving?"

"Aye," I said, my interest growing.

"That's why I remember ye."

"Surely not," I said. "Forgive me, but I have no recollection of a Berton Drink."

"Nor I of a...what's yer name again? Charlie?"

"Chester."

"Nor I of a Chester—what's yer second name?"

"Carter."

"Nor I of a Chester Carter. But I remember yer face."

"Huh," I said. The Mill Creek school was a one-room building—I reckon I'd remember every classmate I'd ever had. Berton was not a former classmate.

"I didn't stay there long, an' I was a few years older'n ye," Berton went on. "Ye had an older brother, didn't ye?"

"Aye. Duncan and Garret."

"I must've been Duncan's age, but nary did I do my lessons with the rest o' 'em, fer I was nary on par with the others me age. Ma said she'd take over me schoolin' right quick, an' then one of the other matrons 'round these parts started giving lessons, and 'twas much more convenient, though hardly did they count as lessons, but that's where I ended up 'till Pa said I was old enough and must've learnt all I could and needn't attend lessons no more."

I nodded along, truly pleased to have found an old friend, in the most liberal interpretation of the word, in my new home. Still, I felt a twinge out of place. I was no scholar, but I'd poised myself for the professional world, which this was not.

"Say, ye wantin' supper?" Berton asked.

I squirmed and hemmed. I would *like* supper, but I wasn't sure 'twas proper to accept a supper invitation when I had no way of returning the favor nor was I even sure I'd been offered an invitation.

"I sure could eat," I finally said.

"Well hows about ye come on to Ma's with me fer some supper?"

"I would greatly appreciate that," I said.

"I'm a headin' there now. Come along."

Berton disappeared from view over the stall door, and I let myself out of the stall and followed him down the barn aisle. He was sinewy and a few inches shorter than me, but he swung his arms by his side as he walked, daring passerby not to jump out of his path. His forearms were bare except for a layer of mud and dust, and his clothes were caked with mud.

We left the barns, heading away from the hill that led back into town when we came upon a rutted dirt road alongside a hay field. A wooded area drew towards the road on our right, and shadows lengthened across the road as the day dimmed into evening.

A cluster of little houses sprung up at the end of the hayfield. They were small and looked shabby, even from a distance. Paint peeled from large swaths of the walls, and every second window wanted a shutter. Little picket fences marked the yards, sometimes leaning against trees, some planks fallen or rotten.

Dogs bounded towards us as we drew near. Berton paid them no mind, though they jumped against us and then fell to fighting each other. The growling and snarling were even louder than the barking had been, and I tripped on legs and tails as I followed Berton towards the houses.

The chicken coops sagged and smelled stronger than the wood looked. Chickens paraded about freely, rooting through the mud and weeds and paying no heed to the rowdy pack of dogs.

Berton turned off the road and onto a dirt trail worn into the grass, leading to the front door of a little house. It'd been painted white once, though now 'twas tan. It lacked a front porch, but the roof overhung the front of the house by just enough to shelter stacked split wood and a pile of muddy boots.

Berton opened the front door and walked inside without announcement.

"Ma! I'm home. An' I brung Chester," he called.

"Hallu!" returned from somewhere inside.

The inside of the home was dim, with chipped and patched walls and an accumulation of mismatched furniture piled with bright pillows and crumpled blankets.

"Chester?" another voice asked. Then the source appeared.

"Me sister," Berton said to me.

"How do ye do," I said. "I'm Chester Carter."

"Me name's Corrine," the girl said. She was a slight figure with dark hair that was thin and curly. Her dark eyes made her face expressive and bright. "I hain't seen ye 'round before."

"Nay, I only just learned of this area a week or so ago."

"Where are ye from, then?"

"I've been living in town. Working at Mr. Tate's bank there."

"Oh! Ye work at a bank, do ye? How exciting!" Corrine said. Her intuition was far from correct, but I held my tongue and bowed my head.

Mr. Drink walked in behind us, the door banging shut behind him.

"Well hallu there, Chester," he said.

"Hallu," I returned.

That was enough talking for Mr. Drink, and he wandered out of the room.

"Do ye ride horses, too?" Corrine asked.

"Aye," I said.

"Oh, I just love the horses," Corrine said.

Berton wandered out of the room after his father. I would've liked to follow him, but he hadn't invited me, and I worried that Corrine deserved a response, though I wasn't sure what to say.

"They're probably gonna eat all the biscuits before we can even set down," Corrine said, following my gaze as I looked after Berton. "Ye stay here, I'll go tell them off."

Then Corrine was out of the room, too, and I stood awkwardly in the parlor, aware of my muddy boots and dusty clothes, though they were none too out of place in the house and among the Drinks.

"Come on, Chester," Berton called from wherever he'd wandered. I moved toward the voice, and then Corrine was back in the room, taking my hand and leading me through a doorway and into the dining room. I sat where she directed me. The others were already sitting, passing around plates, and leaning onto the table to take helpings of the peas, tomatoes, roasted chicken, and biscuits.

"Hallu, Chester," a portly woman said. She must've been Mrs. Drink.

"Pleased to meet ye," I said. The commotion persisted about me.

"Go on, Chester, have some peas. Ye like peas, don't ye?" Corrine asked. I assured her I did.

"And here's some chicken. Do take some more."

We fell to eating, and the conversation dwindled 'till it was back up when Mr. Drink, Hendry, mentioned "that man Bean's horses been bucking at the start and scaring off the others."

"Upset me horses so they broke late. Then lil' May got dirt in 'er face, and 'tis all over fer that gal when she get dirt in 'er face. Closes 'er eyes an' jogs on home, she do. Still think ye could've gotten her home fourth if ye'd laid the whip to 'er a smidge earlier."

"I laid the stick to 'er all the way 'round the track an' she didn' do a thing."

"Nay, truly, Berton! Yer horrible. Ye musn't whip me dear horse like that," Corrine cried.

"She ain' yer horse, an' she won't be mine much longer if she don' start runnin,'" Hendry said.

"I didn' hit 'er hard," Berton whispered to Corrine.

Hendry heard it, as we all did. "Well by Jove, hit 'er hard nex' time. How d'ye think we eat 'round here?"

Mrs. Drink and Corrine rose without ceremony and began clearing the plates.

"Reckon we can play poque, now," Berton said. "An' we won't even need Ma or Corrine."

"I want to play," Corrine called from the next room.

"Ye can play the next round," Hendry returned. He drew out a deck of cards.

I hadn't played poque before, and I was reluctant to learn, for what would my dear ma or sweet Alida say?

"I'm afraid I don't know how to play," I said. "Perhaps Corrine will take my place."

"Don't know how to play poque?" Berton asked.

"Nay."

"How thunderation not?"

"I've never played before."

"Then ye must learn at once. Ye can't stay 'round here an' not know how to play poque."

It sounded like a clear recommendation against staying around the folks of the pleasure gardens, but I overruled it, rationalizing that it could never hurt to learn a new skill.

"Ye'll still be better than Corrine. She only pretends to know how to play poque," Berton said to me, as he began rifling through the cards.

That a girl would have anything to do with a gambling game soothed my inquietude.

Berton dealt the cards and explained the game. We played a few rounds with Mr. Drink grunting a few words here and there on strategy now and again. Corrine returned from the kitchen, and Berton decided I'd had enough lessons for a proper game, only no money, so he dealt Corrine in, and we played a round. I lost first, then Corrine lost, and Hendry won. We played another round, and the game began to make sense.

It grew dark, inside and out of the little house, and we commenced yawning.

"Right time to turn in," Hendry said. I agreed, and I rose to take my leave. I thanked the Drinks for supper and company, and they more or less waved me out of the house. I walked myself to the door, let myself out, was accosted by dogs, and continued on my way back to the barns.

The walk was cool and dark. The cricket song sounded melancholy in the solitude. I walked past the hayfield, the green-gold tassels bent towards me in the gentle wind. I reached the K barn, and the horses shifted quietly in their stalls. A few stuck their heads over stall doors to watch me pass, but I received no real greeting. One of my stall mates was already asleep when I walked into the makeshift bedchambers. He was sleeping in the bunk I'd chosen, which I'd come to think of as my bunk. Upon further reflection, it'd probably been his bunk first. 'Twas an uncomfortable thought, though he'd said nothing ill to me on the subject. As quietly as I could, I climbed into the bunk above him and nestled down for the night.

Mr. Bean knocked on the stall door and called us out of bed the next moment. I sat up and wrestled my eyes open. I was still groggy when Mr. Bean threw me on the first horse, but that woke me up right quick. I gathered the reins and fought with the horse the entire way down to the track, for that horse would rather jog sideways than walk forward. We took a couple of laps and returned filthy. The horse was taken from me as soon as I jumped off, and another was brought out, already saddled. They threw me on the next one, and then one after that, and then I received my morning pay and was bid good day.

I rinsed myself as best I could and put on my more respectable town clothes, which I hadn't yet ridden in. I saddled the pony, wondering at my luck, and jogged him into town, squinting dirt the entire way.

I went straight for the livery.

"Ye bringin' me a horse, now?" Mr. Dover asked, walking out of his barn when he heard the pony clopping up.

"Aye, sir," I said. "Might he rest in your paddock whilst I'm at work?"

Mr. Dover shrugged. "I s'pose." He waved over his shoulder. "That one's fine."

I dismounted, untacked, and turned the horse into the paddock. "How much for that?" I asked.

Mr. Dover shrugged. "A nickel a day?"

I agreed, and I gave him a nickel. I left the tack on the fence and walked to the bank.

The sun was high in the sky when I arrived at the bank, and I felt as though I'd been up for a full day already. But 'twas only nine o'clock, and Mr. Tate and Casey were only just beginning their duties for the day.

Mr. Tate told Casey to tell me to start on some accounting. I don't know what I was accounting for, nor did I know at the time. Casey instructed me on which few numbers to look for in the various columns of the stacks and stacks of records, and I made a note of such things on some line, again and again and again. Terribly slow work, 'twas, mostly for it being so dull. My eyes drooped, for I'd gotten precious little sleep over the last few days, and I'd covered many miles that morning, and the bank was so dim and warm and stuffy, and so quiet.

***

The evening was long in coming, and my spirits were thoroughly depressed, and I was exhausted when it arrived. I revived on the ride home, only to be depressed at the sight of my sorry bedchambers.

A man rose from the pile of raggedy blankets on the bottom bunk.

"Howdy," he said. He might've been double my age, with deeply tanned skin and long, very lean limbs. His graying hair was gathered into a rattail of a braid that fell below his shoulders.

"Hallu," I responded.

"Green Gene."

"Pardon?"

"Me name's Green Gene."

"Pleasure to meet you, Green Gene," I said. "I'm Chester."

"Aye, 'tis wot they done tol' me when ye went an' slept in Ronnie's bed t'other night."

"I'm right sorry for that," I said. "I didn't know which bed wasn't taken."

"Lucky fer ye, 'twas Ronnie's bed an' not mine. I'd not've let ye sleep, but Ronnie done says, 'e's only jus' a lad. Lad needs them's sleeps,' an I said, 'suit yerself, Ronnie, 'tain't me bed."

I nodded. "That surely was good of him."

"Ye sure don' stick round here long."

"Nay. I'm back to the bank every day for my other job."

Green Gene whistled. "Righ' dandy. Only now ye can't ride in the races. Thas where the real money's at."

"Do ye ride in the races?"

"Nay. Used to. Then me horse broke down an' put a crook in me back an' now I only exercise 'em."

The stall door opened and another man walked in. He was shorter, thicker, and paler, and his gray hair was cut short.

"Eh Ronnie. The lad's back," Green Gene said.

"Hallu," Ronnie said, I think to both of us.

"Hullu," I responded.

Ronnie walked up to me and stuck out his hand. "Ronnie. Pleased to meet ye."

"Chester," I returned, shaking his hand.

"Well. 'Nother long day done," Ronnie said, sitting heavily on his bed.

"We playin' poque?" Green Gene asked.

"Reckon we might," Ronnie returned.

"'Tis better wid morn'n two."

"Sure 'tis. Ye playin,' Chester?" Ronnie asked.

"I suppose I might," I said. "But I only just learned yesterday."

"Toodlewho," Green Gene chortled, "I likes me the sound o' that."

I didn't like the sound of Green Gene's comment. "I surely hope we won't play for money," I said. "I can't afford to lose any."

"Oh come 'long," Green Gene said, "I knows ye ain' payin' nothin' ta live here. And there's always food somewhere round here, even if 'tis fer horses. Ye can afford ta lose some."

"Nay," I said. "I'm saving for marriage. And anyway, my girl doesn't approve of gambling."

Green Gene collapsed into laughter, but Ronnie looked solemn.

"Good fer ye, lad," Ronnie said. "Yer settin' out the importan' stuff."

"Yer girl's already tellin' ye what ta do an' ye ain't even married yet?" Green Gene asked.

"She only made known her thoughts on gambling," I said. "And I happen to agree."

"Chester makes a good point," Ronnie said. "Anyway, 'tain't fair ta stake money when the lad's only jus' learned to play. We'll play without stakes."

"Nay, there's no fun when there's no stakes," Green Gene said.

"How's about filling water buckets?" Ronnie asked.

Green Gene shrugged. Ronnie turned to me. "I suppose," I said, wondering if I were opposed to gambling on principle or only the prospect of losing good money. In the end, I figured camaraderie with my stall mates was worth something which ought to excuse a minor moral violation, should there be one.

The only issue, which didn't occur to me until we started playing, was that I had no responsibilities to fill water buckets, and thus nothing to win by shifting that chore to another person. Luckily, this didn't become an issue, for I lost every game and ended the night needing to fill three buckets-worth of water the next morning.

"Who taught ye ta play, anyway?" Green Gene asked, as he took the cards and I lost, again.

"The Drinks," I said. "Hendry and Berton."

"Done course," Green Gene said. "Berton can only win when he's cheatin', an' he's always cheatin' when there's anythin' ta win."

"Surely not," I said. "He seemed to play honest."

"Probably cus there weren't no stakes," Green Gene said. I allowed that we hadn't played for stakes. "Ye mark me words, don' ye never play gains' with Berton if ye got anythin' ta lose."

"He seems like a nice enough lad to me," I said. He had, after all, invited me to supper.

"Oh sure, he surely is nice enough," Ronnie said. "But he's a rapscallion. Little things, but enough to send him to jail a few times."

"Really?"

"Aye. An' any time anythin' goes missin,' ye can bet Berton had sommin' ta do wid' it," Green Gene added.

"Oh, plenty o' other folks might've done it. How's 'bout Don? He's known fer sticky fingers," Ronnie said.

Green Gene shrugged. "Don's bad news, too. Don' bother with him, neither."

"And Benny's been banned a spell on account of his cheatin' the books in the races," Ronnie added.

"Sure, he's crook'd, too."

"Really, ye do best ta keep yer eyes open. Fair few folks here will pull the wool on ye if ye let 'em."

"Ye stick wid' Ronnie an' me. We know the lay o' the land."

Ronnie nodded. "That's right. Ye best be careful. An' ye can ask me fer help any time."

I thanked them both, and I was quite happy to be sharing a stall with perhaps the only two honest fellows in the racing industry.

***

Despite the insufferable dullness of my work at the bank, the week passed quickly. All the riding back and forth, into and out of town, seemed to shrink the hours in the day until there were hardly any left. Rising at dawn and playing cards into the night left little time for sleep. By Friday evening, I was nearly too tired to attend the Lewis's barbeque, though I never doubted I would attend.

Chapter Eight

There weren't nearly enough of these barbecues. Mr. Lewis gave one every summer. He lives just on the edge of town in a nice, tidy house with a hay field behind and great oaks with gracious limbs shading the front. It was a shorter trip for me, rather than going all the way home to see my family, and the TenEykes would be there, too.

Mr. Tate let us leave the bank an hour early on Saturday so we could show up to the barbeque along with everyone else, which was as early as was seemly. It must be past the calling hours of the morning, but too late may offend the host, and, it'd be better to be at the barbecue than anywhere else.

Mr. Tate, Casey, and I left the bank together and walked to Mr. Lewis's property. Mr. Dover, driving his bay horse, passed us on the road. He raised his hand in greeting, and Mr. Tate grumbled about the dust Mr. Dover had stirred up for us to walk through.

We arrived in good time.

"Suzie!" I called. My little sister looked remarkably polished, wearing a light pink dress and a bonnet with a matching pink ribbon.

"Oh! Hallu, Chester," she said. She walked over to us.

"You look well," I said. "You and Timmy have convalesced well?"

"Oh yes. We had to, for we have a barbeque to attend."

This sounded exactly like Suzie, and I wondered how sick she'd really been. Probably only sick enough to not want to attend to her lessons.

"Suzie, ye remember Mr. Tate and Mr. Tucker," I said, motioning to my two companions, though I wasn't sure she'd met them.

"Of course. How do ye do?" she said, sweeping into a curtsy.

Mr. Tate and Casey bowed.

"I don't believe I've had the pleasure," Casey said.

"Oh no," Suzie agreed. "But I've heard ever so much about you."

I felt obliged to my sister for saying it, though 'twas a fib, for I hardly ever mentioned Casey when discussing the bank at home, and I further doubted Suzie's propensity to listen when I did speak of the bank. She preferred to hear of Alida and Simeon and other such social gossip.

"Do excuse me, sirs," I said. "I ought to find my family."

"Go on. Enjoy your weekend," Mr. Tate said. Casey bowed at Suzie, and I offered her my arm so she could direct me to our family.

"Why on earth didn't ye invite yer friend to come with us?" Suzie asked, when we were a few paces away.

"Who, Casey?"

"Mr. Tucker."

"Yes, that's Casey Tucker. I s'pose I've never regarded him as a friend."

"I should like it if ye'd start."

I looked sideways at Suzie. I couldn't imagine she'd actually like Casey, should she spend any time with him. I told her so.

"Oh, ye don' know a thing 'bout who I like," she said, and I was saved from answering—for she was probably mostly right—when we arrived in the little slice of shade where Ma had spread blankets and she and Pa were reclining.

"Hallu, hallu," I said, dropping to my knees to kiss Ma and Pa.

"Hallu, dear," Ma said. "The boys are off, socializing."

"Well perhaps I must do the same," I said. I was thinking of finding Alida, of course.

"Nay, before ye do, I've been worried sick, and I must have a moment to converse with ye."

"Whyever have ye worried?" I asked my Ma, even as my stomach dropped remembering my new homestead.

"Well, dear, Mrs. Miller wrote." I'd forgotten about Mrs. Miller's threat. "And she tells me ye up an' left her establishment. Now I don't like this, fer your Pa specifically trusts the Miller residence, and, of course, I prefer to have ye where I have connections, as well. And—now, she surely might've been mistaken—but she tells me ye've gotten into horse racing?"

I hardly knew where to start, but Suzie, who'd been looking like she was about to wander away, was now very much interested in hearing this conversation and had settled herself on the blankets. Pa held me in his steely gaze.

"Yes, Ma," I said. "I no longer stay at Mrs. Miller's. Ye see, I'm saving up money, for I've found accommodations just out of town."

"And where are they?"

"Well, to be truthful, they are in the pleasure gardens. But, ye see, 'tis only a place to sleep, and then I'm back to the bank each day. 'Tis hardly any different, except now my expenses are significantly lower."

"Where a body rests is truly one of the most important things, lad," Pa said. "'Tis home for a body, and ye can't escape the influences of home. Ye'll not do well ta be makin' yer home among the pleasure gardens."

"They really are nice, decent people there, Pa," I said.

"Do tell me yer not racing horses," Ma said.

"Nay. I'm only riding them in the mornings. I've got not a thing to do with the racing of 'em. Not riding 'em in races, and surely not gamblin' on 'em. Trust me, Ma, 'tis only like riding any other horse. I always liked to do that at home, when I was a boy."

"Aye, but now yer making the pleasure gardens yer home, and ye ain't only a boy." Ma looked close to tears.

"Please, Ma, trust me when I say I'm staying out of trouble," I said. "Please." I offered Ma my hand. She took it and patted it and blinked a few times. Pa frowned but was silent.

We sat quietly, until Suzie lost interest and took her leave, and I followed. As uncomfortable as the conversation had been, 'twas made worse by being at the barbeque. I couldn't allow the whole of the barbeque to slip away by having no fun.

I wandered around, bumping into old school friends and playing a game of horseshoe before I finally glimpsed Alida. She sat at a bench beneath a shade tree, speaking with none other than Casey Tucker. I meandered over.

"Good day, Alida. Casey," I said, bowing to each in turn. They each offered but a small nod.

"How are you this day?" I asked. Of course, I was speaking to Alida, but she hesitated and looked to me and then Casey as though she wasn't sure who should answer.

"Just fine," she said finally.

"Very good to hear," I said, for I had nothing better to say.

"And I hear you have moved to the racetrack," Alida said.

This was rather surprising. "Where on earth did ye hear such a thing?" I asked, rather than confirm it.

"What, so did you hope 'twould remain a secret?" she asked.

"Not at'all. I only wonder at who is talking about me like this."

"Like this? It's not as if it's idle gossip, or untruthful and malicious. But perhaps you are rightfully ashamed."

"It's only but temporary," I said. "Another source of income and lower cost of living. And, of course, I do still work at the bank."

"Yes. Well, clearly you will do as you will, so I will withhold any future advice, for clearly you don't care."

"Alida, I always do care what ye think," I said. I sincerely hated that Casey had not excused himself from my verbal lashing.

Alida rose. "I should be getting back to Mother. Good day."

I bowed. "Good day."

Casey bowed as well, and Alida offered him her hand in parting. And that scamp of a lad took it! My, I was angry enough to allow only Alida to leave before I turned on my heel and stalked away without taking leave of Casey. I would've thought it was he who told Alida about my moving to the pleasure garden, but I was quite sure he hadn't known.

When I returned to my family's blanket, Duncan and Tim were there with Ma and Pa. Suzie appeared shortly after. Duncan warned me that the legislature was considering outlawing horse racing. I reminded him, and everyone else for good measure, that 'twas only a temporary move and all would do well to forget about it or at least stop worrying.

Tim wouldn't let the subject lapse at that, though he, at least, spoke favorably.

"Ye think I could ride?" he asked.

"I don't think Ma would have it," I answered. Bringing my younger brother to the pleasure gardens was about the only thing I could think to make Ma sadder.

"Do the ladies wear nice hats?" Suzie asked. I realized then that bringing my younger sister to the pleasure gardens was even worse.

"No," I responded. "They wear the same hats as everyone else. And riding horses at the farm is much more enjoyable than riding at the track, Tim." Neither response was entirely truthful, but both were worthy fibs which may save my poor parents some grief.

Finally, the barbeque was ready for eating. I ate, without enjoying it quite as much as I might, and then I excused myself to return to my humble abode. I wasn't returning with my parents for a Sunday at home, partly so I could ride horses in the morning, and partly because I felt rather unwelcome with the constant berating about my new employment.

I retrieved the pony, and we rode home. Berton stuck his head into the barn as I untacked.

"Up fer a game of poque?" he asked.

I felt not at all up for a game of poque. I was rather depressed.

"Truly, I feel I'm all but too tired for it," I said.

"Right, well, tomorrow, then," he said, and was back on his way.

My stall mates weren't in when I entered, so I lay down and slept a delicious sleep. I awoke to Mr. Bean's yelling with a smile on my face and a song in my soul, which was only expanded by the exhilaration of galloping around the track.

My second week in my new home passed much the same as the first: in a flurry of work and travel and exhaustion, interspersed with playing poque with my stall mates and the Drinks.

The working week drew to a close, and I turned once again towards the TenEyke house for my Saturday dinner and stroll with Alida.

I rang the doorbell. Miss Rosie bustled to the door, but instead of admitting me, she walked onto the stoop and closed the door behind her.

"Chester, dear," she said, frowning over me. "Really, your shirt looks rather dusty, dear. Ye must take better care."

I patted at the front of my shirt, knowing it would do no good, only to demonstrate I valued her advice.

She frowned some more as I fidgeted on the porch. "Mr. TenEyke has said ye are most welcome to dine with us, as always," Rosie said.

I bowed. "I'm most grateful for his hospitality. As always."

"However, Alida does not wish to walk in the garden today."

"Does she wish to converse in the parlor, do you think?"

"Nay. She rather doesn't wish to speak with you alone."

My cheeks grew hot, and my stomach curled up inside of me.

"Is it because of the pleasure gardens?"

Miss Rosie nodded.

"I wonder that she can't trust me. 'Tis but temporary," I said.

"Chester, ye must think of this as Alida must. No good comes to a lady when she trusts a beau."

I thought surely some good might, and certainly the beau would be better off trusted. I sighed.

"Will ye yet dine with us?" Rosie asked.

I shook my head. "Nay. Thank ye, Miss Rosie."

She watched as I turned to walk away, keeping careful sight of the bricks in the walk as I tread upon them.

I walked back to the livery, retrieved the pony, and rode him home. I was all out of sorts, but we still arrived at the chestnut-lined path far earlier than normal. Pa, Duncan, and Tim must've been out back, working. It would be harvest soon, and I wondered if they'd have to hire hands to bring in the wheat and barley, what with Garret and me gone. Not if Duncan could help it. He'd do the work of three hired hands himself to save funds for project parcel.

I had the pony grazing in the paddock and had rinsed my hands and face and climbed to the stoop of the house before Ma or Suzie saw me. Suzie swung open the door just as I was about to walk in.

"You mean thing!" she said, hugging me. "Arriving early and then sneaking up on us?"

"I wasn't sneaking," I said. I patted her shoulder and then walked around her to get into the house. "Hallu, Ma."

Ma didn't answer, so I supposed she hadn't heard, but I didn't bother to raise my voice and try again.

"Well then, how is Alida?" Suzie asked.

"I reckon she's just fine."

"What do ye mean ye reckon? Didn't ye see her today?"

"Nay."

"Whyever not?"

"She didn't want to talk to me."

"Why not?"

"Because she disapproved of me living in the pleasure gardens."

"Her and everyone else," Suzie said, laughing. I nodded. "You could move back, ye know. Make everybody happy."

"I don't want to do that."

"Why not? Ye ought ta quit being selfish, and I reckon things will look up for ye."

"Mayhaps."

"So what did she say?" Suzie asked, unable to let the subject drop.

"Naught to me. The maid said she didn't want to talk to me."

"And ye just left it at that?"

"Aye."

"Why Chester! How could ye ever be so cold?"

"How do ye mean? She's the one who won't talk to me."

"And ye'll just let it drop as if ye never had more than a passing thought for her? Surely you must fight for the one you love. Tell her you'll live anywhere and do anything if it means you can be with her."

"I don't reckon that's the truth, though."

"Ye cold, heartless boy! Ye don't love her? After all that time wooing her? Or you're just too selfish to set aside yer own whims for her benefit?"

"I reckon I don't love her."

"My! I'll be! Well I sure am glad she figured ye out and was done with ye, you heartless boy."

I agreed. It didn't make me feel better, discovering I didn't love Alida. I only felt more like a fraud.

Suzie ran out of the room and left me with my sorry thoughts for but a moment. Then she was back, with Ma, telling Ma about how heartless and cold I was, how I had wooed poor Alida for months without love.

"I sure did *like* her a lot," I said. "I wasn't trying to trick her."

"Chester, dear," Ma said, "I worry you're only reacting to disappointment. Perhaps ye love her and are only angry and sad, now. Ye'll realize in a few days."

I shook my head.

"Well how on earth do ye know ye don't love her? Ye had all these plans to marry her. She'd make a fine wife. Hard to do better than a sweet and pure girl like her."

"I don't know. Isn't it something you should know, if ye love a person?" I asked.

"'Tain't something ye always feel," Ma said. "Not when ye've got other feelings to feel."

"Do take heed, though," I said, "Alida was the one who ended things."

"A lady must look out for her future," Ma said. "Ye must now show her she can count on ye."

"But I don't want to," I said. "I don't want to marry her anymore. Why do ye both seem to think she's the only girl in the world?"

"Well it surely t'ain't like ye can take yer pick of 'em," Suzie said. "Ye can't go throwing away ladies like this. Ye treat one poorly and ye'll never get another."

"Alida is a lovely, dear girl," Ma said. "She's ever so accomplished, and she comes from a good family. That she's displeased about your new residence only demonstrates her good sense. Not many girls her age can put sense above their hearts."

I thought perhaps it demonstrated that she'd never had a real heart for me, either, but I didn't say it. I kept quiet and hoped the subject would drop.

But at supper, Suzie had to bring it up again, for Pa, Duncan, and Tim had to know, of course. Duncan was quiet and gave me a sympathetic look, and Tim didn't blink at the news.

"Tis truly a shame," Pa said. "Always good fer a lad to find a good, sensible girl and settle down. Ye don't need ta be chasin' adventure yer whole life. An' the sooner ye realize that the better."

Chapter Nine

I rode the pony back to the pleasure gardens Sunday evening so I could exercise the horses bright and early Monday. 'Twasn't pleasant telling Ma why I couldn't stay the night. Of course, Ma told Pa, who frowned, shook his head, and wondered, 'mightn't it be better to apply myself fully to one job, rather than always running off betwixt two?' But banking was far too insipid to earn my full efforts, even had I no other claims to my attention. Even the excitement of the robbery had worn away. Mr. Tate was reasonably satisfied that his fellow bankers were looking for Tate's bank notes, and that was all he could think to do, so he left it at that.

I left straight after supper, and I wasn't sad to leave, either. Suzie kissed me and whispered that I must run along home and make it up to Alida as soon as possible by professing my foolishness, preferably with a nice little gift—a ribbon or a dainty pastry would do—and a promise to move back into town at once. Duncan shook my hand and told me to keep my chin up, and Tim asked me to write directly if I needed help riding horses.

The pony and I made good time, and it was only just getting dark when we arrived at the barns. I heard raised voices emitting as we approached. Ronnie ran out.

"Ye seen Berton?"

"Nay," I responded.

"He's supposed to ride the next race, but ain't nobody seen him 'round."

Mr. Bean appeared at my shoulder as I led the pony inside.

"Ye seen Berton?"

"Nay. Not since Friday last," I said.

Mr. Bean swore. "Will ye ride this race?"

"Ride in a race?"

"Aye. I needs a body on the back o' my horse at the startin' line in five minutes, an' yer the lightes' body I seen."

I would've liked to have a greater recommendation than my size, but I was still pleased.

"I suppose," I said. "But-though I've never done it before."

"'Tis all the same. Ronnie, get 'em silks. Bring tha' horse out. Come 'long."

A lad walked the horse out of the stall in front of us. His glossy roan coat still shone in the fading light. Mr. Bean walked out after it, motioning for me to follow.

"All the same. Ye jus' have to stick on fer the firs' part. Don't need to do nothin' else. The lads'll lead ye to the start and keep 'em there, an' the horse'll break when the flag goes down. Ye jus' keep 'em straight in the open stretch. Get out ahead if ye can, if not, keep 'em comfortable. Stay low over his neck, eh. No standin' straight up like ye ride 'em in the mornin'. An' remember ta hit him down the backstretch, and if yer ever fallin' behind. Don' let 'im fall mor'n five lengths behind the leader, an' really push 'im down the stretch. He can win this one."

We were nearly to the paddock, and my supper was curdling in my stomach. Ronnie ran up with the shirt and cap in Mr. Bean's colors: orange and black stripes. I wondered that he'd chosen such colors for himself, but I numbly allowed Ronnie to assist me in putting the shirt on over my own, buttoning up the collar, and tucking in the tail.

Others were tacking up the horse in the paddock. His eyes were wide, and he shook like a leaf.

"Makin' me horse nervous," Mr. Bean grumbled. "Walk that horse 'round. Get 'em loose," he yelled.

The grooms paid him no mind. One twisted a handful of the horse's skin while the other threw his weight into tightening the girth. The horse cocked a back leg, and the grooms jumped back.

"Scared of a kitten, they," Mr. Bean grumbled. "Someone git the kid a whip!"

I had a whip in my shaking hand the next moment.

"Right. We'll throw ye on here. Don' worry 'bout the stirrups nor the steering nor nothin' till ye get to the startin' line. An' hold on to his mane at the start. They're out quick if yer not ready fer it."

I nodded, for I couldn't open my mouth. The grooms began leading the horses out to the track. Mr. Bean motioned me over. The horse I was to ride was prancing in circles in the paddock.

"Right, when he comes back 'round," Mr. Bean said. I jogged to catch up. Then the horse was drawing in front of me. I grabbed a chunk of mane with my left hand and the saddle with my right and hopped around with my left leg bent at a right angle. Mr. Bean finally grabbed my shin and pushed me up, and then I was on my stomach on the horse. I slid my right leg over, and I was astride as the horse shimmied in the paddock. Somehow, I still had a hold on the whip.

"Don' worry 'bout the stirrups 'till ye get to the start line," Mr. Bean called. "Send, hold, send."

I hardly knew what any of it meant anymore. We were walking onto the track now, the groom hanging on to the rein as the horse pranced and jigged.

We were at the starting line too soon, and then I had to worry about the stirrups, which were too short. Nay, they weren't really too short for the riding I was supposed to do, but they were far shorter than anything I'd ever ridden in before. I tried to stand in the stirrups as the horse snorted and hopped around. 'Twasn't clear to me how a body was supposed to balance doing that.

"Might I let the stirrups out a smidgen?" I yelled down to the groom above the snorting horses, the cheering crowd, and the other folks calling and pushing and pulling and such carrying on.

"Nay. They don't go any longer, and even if they did, that'd be far too long fer racin.' Yer needin' to stay off his back, eh?"

"I might truly end up off the horse," I mumbled.

The groom had us lined up in the middle of the pack. There wasn't a best direction to fall, so far as I could tell.

"Right, hold on tight, now," the groom said. "There's the starter." He nodded to a man inside standing track-side of the inside rail, holding a white flag.

"Line 'em up. Two horse, yer way out in front. Back her up."

There was a great deal more jostling as the horses bumped into each other and the grooms attempted to hold the horses behind the starting line, and as still as possible, while staying out of the way of the start.

The starter lifted his hand. I grabbed hold of the mane in both hands, even as I held tightly to the reins and the whip.

"On yer marks. Get set. Go!" The flag was down, the grooms let go. Everyone was shouting, and everyone was flailing. The grooms were shouting for speed and flailing their sticks at the disappearing rumps of the horses, even as they cowered from the clods of dirt the horses kicked up. The jockeys were shouting at their horses, and the other riders, and making big cracking noises with their crops. The crowd was shouting and waving ribbons and flags. The horses were snorting and squealing and breathing like dragons as their powerful legs churned through the air and kicked up the dust. And I was shouting from the surprise of nearly coming off the back end of the horse as he shot forward from under me, flailing as I attempted to stay aboard. My hold on the horse's mane jerked me forward and gave me a good crick in the neck, and the horse was still running, running forward as I held on for dear life. I fought the wind and pulled myself forward to crouch over the horse's withers.

I finally gained enough composure, as the field left us behind, to lay my whip to the good horse's rump. He jumped forward and drew up to another horse's flank, where I was content to let him run. There was nothing but the sound of hooves now, so loud over the dirt. The horses in front kicked dirt into my face. I squinted and blinked the mud and dust out of my eyes and kept sight of the inside rail.

We flew over the track, the horse pulling my body forward with each stride. We were rounding the turn, and I pulled the horse left, hoping he'd hug the rail. Too far, and he almost bumped into another horse, so I gave him another clop with the whip, and we were in front of a horse within two strides. We neared the final curve. I reached back with my whip a few more times and crouched lower over his back. The horse was really running, but we had to go wide to get around the others. He leapt forward, and we were gaining. We ran on and on and on. 'Twas too late to catch the others, though. We passed beneath the finish wire, and I pulled back and requested that the horse stop. 'Twas hard to do with my shaking limbs, as I balanced precariously high above the horse's back, but the horse might've been about as tired as I was, for he slowed with the rest of them, his breathing ragged, and turned back to take his place among the others heading for home.

Finally, the groom blessedly appeared on the track. He grabbed hold of the horse's reins so I could drop them. I slid to the ground, my legs shaking. I was filthy, covered head to toe in dirt and mud, and I had to smear the dirt from my eyes to see Mr. Bean frowning at the paddock rail. I stumbled towards the fence.

Mr. Bean pumped my hand, which was limp and clammy.

"Ye sure let 'em git away from ye at the start. An' then ye rushed 'im towards the middle and all the way home. An' what de ye mean standing that tall down the homestretch?"

I had no idea what I meant by it, no more than I understood what Mr. Bean was saying to me.

"Tha' horse was ready to run. He was ready to win." It sounded rather like an accusation. "But hey, first race, eh?" he said, clapping me on the back. "Whaddye think?"

This question seemed to change my entire perspective on the ordeal. A smile came slowly to my lips, and then I was beaming like a fool.

"Reckon I had a good time," I said.

"Looks like it," Mr. Bean said, grinning at me. He reached into his pocket and counted out some coins. "Reckon this is 'bout how much ye earned," he said, handing me a handful. "It's more if ye win, mind ye."

Even so, 'twas more money than I'd ever been given at a single time, if I don't count the gold customers slid across the counter at me for deposit at the bank.

Mr. Bean ambled away, and I finally made my way back to the barns. I washed as well as I could from the barn spigot and dried myself with the little towel hung there, and then I made my way to my stall.

Ronnie was there, sitting on his bed and shuffling cards. "Well there's our lil' jockey," he said, grinning. "How'd ye fair?"

"I reckon I lost the race for 'em, but I sure made out alright," I said. I'd mostly recovered my sensibilities and my ability to speak.

"Only think of how well ye'd do if ye went an' won it," Ronnie said. "I'd race if I weren't so old and so heavy. Not a body wants me on 'is horse."

I nodded in sympathy. Green Gene sauntered in.

"We playing cards tonight?" he asked.

"I am," Ronnie said.

"I will," I said.

"We're bettin' tonight," Green Gene said.

"Nay, I'd rather not," I said.

"Ye've had yer practice. Yer ready ta play fer stakes," Green Gene said.

"I'd still rather not lose any money," I said.

"We all knows ye can stand it today," Green Gene said.

"Truly ye were jus talkin' on how rich the ride made ye," Ronnie added.

"Oh come, now," I said. "It hardly matters how much money I have, I'd still rather not lose it, and my dear Ma would faint if she heard of me gambling."

"Yer a grown lad. Ye hardly need ta worry 'bout yer ma," Green Gene said.

"Hows 'bout that little lady of yers?" Ronnie asked.

"Nay, she'll no longer see me."

"'Tis all fer the best, I'm sure. Ye want a lass ta stand by ya in richer and poorer," Ronnie said.

"I never liked her one bit," Green Gene added.

That was enough to distract me whilst Green Gene delt the cards and extracted a few coins from my purse on my behalf for the stake. The money was already out, and my hands were clean enough, so I went and played the round. And what do you know, but I won. It might've been my first ever win at poque, and 'twas for stakes, no less. By the time I slept, I really had done well financially that day, though I wasn't sure any of it was honest money. Nor was I confident on the propriety of working on a Sunday, though, coming from farming folk, I knew caring for animals and delicate sprouts was permitted on Sundays. I only hoped the exception extended to other animal work as well, say, riding horses.

The next morning, I arose unwillingly. But I was on a horse a few moments later, which woke me up, as did the congratulations on the night before.

"Ye a regular jockey, now?" a few wanted to know.

I couldn't say I was, but I let on that I wouldn't mind being called to service again.

"Ye can ride me horse," Mr. Drink said. "Berton came back this morn' and tol' me he's hightailing it at the end of the week. Won' say why. But now I needs a body ta ride me horse on Saturday."

"Morning?" I asked.

"Sure."

"I can't ride Saturday morning, on account that I'll have to be at the bank."

"Well see if ye can't get a pass from the bank fer half a day, eh?"

I offered a noncommittal response.

"I only pay the newbies eight per cent. Haven't earned yer ten per cent yet."

"Yessir," I said, not knowing nor caring how Mr. Drink calculated these percentages. I slid down from my lathered horse, was thrown up on the next one, and rode back out to the track.

The sun was high by the time I finished, and I was drenched in sweat myself. That gave the dust forever floating in the shafts of sunlight slanting through the barn windows something to stick to - my skin, which turned muddy.

I cleaned myself as best I could, and then I saddled the pony and rode into town.

I was a few strokes late to the bank that morning. Mr. Tate was behind the counter, counting bills, and he frowned up at me when I entered.

"How am I supposed to run a bank when me boy doesn't show up?"

"I reckon Casey is here," I said, though that wasn't a smart response in defense of my own utility.

"Half of the help is hardly something to be happy 'bout," Mr. Tate said.

"I'm sorry, sir," I said. "I was delayed."

"Well don't be delayed no more," Mr. Tate said.

"Yessir." I hung around, loitering in the lobby, waiting for Mr. Tate to give me something to do. It looked like he had returned to counting, and I was loath to disrupt him in such a task. But after several minutes, I felt that would be the lesser evil than to remain idle.

"Sir," I said. "What shall I do today?"

Mr. Tate finished his counting, I suppose, for he kept his head down another few moments before he looked up at me with a perfectly blank face. Then he gazed about the room.

"'Tis terribly dusty," he said. "Dust it up, will ye?"

I would, but I would not like it, and I would feel it below me, notwithstanding my tardiness that morn. Nor was I any good at dusting. I looked around for a feather duster, and eventually I happened upon an abandoned cravat in a cupboard which I used to wipe the surfaces in the bank. My efforts didn't make a visible difference, even when I applied some pressure. Aside from dust, I found clods of mud, dead roaches, and spider webs, and I removed those with more facility. Every nook I examined lent itself to more cleaning. The old cravat was soon soiled, but I had no other. I walked around like a blind maid, without order nor direction and making no discernible progress, entirely ignored by Mr. Tate and Casey and every patron who happened into the bank.

Chapter Ten

The day finally dragged to a close.

"Mr. Tate," I said, as he flipped shut his heavy ledger and leaned back in his chair. "Ye wouldn't mind if I made off a wee bit early this Saturday, would ye?"

"Made off early? Goodness, why on earth would ye do such a thing? I hope yer mama isn't sick?"

"No, no sir," I said. "It's only to ride a horse in a race, you see. I don't get too many offers like this, but it sure pays well."

"You think it pays well, now that ye see the money, but they're paying ye fer riskin' life an' limb. Ye git unlucky an ye'll have to make what they paid ye last the rest of yer life on account that ye won't be workin' no more. Not good pay when ye factor in the risk, see."

I hadn't thought of it that way. But Mr. Tate had begun a lecture, and he would continue, and Casey wandered into the front room to listen in.

"An ye only thinks it pays well because yer young and don't know no better. Ye stick in the professional field, and own yerself a business, and that's when ye really start earning well. Ye can make money with someone else doin' yer work, if ye stay in the business long enough. That's the way to do it, not with gamblin' yer body in a young man's pursuit without a thought of how you'll survive on the morrow."

"Yessir."

"Not to mention what ye owe yer fellow men. Young men aren't meant to earn well, nor be preeminent in their fields. 'Tis only years of work that brings honest success. Young men are meant to learn their trade to serve their society. Take bankers. Bankers help others set aside their money and grow it, and build houses and businesses, and make investments. Bankers are in the business of building societies. Horse racers are in the business of swindling people out of their money. Gettin' people to gamble it away. An' breedin' fast horses that have no use pulling plow nor cart, only runnin' fast. Too fast fer ladies an' proper folk."

He spoke convincingly. He convinced me.

Mr. Tate stood up and gathered his belongings in his satchel. "I'll be seeing ye Saturday, then?"

"Actually, sir, I've grown a mind that perhaps I'm not cut out for the professional field." I started haltingly, and finished all in a jumble of words, and then I wished I could recant, but I couldn't.

"Dear boy," Mr. Tate turned to me and crossed his arms over his chest. "I, too, hail from a farmin' family. That's why I had no reservations with bringin' ye on as an apprentice. An' I've no reservations of keeping ye on. Ye could be a partner one day. Don't be a fool and throw it away because ye've got a passin' fancy and feel yerself out o' line with the professional world."

"Nay, sir, I've decided I don't want the professional path."

Casey watched on in unfettered interest.

"Ye can't know that so early on."

I would've been inclined to agree with him, had I been thinking properly, but the disagreeable colloquy and the audience prevented cool reflection on my part, and I fancied myself most sure, most settled, and most correct.

"Perchance I will return at some later date with a better head upon me shoulders," I said.

"Well if ye think ye'll be returning here, ye better think again," Mr. Tate said. "Ye walk out like this, and I surely won't hold yer position open fer ye."

"Of course not, sir," I said. "I know ye cannot hold the position."

We stood there, for a moment.

"Well?" Mr. Tate grunted.

"Thank ye fer everything, sir," I said, extending my hand to shake Mr. Tate's. "I do appreciate the opportunity ye've given me."

Mr. Tate waved me away and brushed past me. "After I's practically gives ye the keys to the kingdom, eh? Ye travel 'round with me, seeing all the sights, ye knows exactly how the business works. I've treated ye like me own son, raising ye up to take over the business. Not good enough fer ye, eh? Not enough excitement? Well, I'll tell ye what, young man, there comes a time in life when ye dread excitement. All ye want is a home an' a hearth an' a good, reliable income to bring home to it. Ye'll learn one day. I only hope it's not too late fer ye."

"Yessir," I said, feeling sick to my stomach and walking out of the bank as Mr. Tate latched the door behind us. Casey hurried out and stood awkwardly on the stoop. I wondered if he was also Mr. Tate's adoptive son (which I hadn't known myself to be), or if I was vacating the spot for him. I shook his hand, turned, and walked to the livery, hoping the distance would ease my senses.

I was dread-filled. If I'd known I might've one day owned the place, I might have stifled my hot-headed escapade. 'Twasn't a thing I could ever tell my father, and I only hoped Mr. Tate hadn't mentioned that when he'd been in negotiations with my father. And that it wasn't true.

Luckily, Mr. Dover wasn't in a conversing mood, and I retook possession of the pony with only a nod in his direction. We trotted on home. A gallop would've done wonders for my depressed spirits, but I hadn't the gumption to ask for it, and the pony had been ridden enough of late to feel no need for the faster pace.

***

We arrived back at the barn to a flurry of activity.

"Good thing yer here," Ronnie said. "Willy fell off the last race, an' they're lookin' fer someone to ride his horse the next. Ye wan' it?"

"Yessir," I said, though I didn't think news of a fall boded well for my future. Ronnie was gone at once, and then a groom was handing me silks and a helmet and a stick while another was leading the pony away and bidding me to hurry and get to the paddock.

I jogged over to the paddock. The trainer saw me, shook my hand without a second question, and the next thing I knew, I was looking down at him from atop the horse as he gave me directions I can't recall, and surely couldn't carry out.

No matter. The horses were prancing to the starting line, the grooms straining to restrain the steeds from bolting, and my mind was empty of all else but grabbing hold of the mane and putting my feet into the stirrups and staying astride the horse. The starter was holding up the white flag. I looked at the track ahead, through the horse's ears, as he tossed his head and shook his mane, tapping his front feet and sending up clods of dirt.

Then the pistol fired, the flag dropped (I know, though I didn't see it), and the horses were running. The grooms bent away and covered their faces as dirt flew up behind the horses' heels. I remained atop my horse only by the strength in my fingers wound around mane as the horse tore forward and jerked me along with him.

We broke well, I know because I could still see the track a few heartbeats in, and I didn't get a facefull of mud. We were running side by side with two others, pulling ahead of two more. Five more bounds in, and I chanced a glance behind me. I pulled the horse to the inner rail and checked his stride. We matched the horse to my right stride for stride. My stirrup rubbed against the other horse's shoulder, and I nearly died of fright for thinking he'd push us into the rail or smoosh my leg. I gave my horse a tap on the rump, and we jumped ahead, clear of the other horse, who moved in behind us.

We moved around the turn in the lead, neither gaining nor losing, and we neared the final furlong. The jockeys were yelling behind me, and I heard the smack of whips, horses heaving, and hoofbeats pounding franticly. A horse moved in beside us. I crouched low over the horse's neck and nearly unseated myself as I hit him with the whip. And then we were below the wires, and I could catch my breath and let the poor horse catch his, and we were trotting again, and then the groom was on the track to catch the horse. We both clapped the good horse's neck, and the groom pumped my hand,

and then we were back in the paddock, and I slid off the horse, and the trainer pumped my hand and clapped me on the back, and I scarcely heard a thing, though everyone was talking and laughing uproariously. I couldn't remember what had happened an hour earlier. My thoughts were empty. There was only a fuzzy, warm feeling draped over my mind after the danger had picked up and walked off.

Somehow, I ended up back in the barn with a pocket-full of coins, which Ronnie wanted to count and admire.

"Nicely done, lad," he said. "That was quite the race. Ye ran it well. Looked like ye knew what ye were doin.'"

"Thanks," I said, sinking on to an overturned bucket and leaning my head back against the dusty wall. I looked into the rafters, covered in inches of dust and cobwebs that must've been accumulating for as long as the barn had been standing.

"Now, he was a favorite, to be sure. Ye can always do better by winning on a longshot than a favorite. But 'tis always best of all to win rather than lose, so most jocks fight ov'r riding the favorites. Ye did get lucky gettin' on 'im today."

"Say, how's Willy?" I asked. I'd completely forgotten about Willy.

"Oh, he'll be fine in a few days, I reckon. Got himself a nice little bump on the ol' noggin an' a few good bruises, but nothin' that don' mend itself."

I hoped that were true.

"Matter o' fact, I reckon he's kicking himself fer not jumpin' back on tha' horse an' winning that race himself. Can't win if ye don' ride, ye know."

I leaned back against the barn wall, reminded of my thrown-away job. Luckily, Berton sauntered up to shoo those thoughts away.

"How'de'do," he said, kicking over a bucket and settling upon it with lazy grace, composed and comfortable without sparing a thought to a thing. He was covered in mud—he must've just come back from a race, more likely several of them, but he displayed none of the jittery exhaustion I felt.

Ronnie passed me my winnings back. I wished he'd waited or had been more discreet. Berton whistled.

"Turning into a reg'lar rider yerself, eh? If ye weren't so new, I'd cane ye fer cuttin' me off last race."

"He did no such thing," Ronnie said. "He was a good len'th in front when he went ta the rail."

"Was not," Berton retorted, "An' I reckon I'd know better'n ye. I was a lot closer, I was."

"I sure didn't mean to cut ye off, if I did," I said.

"Ye didn't, neither," Ronnie said.

"Did too," Berton retorted. "An' 'tis against the rules, an' yer liable ta git a body kilt that way."

"Now I know better."

"But he didn't cut off nobody, neither," Ronnie said. "Yer jus' tryin' ta make 'im into a sissy rider so ye can whup 'im easy. 'Tain't right."

"Am not. Tryin' ta make one rider who will actually ride by the rules is what I'm after."

"Is ye admitting ye can't abide the rules yerself?"

"One *more* rider is what I mean."

I'd gone back to resting my head on the wall, and my eyes drooped shut.

"Got yerself some good earnin's, though," Berton said. "An' I hear yer a bettin' man, now. Let's at it."

"I'm no betting man," I said.

"Then a drink, eh? Ye'll buy me a drink?"

I rathered not buy Berton a drink, and I'd really rathered go to bed, but Berton had shown me too much hospitality for me to refuse this request when we all knew I'd recently come by funds.

"Very well, then," I said.

"Come 'long. Ye comin,' Ronnie?"

"Nay. Have a good time."

Berton pulled me up and we left the barn. I followed Berton. 'Twas dark, and I didn't know where we were going, and I was exhausted, and I felt we walked a long, long time. Finally, Berton turned into a little tavern.

The lamplight inside was warm and bright and brought me back to wakefulness. I glanced around and recognized the place.

"This is the seed company, isn't it?"

"Huh?"

"Simeon TenEyke's seed company."

"Oh, sure, Sim owns it. I think he do run a seed company out o' it," Berton said.

It looked different as a tavern. Tables stood on the dusty floor, and seed bags and feed sacks sat stacked against the walls. Barrels of whiskey and jars of ale and wine shunted the seed sacks to the side on the crowded countertops. People milled about, drinking and dealing cards, and someone plucked at a fiddle in the corner.

Berton led me to the counter. Simeon turned, and I nodded politely, hoping Alida wouldn't hear about it.

"What're ye lads drinking?" he asked.

"Whiskey," Berton said.

"Rum," I responded. I slid a coin on the counter, and Simeon set out two glasses a moment later. I followed Berton to a table, for I had nowhere else to go and I couldn't leave, at least not before I finished my rum.

An ancient man with a beard a lifetime long was dealing cards. I refused to play, but I reckon his hearing was bad, for he dealt me in, anyway.

"No thank ye, sir," I said again. "I don't care to play."

He paid me no heed. Not a soul did. I wondered if anyone could hear me, if I were speaking aloud. I took a sip of the rum, and it went straight to my head, on account of my empty stomach and exhaustion. The cards lay before me, so I picked them up. We were a round in before I realized I was playing.

I won a round and a few coins with it, so I must've laid something on the table. Somehow, I had mind enough to refuse another drink, though I couldn't refuse another game of poque. Several rounds later, I looked up and saw there was only myself and one other man left playing across the table. He was old and grizzled, and I reckon he'd lost all the silver he'd brought to the bar, for he upped his bet with a horse.

"A horse?"

"Wins races. Black. Stallion. Big-boned. Good blood."

"I know the horse," Berton whispered in my ear. "Good one. Worth it, that horse. Ye'd never afford to buy it."

"Then I can't afford to bet on it," I said.

"Nay. Yer winning, and this is a bargain. Ol' man's let the whiskey go to his head."

I reckoned I had, too, though my thoughts were returning, and I felt a touch sharper in the lantern light. Not sharp enough to refuse the bet, though, and I pushed my coin purse into the center of the table. 'Twas much heavier than I remembered, though I don't know how much it held.

I don't know how the game played, only that it ended with Berton clapping me on the back, a stranger pumping my hand, and the old man stalking away. The coin purse was back in my pocket, and I was high-tailing it out the door, hoping Simeon wouldn't tell Alida she'd been right about me.

I made it back to my stall and shut myself inside, fumbling in the dark. The walk home felt much shorter than the walk to the tavern. Ronnie and Green Gene were sleeping, and I climbed into my bunk as quietly as I might. I wonder how I managed to sleep that night, but it came as natural as the game had, with as little thought or planning. My head hit the pillow, my eyes closed, and when they opened again, I had a pounding head, a hollow stomach, and an earful of Mr. Bean calling for up and at'em from the barn aisle.

Chapter Eleven

I rolled out of bed and stumbled out of the stall. I gulped down half a pailful of water and felt grateful that the dawn sun was dim and soft. I felt unsteady on my feet, and even less steady atop the horses, but somehow, I made it around the track and back to the barn nearly a dozen times that morning. I needn't run off to town, so I rode more horses that morning than I ever had before, on less sleep, less food, and a woozier head than I'd ever like again. I was shaking like a leaf when I slid down from the last horse of the morning.

"Where's yer horse?" Green Gene asked. He was pushing a wheelbarrow down the barn aisle, and he passed me as he spoke.

"What horse?" I asked. A small boy wearing a soaked-through shirt that clung to his slight frame led the sweaty horse I'd just ridden away.

"The horse ye won," Green Gene called from inside a stall. Manure flew through the door, and most of it landed in the wheelbarrow.

I'd all but forgotten about the horse I'd won, and now I was ashamed to remember it.

"How'd ye know 'bout my horse?" I asked.

"Berton done tol' the whole town," Green Gene yelled. "An' good thing he did, or tha' man would say it nary happened an' swindle ye outta yer horse."

I approached the stall so Green Gene wouldn't be obliged to shout about my gambling, and I was almost hit by a flung clod of manure.

"Where do ye reckon my horse is, then?" I asked.

"I reckon ye best go on an' find it 'fore the ol' man sells it from under ye or sends it away. Ye got ta take possession quick in such matters."

"Well, where should I look?"

"Ask around, eh?"

I turned and found Mr. Bean examining a horse's shoes not more than a few paces away.

"Do ye know where..." I started, realizing I didn't even know the name of the old man from whom I'd won a horse. "...er...well, I'm looking fer a horse, ye see."

"Yer lookin' fer yer horse, is ye?" Mr. Bean asked.

"Yessir."

"Ye won 'im from ol' Lincoln, eh?"

"I don't know."

"Thas' righ,' Green Gene yelled.

"He's in the B barn."

I thanked Mr. Bean and wandered outside. At length, I found the B barn, though the letter painted on the front was so faded it might've well been the "P" barn. I walked inside and wandered the length of the aisle without finding a person. I turned around and walked it from the other direction, this time looking at the horses. They were almost all black, it seemed, and I wondered which could be mine.

A lad walked into the barn, eyed me up and down, and looked as though he would pass by without comment if I didn't stop him, so I did stop him.

"Pardon, sir," I said, "but do ye know where the man who owns these horses is?"

"Who's asking?"

"Me," I said.

"Who's you?"

"Chester. I won a horse of his last night, ye see." My face grew hot.

"Oh sure," the lad said. "He wagered the confounded stud. Sure, I ain' never liked the horse. Mean as a rooster, but we be needin' a new stud now an' I ain' happy 'bout that. Not that I've got a place to say nothin' 'bout it, only he might've wagered any o' the yearlin's an' made out better because o' it."

I nodded along.

"He's right over here." The lad led me to a stall. I looked inside at a black horse with a white blaze. The lad slid a halter over the horse's face, then fitted a chain around the horse's nose.

"I'll need this chain back," he said. "'Tis the only one I've got."

He opened the stall door and handed me the end of the lead rope.

"You're just giving me the horse?" I asked.

"It's yer horse, ain't it?"

"Well—yes," I said, supposing it was, though I wasn't really sure this was the wagered horse, nor was I convinced the wager had truly happened, or that I'd won.

"Ye can go an' take yer horse, then," he said. "I'll tell Duey ye came an' picked 'em up."

"Thank ye, sir," I said. I tugged the rope, and the black horse followed me out of the stall.

"Oh—" I said, stopping, "What do ye call him?"

"Fisheye."

"Fisheye? Why on earth?"

"Look at 'is eye."

I looked. "Looks like a normal horse eye to me."

"'Tother eye."

I looked at the other eye. The whites of his eye showed around his dark brown iris, even as he looked calmly back at me. It's not often you see the whites of a horse's eye, unless he's spooked. It reminded me more of a person's eye than a fish eye, though 'twas a tad disconcerting all the same.

"Right, then," I said. "Thanks again."

I led Fisheye back to the K barn, only then beginning to wonder where I'd keep my new horse. Fisheye took to prancing. I gave him a few tugs with the chain, which he ignored, but he didn't look ready to bolt.

Berton fell into step beside me.

"Nice horse, eh?"

"I like him so far."

"Good horse, 'tis. I knew ye'd like 'em. He'll run well fer ye. Won a few, an' he'll still stand stud."

"But where am I going to keep him?"

"Jus' plop 'em in an empty stall. Plenty o' room in our barn."

"I can do that?"

"Sure, why not? No one owns those barns, nor at least no one remembers who owns 'em, an' no one's keepin' books on the stalls."

"What does it cost to rent a stall?"

"Don't cost ye nothin.' Ain' nobody paying nobody rent 'round here."

This astounded me. "How can it be that all these barns exist, and no one claims them? Someone had to build them, for sure."

"Oh, sure, an' I reckon if ye ask around enough ye'll fin' someone who knows who 'twas. I's thinks it's some ol' family that lets out the stalls fer free ta keep trackers here so he can make all his money on the bettin.' Whoever owns the track, that's who owns the barns."

"I reckon ye don't know who owns the track, neither."

"Nay. Never come up. Never been an issue."

We walked into the close, dusty air of the barn. Horses put their heads over the stall doors and nickered to Fisheye, who responded to them all and would've taken a detour to nuzzle each one's nose and screech if I'd've let him.

"This here's a good spot fer 'im," Berton said, pointing to an empty stall. The floor was nearly bare—instead of a soft layer of straw, a few patches of moldy hay lay upon, without obscuring, the dirt floor.

I opened the door, led Fisheye inside and turned him around.

"Well ye git 'im settled in, then," Berton said. "But ye'd best come 'round fer supper tonight. Corrine's been on my case fer not bringin' ye over near enough."

"Thank ye, I do 'ppreciate it," I said. "What time?"

Berton waived the question away as he sauntered off down the barn. "Oh, sundown, 'round then. Or before, ye can head over whenever an' they'll be happy ta see ye."

I wondered if Berton was planning to skip town again or simply not including himself among those who'd be happy to see me. I busied myself looking for buckets for Fisheye's water and straw for the stall floor. Then I wondered how I'd feed my new-found horse, and I eventually decided upon taking the pony out to the seed store, for that's the only spot I could think of to buy horse feed.

The sun was high overhead, and hot. I donned a hat and let the pony meander at his own pace. I was flushed and sweaty when we arrived.

Simeon TenEyke was at the counter. He didn't always work the counter at his shop. I suppose I was just unlucky. I nodded to him and avoided eye contact as I walked to the counter.

"I'd like to buy a bag of horse feed," I said, before he could greet me. I wanted to avoid pleasantries.

"What kind?"

"What do ye sell?"

"The racetrackers like the high-energy feed. Add some extra molasses in there to get the horses running like they should."

I resented that Simeon should think of me as a regular racetracker, but I could hardly correct him.

"As I understand it, you've recently—shall we say—come into a racehorse of your own?"

My face glowed hot. He'd been privy to my gambling, and he knew now that Alida had been right to turn the cold shoulder to me. I nodded curtly.

"How nice to hear," Simeon said. Mockery.

"Heartbreak doesn't always make a man better," I said, though 'twas a foolish thing to say and I hated that I'd said it.

"Dear sir, please don't think me insensitive. I was pleased to see you looking so well. Hardly looking heartbroken."

I said nothing.

"It's a nickel for the high-energy feed."

I took out my coin purse and counted out the coins.

"Are ye carrying it home or returning with a cart?"

"I'll carry it home."

Simeon threw the feed sack over his shoulder and followed me outside. I untethered the pony and swung astride. Simeon handed me the feed sack, and I balanced it across my knees. The poor pony smelled it and was most distressed that I should not be feeding him at that moment. I insisted he walk on, and he did, grudgingly. I waved goodbye to Simeon, who was hardly more upright than I, as one whose establishment enabled and facilitated gambling among the ne'er-do-wells like me.

I made it back to the barn and fed and watered my horse, and then I cleaned the stall, and then I cleaned the horse, and then I took him for a bit of a walk around the barn area, and then it was growing dusky outside, so I walked to the Drink's house.

The hay fields rustled gently, ready for harvest. It had been a good year for hay. Pa and Duncan were probably worrying over harvest every day, back home. The dogs came bounding up to me, snarling and barking. I briefly feared I'd be attacked for walking up, unescorted, but the dogs simply fell to fighting amongst themselves and falling over each other in pitiful pursuit of my affections. I liberally offered pats to each of the dogs, until my hand got in the way of their fighting and one bit me rather hard. I withdrew, and after that, those dogs could fight with each other as much as they wanted, and I'd not pet a single one.

Corrine appeared in front of her house, where the front stoop would be if the Drinks were prosperous enough for a front stoop. She walked towards me as I continued in my halting manner, trying to avoid stepping on, kicking, and tripping over the dogs.

"Chester! So good of ye to call!" Corrine said. "Berton told me ye were coming, but I weren't sure whuther to believe him. He does like to play tricks on me, that naughty boy."

"I was pleased to be invited," I said.

"Oh, you're always invited, do know that," Corrine said. "We do so love having guests, but there are so few people to have over. Most of them are not the right type for inviting over, you see. But I'd best leave that as 'tis, for I don't understand what makes that so and I'm liable to say something regrettable."

I couldn't think of a response, so I kept my mouth shut.

The dogs were still clambering, but Corrine picked up a stick from the side of the path and made as though she'd hit the dogs with it. They ran off in a hurry. It seemed *someone* must've hit those dogs with a stick at some point, but I'd be surprised to learn it was Corrine.

I walked to Corrine and shook her hand, though I later thought she hadn't offered it. She blushed and took me by the arm, and we walked inside.

Mr. Drink was sitting on the sofa, smoking a pipe. Terrible habit, pipes, and even worse inside. He scarcely looked up when I walked in, though he grunted when I greeted him and asked after his health.

Mrs. Drink poked her head in from wherever she'd been. "Howdy, there, Chester," she said.

"Hallu, Mrs. Drink."

"Good of ye to stop by. Berton should be 'round shortly."

"Nay, Ma, he went all the way to town," Corrine said.

"'Tain't what I heard," Mrs. Drink said. "He said he was only going to pick up some seeds and sweet feed."

"Nay, he's back racin' those mules up the hill again, mark me words. Ye'll have to have a word with 'im, Mrs. Drink," Mr. Drink said.

"Me? A word with him? You're the one who says he's off racin' mules again."

"Because 'tis true, whuther nor not ye like it."

"Well if ye know so well what e's doin,' all the better fer it ta be ye who tells 'im straight."

"Ain' nobody gone tell me what I's better do in me own house, not even ye," Mr. Drink said.

"I'll tell ye what to do, and ye'll like it, moreover."

Corrine was chortling, but I was mortified to witness such an intimate argument. 'Twas as if they had forgotten my presence, or simply didn't care what I heard. I'd never heard my parents argue, much less stranger spouses. Nor was Corrine embarrassed by my hearing a domestic argument, nor did anyone seem to care for the privacy of the absent Berton, who couldn't have a word on his own behalf.

"Do ye know anything 'bout this mule racin,' Chester?" Mr. Drink asked.

"Nay, sir," I said, even more mortified now that 'twas clear Mr. Drink acknowledged my unseemly presence.

"Tis best ye keep it that way. Truly is illegal, that, and a danger to everyone involved. Mrs. Drink will need to have a word with Berton about this."

Mrs. Drink had disappeared back through the doorway, but she wasn't gone from earshot.

"Berton's father really ought to flay the boy if he knows what's going on," she yelled.

Corrine had a fit of laughter, and I wished I hadn't been invited to supper, or that I'd rejected the invitation, or that I'd been lost or delayed, anything that meant I wouldn't've been there at that time to listen to such improper conversation.

Corrine must have heard someone approaching, as she said while taking my arm and leading me away, "Come along, mayhaps that's him." I didn't know to whom she referenced, but I was happy for an excuse to leave, and so I followed her out of the house.

Sure enough, there was Berton, by the pump at the side of the house. He was dousing his face with water, and it ran down his chin and dripped to the ground in a brown stream.

"How-de-do," Corrine said. "Yer as good as flayed."

Berton didn't answer right away. He took a filthy handkerchief from his pocket and wiped his face. I offered him my handkerchief, which was much cleaner, and he took it and muddied it on his face and neck.

"I ain' been flayed fer goin' on a decade," he mumbled, dabbing at his eyes with my handkerchief.

"Well, Pa knows ye've been racing mules again, so I reckon ye'll get good an' flayed this time."

"I ain' never get flayed, but ye don' need to go on saying a thing 'bout no mules. We'll have no talk of it."

"I'd like to talk of it, though. Ye never let me come along. The least ye could do is tell me 'bout it."

"Ain' no place fer a girl."

"Fie diddle dee, I reckon 'ain' a place ye ought ta be, neither. Mayhaps ye should just stop before ye get locked up again."

"Lookie here, what I won," Berton said. He drew a charm out of his pocket, a beautiful blue stone set in a silvery frame. A ribbon wound around the opening to the chain.

"Oh my, how pretty," Corrine said, reaching out and taking the charm from her brother. "My how pretty." She began to untie the ribbon.

"What do ye think yer doin'?" Berton asked.

"I'm going to try it on."

"No yer not, give it back."

"Why can't I wear it? Yer not goin' to wear it, an' ye've got no one else to give it to."

"I'm going to sell it."

"Well hows abouts I wear it until ye sell it?"

"Nay, I'll not have ye start a conversation 'bout where ye got that."

"Do let me just try it on, then."

"Nay, give it back."

Berton wrested the charm from Corrine and dropped it in his pocket. I hoped his pockets weren't as holey or filthy as the rest of his clothing.

"Oh, ye hateful thing. It wouldn't hurt ye to be nice to me every once in a while," Corrine said. "Come on, Chester, let's go."

"Hang on, give me a chance to talk to Chester," Berton said. He returned the handkerchief to me a filthy mess that muddied my fingers as I took it. "How'd ye like to come next time?"

"Where?"

"Mule racing."

"I'd not like it at'all," I said. "I've heard it's illegal."

"Eh, soft illegal," Berton said. "Not a body really minds. It's not illegal like stealing nor murder."

"Oh, stop corrupting him," Corrine said. "He's got no use for mule racing. He's much too good fer that."

"Right," Berton said, winking at me. "Just let me know, anyways."

We followed Corrine back inside.

Mr. Drink didn't look up as we trooped in. Mrs. Drink popped her head back into the parlor when she heard Berton and me chattering. "Supper's up."

We moved into what they called the dining room and sat around an uncovered table. Corrine went to help her mother carry in the plates and pans, and then she called to Berton for help with the same. I rose to offer assistance, though my sensibilities counseled against trespassing into another family's kitchen. I was shooed away, anyway, and the food was laid upon the table with us all seated around it in short order.

Supper was delectable, and it was a real treat to have a home-cooked meal and a table to eat it on. I'd been resorting to corn on the cob roasted, husk-on, over coals and sausage fried on skillets over open flames, eaten wherever we'd cooked it. 'Twas great frontiersman fare, and it pleased the boyish soul in me, but 'twasn't any comparison to fluffy biscuits with butter, potatoes whipped into cloudy mashes, and beans in a creamy casserole.

'Twas a meal with pleasant company, too. Not a body said not a word about mule racing, and the conversation instead turned to the weather and the upcoming harvest, etc.

"We're going to the dance tonight, aye?" Corrine asked.

"I don't know 'bout such a thing," Berton said.

"Yes, ye do!" Corrine said. "I was there when Aggie told us about it. They'll all be there."

"I don't remember."

"You do too. Don't ye remember it when Aggie spoke to Berton and me after ol' Sadie won, Ma?" Corrine asked.

"Sure I do," Mrs. Drink answered.

"I don't," Mr. Drink said.

"Course ye don't," Corrine said. "I didn't ask ye. But Berton, she invited everyone."

"Well if ye remember so well, why are you asking me 'bout it?"

"I was only asking if ye were going. You're going, aren't ye, Chester?" Corrine asked.

"I surely wasn't invited," I said.

"Sure ye were," Corrine said. "She said everyone was invited, even if she didn't tell ye specifically."

"Are ye sure *everyone*?" I asked. "I've nary even met the lass. It hardly seems likely she'd invite me to her get-together."

"Oh, that's what she does. How else would anyone meet anyone else 'round here, but by inviting *everyone* to get-togethers?"

I didn't have an answer for that.

"So I reckon we're all going," Corrine said. "We'll have to leave soon."

I hadn't remembered Berton nor me assenting to going, but Berton made no objection, so I didn't either.

"I'm not," Mr. Drink said.

"I know you're not," Corrine said, "ye weren't invited."

I shan't pretend to understand how this method of invitation worked, but I didn't press the subject with Corrine.

Chapter Twelve

Corrine had us out the door in short order. I was most surprised when she took Berton and me arm in arm, that we might escort her properly, for I hardly imagined Corrine would put on such airs. Berton had none of it.

"I ain' held yer arm since ye were a toddler. I don' reckon I's needs to start now," he said, shaking his arm free from Corrine's grasp.

"Oh po!" Corrine said. "You're such a sour melon. Why can't ye be sweet like Chester?"

"Oh we all knows yer sweet on Chester," Berton said.

"I said sweet *like* Chester, and ye know it!"

"An I knows what we all knows 'bout ye being sweet on Chester."

"Oh hush yer loathsome mouth!" Corrine said, swatting at Berton without losing her hold on my arm. I didn't dare shake free from her now, though I was dreadfully uncomfortable.

It was dark at least, so I didn't have to worry about where to look. Corrine led me with her hand through the crook in my arm, and Berton traipsed along somewhere ahead of us, only just visible in the darkness. The sky was low, and the night was warm and humid.

Soft strands of music wafted towards us over the breeze. As it grew stronger, a soft glow emerged from the trees. We approached, and I made out an old farmhouse, its windows aglow. The soft slur of voices, laughter, and singing met us next, mostly coming from a fire spit off to the side in the clearing. Berton drew farther away, and he was sipping moonshine amidst a crowd by the time Corrine and I arrived.

Corrine finally dropped my arm to hug her friend in greeting.

"Aggie!" she said. "Hello, hello!"

Aggie made a similar exclamation. She was a plain girl with mousy brown hair that looked like it might've been pinned up in the morning and fallen out gradually so now 'twas mostly a tangle at the nape of her neck. I couldn't be quite sure in the dancing firelight, but it looked like she was wearing rouge.

"Dear Aggie," Corrine said, "this is Chester."

"Good to meet ye," she said. I returned the greeting, wondering if it was proper to thank her for her hospitality, having never been invited in the first place.

"Have some punch and cake. We'll start dancing soon enough," Aggie said. "Just as soon as I can get those fiddlers to play dancing music. They keep going back and forth with the new ballads they think are so smart, but not a body can dance to those, not the least because Johnny and Kev can't hardly play them, though they'd never suffer me to say it."

"Oh please do," Corrine said. "You'll dance with me, won't ye, Chester?" she asked.

"Oh. Aye," I said. It wasn't within me to deny a girl a dance, even if I'd wanted to, and I really didn't want to, I don't think.

Aggie was called away to attend to other matters, and Corrine asked me to bring her punch and a slice of cake, so I wandered off, too.

I found Berton near the same. I ladled a bit of the punch into a glass.

"Nay, have the real stuff, not a mite o' that fruity nonsense," Berton said.

"'Tis fer Corrine," I responded.

"Good gravy, lad," he said. "Ye needn't go on doin' all that fer her. Someone's bound ta think yer sweet on her, too."

"'Tain't right to turn down such a modest request, I don't think," I said.

"Don' tell me!" Berton slapped his knee and smiled incredulously. "She's gone and *asked* ye to bring her punch? My, that girl's got no shame. Keep yer wits about ye, lad!"

"Nay, ye needn't worry at'all," I said. "I'm a perfect gentleman towards her, always proper, I do promise."

"'Tain't her I'm worried fer," Berton cried, when he had recovered enough from a fit of laughter to speak again. "Yer the one who's got ta keep his head on tight to keep from gettin' tricked into fallin' in love. Do take care, now."

"I hardly think you're doing right by your sister, sir," I said.

Berton thought this was rather funny as well. I decided he was a hopeless case, so I took a slice of cake and the cup of punch and returned to Corrine.

Or I tried to return to Corrine, at least. She wasn't where I'd left her. The clearing was crowded, and not a soul among them looked familiar. The flickering firelight barely warded off the darkness surrounding us. I wandered around, pretending I did not feel lost.

The fiddlers started up a reel, and suddenly Corrine was at my side again.

"Come now, let's dance!" she said.

"How 'bout yer punch?"

She took it and drank it in a gulp that would've made Tim proud. I, however, was taken aback by the display. Corrine set the glass aside, took my hands, and led me into the crowd so I could dance the reel with her.

I was no expert dancer, and I learned that neither was Corrine, though she was perfectly willing to lead me through the steps.

The music sped up, and the dancing sped up, and I learned the steps just well enough to keep up with the rest of the circle and mostly avoid bumping shoulders with them. Everything was a breeze of movement and laughter, and I hardly noticed that we'd been dancing for hours, except that my feet were tired and my throat parched. At last, the circle dancing began thinning, and so too did the band.

"Come, Corrine, don't ye think we'd better get going?" I asked. "It must be getting late."

"Oh, I suppose," she said. I wondered at her uncommon stamina.

"Where is Berton?"

"I reckon he's run off already. He falls in with his friends and does that."

"Huh."

"You'll walk me home, though?" Corrine asked.

"Of course," I said. I wouldn't've allowed her to walk home alone, though the prospect of walking alone with Corrine frightened me.

"Then I 'spose we can leave," Corrine said, taking my arm.

"Shall we say goodbye to your friends?"

"Nay, we'll see them all tomorrow."

They weren't my friends, so I allowed it.

I led Corrine away through the small stand of trees and down the road. She was amenable to a moderate pace, now. I had nothing to say, and I was pert near falling asleep, so the walk was quiet. The drying corn rustled softly to our side, a dark mass amid the darkness. The trees were black, the sky gray. We finally saw the gleam of the Drink windows ahead. We approached, and the dogs ran out lazily, scarcely yipping in the hushed night. They mostly parted ways for us as we continued towards the front door, probably out of respect for Corrine.

We reached the stoop and stopped.

"'Twas a pleasure tonight," I said. "Thank ye for taking me along."

"Thank ye, Chester," she said. And then she leaned over and kissed me on the cheek.

Never in my life had I even considered a lady might do such a thing. I'd only ever heard of the ladies who cried and required a marriage proposal if a gentleman were so presumptuous. I was most taken aback, and I stumbled backwards, bowed, mumbled goodnight, and hightailed it away too fast for the dogs to follow.

***

I was groggy as all get-out the next morn. But there's nothing like a brisk gallop to cure such defects, and I was awake by the time it was well and hot out. I rode Fisheye last, and a good lad he was. I thought him much stronger than all the rest, though most likely 'twas only that I loved him so on account of him being my own. The lad did eat, though, and I was already running low on the bag of feed I'd bought from Simeon's store. I'd need another soon enough, and Fisheye hadn't yet begun to earn his keep.

I bathed Fisheye in the wash stall, dumping sudsy water over his back. Mr. Drink sauntered up and I glowed red in the face. Surely he didn't know what had happened last night. And if he did, could he truly hold it against me? I felt an innocent party.

"Ye want ta ride this Thursday?"

"In the races?"

"Mmhmm."

"Sure I do."

"I got three horses in. Ye want 'em all?"

"Well sure, but what about Berton?"

"Done gone and got 'imself in jail again."

"Really?"

"Mmmhmm. I've already been down there this morn,' bringing 'em food from his ma. His ma can't stand the thought of Berton goin' hungry, though it'd probably do 'em some good. Might keep 'im honest. He could stand to be lighter, too, if he's gone try to win some races."

"What did he do?"

"Oh, more o' the same. Bettin' an' drinkin' on street corners. The boy's jus' too loud 'bout it, 'sall. I done tell 'im, if 'e don' carry on 'bout it, none will be the wiser an' 'e won' git in no trouble."

"Oh."

"He'll be out in a few days. An' ol' Ernet treats 'im too well fer his own good. Jails ain't what they used to be."

"Really?"

"Nay. Back in me day, they called it capital punishment by chance, on account you might jus' as well die as not after gettin' sent to prison."

"Huh."

"Still, best fer everyone to stay on out o' there. Too far fer me to be makin' trips every day."

"Aye."

"Ye ever gone run that horse a' yers, o' jus let 'im eat?"

"I'd like to run him," I said, brushing the water from Fisheye's coat. The water ran to the floor in tan rivets and formed muddy puddles. "I was only just wondering how I'd go 'bout signin' 'im up."

"Oh, yous only have to talk to the bookkeeper. She'll get ye settled. But don' enter 'im in any agains' me horses, on account that yer ridin' me horses 'till Berton's out."

"Aye sir," I said. "Thanks."

"Ah well, better be gettin' home to dinner."

"Good day."

Mr. Drink grunted and ambled away, and I stood back to admire Fisheye. His coat was still wet, though not dripping, and it was a shiny black even in the dim barn. I untethered him and walked him out of the barn, his shod hooves making a jaunty clopping on the hard-packed earth. He was a raring fellow, always walking along with a bob in his head. The sun was bright, and he only required about a quarter hour of walking 'round the grounds before his coat was dry and gleaming. I took him back to the barn, sent him into his stall, and watched as he drained half of his water bucket in a single gulp. I filled it back to the brim before I left in search of the bookkeeper.

I went to the office, a squat building almost as dusty as the barns and sorely wanting paint. The bell tinkled as I walked inside. A half wall divided the room long-ways, separating the lobby from what I imagined were the official things going on behind the counter. It reminded me of the bank, and I felt a wave of aversion grow in my stomach. Still, I wandered over to the counter.

A white head popped up and nearly startled me out of my skin.

"Hallu?"

"Hallu," I responded. "I'm looking for the bookkeeper."

"Well she's not in now."

"Aye, sir, thank ye."

"What'd'ye think? She lives here? Plenty o' people seems to think this, always wanderin' in at odd hours an' wantin' their pay. Come to think, I don' think we got no pay fer ye."

"Nay, sir, I don't reckon ye have pay for me. I was wanting to see about entering my horse in a race."

"Well ye don' need the bookkeeper fer that. Why on earth were ye lookin' fer the bookkeeper?"

"I was told to look fer the bookkeeper. But pray tell, who must I see?"

"Well *I* can git yer horse entered. Who's yer horse?"

"His name is Fisheye. The black stallion."

"Eh. Yer the lad who won a horse at cards, eh?"

"Aye, sir," I said, red creeping into my face.

"Ye ain' the firs' nor will ye be the last. Jus' don' lose 'em to a game, eh? If ye can manage ta keep yer horse, ye will be the firs.'"

"Aye, sir, I'll do it."

The man laughed a big belly laugh. "I'm rootin' fer ye. Truly. Now, I don' reckon ye've been here ta pick up yer horse's papers?"

"Nay, I don' reckon."

"Well that's a problem, on account that now it don' look like ye own the horse from our records."

I bit my lip. "I do own the horse, ye see. He's been under my care fer goin' on a week now."

"Now I's a happens ta know how it went down, an' plenty o' witnesses, so I know ye jus' didn't get yer papers transferred. I'll do it righ' now. Jus' know, laddie, next time ye acquire a horse, firs' thing ye do is come here with the old owner an' get yer papers switched to yer name. Even before ye take the horse, eh? Ye don' want no allegations of thievery."

"Yessir."

"Now what is yer name?"

"Chester Carter."

The old man took out a manila envelope and wrote 'Chester Carter' on it in big block letters.

"Let's see. An' ye won Fisheye from ol' Duey, eh?"

I thought that name sounded right, so I kept quiet. The old man rummaged around in some huge drawers, found an envelope titled 'Duey Lincoln,' and drew it out. It was stuffed with sheets of paper, which he rifled through.

"Here we are. Fisheye. Born 1815, dark brown colt, four white socks, each ending below the knee, and with a white blaze."

"Aye, sir, that's him."

"Well now we'll go on an take this an put it in yer file. There, now ye own a horse on paper."

"Thank ye, sir," I said.

"An ye wanted ta run 'im, eh?"

"Yessir."

"Which race?"

"Not one that Mr. Drink is entered in."

"Are ye ridin' his horses?"

"Aye."

"Good fer ye. But don' expect no loyalty from Hendry. Soon as Berton's out, he'll drop ye fer Berton."

"Understandable."

"'Tain't hardly. Berton hasn't earned it. Be better if he learned that if he's not available, he'll get dropped like that."

I didn't have a comment. Luckily, the old man was still busy thinking about races.

"Ye could enter the 5th. Hendry don' have no horses in that one. 'Tis a mile. Fisheye's done well in the miles before."

"Alright," I said. "I'll do that one."

"It's a quarter to enter. You'll get it back if the horse finishes, an' if the horse does well, you'll get yer winnings on top o' that."

I nodded and handed the old man a quarter. He dropped it into an iron tin where it made a pleasant clanging, and then he wrote 'Fisheye' on a sheet filled with cramped letters.

"Easy as that, young man. Yer horse is entered."

"Thank ye, sir," I said, and I bowed. The old man disappeared again under the counter. I wondered if he were sitting on the floor—strange, as he could sit on a stool. But I didn't dare peer over the counter to investigate, so I left the building to the door tinkling behind me.

I wrote a letter to Ma and Pa to tell them I wouldn't be back for the weekend, nor for harvest unless they really and truly needed me, and I begged they tell me if so. I had a full docket of races lined up to ride and a horse of my own to condition and race. I felt busy and almost as though I were making something of myself. I sent the letter off that evening, to be taken by post the next morning.

And the next morning, who was back in the barns but Berton? I couldn't help being disappointed to see him.

"Hallu," I said, upon exiting my stall and seeing him replete with hardhat and whip, ready to be tossed onto a horse that was now walking down the barn aisle in hand.

"Hallu."

"You're back, eh?"

"Aye. Not a moment too soon. No good being caught up in nonsense."

I thought 'twas his own fault, and I might've mentioned something along those lines, but he was already taking the horse's reins and mane in his left hand. He bent his left leg to bring his shin parallel to the ground. "Give me a leg, eh?"

I complied, reluctantly. Berton tipped his helmet to me from astride the big chestnut horse as the latter clopped out of the barn in a hurry.

Mr. Drink walked out of his office.

"Aye! Chester. Me boy's out. He'll ride me horses. He says he's light on account of having to share all the food I brung him with the guard. I always knew that guard had taste."

"But—ye gave me the races, and I entered my own horse in a race on account of not being able to enter against you."

"Things have changed, ye know that. Me boy's back, an' I've got to do right by me horses. He's a better rider than ye, 'tis not just that he's my son."

"Fer all the races down the road, I can understand ye want Berton to ride. But these races you already gave to me, and I didn't do a thing wrong."

"I'm sorry lad. 'Tis the way things work. I'd bet ye can pick up some more races if ye ask 'round."

If I hadn't had a fidgeting horse to hop onto, I'd've had a biting response. Luckily, Mr. Bean walked away while I grabbed up the reins.

Galloping drained the sharp part of my anger away, though I was left frustrated and tired. After riding Mr. Bean's horses, but before exercising Fisheye, I paid a visit to all the barns and looked around for the trainers. Most were elusive, but I recognized a few. Unfortunately, the race was the morrow, and there was nobody looking for a rider on such short notice, though I picked up a few races in the following week.

I took Fisheye out for a gallop and was struck by such inspiration that the subsequent bathing, walking, cleaning, feeding, and watering I did for once struck me as a terribly long, tedious, and arduous process.

Finally, I finished, and I turned towards the racing office.

The old man was standing behind the counter when I entered.

"If 'tain't Mr. Chester," he said. I realized I'd never thought to ask his name.

"Aye, sir. And pray tell me your name."

"Don Ware."

"Pleasure, Mr. Ware."

"Call me Don. Now, what can I do fer ye?"

"I was wondering if I could switch Fisheye over to race one of Mr. Drink's horses."

"Ah, Berton's back, I did hear."

"Aye."

"I did warn ye 'bout this."

"Aye, sir."

"Well, let's see what we can do. Were ye hoping to win the race, or just run against a Drink horse?"

"I reckon I'd like to win it."

"That's a smart lad. Well, you could always try the fourth race. Mr. Drink's got Patty Longstockings in, and I don't know why, as that horse hain't nary run a good race. The field's pretty strong, though. An' Fisheye hain't run in a few months. 'Tis always a question how they'll come back after a few months off."

"Is that your recommendation, then? The fourth race?"

Don looked over his ink-splotched document and nodded slowly. "Mmhmm. Carries no guarantees, though, lad."

"Aye, sir. Might I switch Fisheye to the fourth race?"

"I suppose so. Now, I really should keep yer quarter deposit for the other race and charge ye another quarter fer this next race, but on account that no one's here, I'll switch 'em over just this once."

"Thank ye, sir."

Don nodded and very carefully, though not very neatly, scratched out Fisheye's name under the fifth column and placed it under the fourth. "Good luck, young man."

"Thank ye."

I left the racing office in better spirits, but with a big knot of worry in my stomach.

Chapter Thirteen

There was no exercising the next day, on account of the races. I brushed Fisheye till he shone and even polished up the old saddle I'd begged use of from Mr. Bean. I didn't eat all morning, nor the night before, to give my horse his best shot of winning.

"Ahoy! Chester! Ye've got some visitors," Ronnie called from outside the barn. He came tramping in, and I stuck my head out of Fisheye's stall.

Lo and behold, silhouetted against the bright light from outside, were the forms of Tim and Suzie, my two younger siblings. I thought the hunger had gone to my head.

"What're'ye doing here?"

"Hallu to ye as well," Suzie giggled. "'Tis good to see ye."

"Aye, most good to see ye as well," Tim agreed.

"But truly. What are ye doing here?"

"Visiting ye, what else?" Suzie said.

"An' maybe bettin' on some horses," Tim added.

"Ye'll do no such betting. Goodness, Ma an' Pa would kill me if I let ye do that. How did they even allow ye to visit?"

"Truly Pa sent us out fer some seed at the TenEyke shop, but then we asked around and realized this place 'tain't so far out o' the way. An' Duncan was supposed to come with us, but he got to be busy looking at the neighbor's plot, so we came by our lonesome," Tim said. "An' then we were only just bumbling around and looking fer ye, but no one seems to know ye save our new friend Ronnie." I only then realized Ronnie was still there, and party to our conversation. I stepped fully into the barn aisle and shut the stall door.

"Aye, Chester an I are stall-mates," Ronnie said. Suzie thought that was funny but stifled her laughter as best she could.

"Well, 'twas good of ye to visit, but ye really musn't stay long. Ma will expect ye back an' I can't have it out that I'm introducing ye to racetracking," I said.

"Come, now, we've a mind to see ye ride," Tim said. "Suzie read yer letter an says ye've got lots o' rides, now."

"Nay, I've but only one, now," I said. "The others were given to another rider."

"Well we'll have to see yer one race, then," Tim said.

"I wish ye wouldn't."

"Well we shall, and I daren't think ye can stop us," Suzie said. I truly didn't like this newfound spirit in my siblings. I suppose I'd never really encountered them so far removed from our parents, for they surely wouldn't speak with such liberties on the family farm.

I felt sick to my stomach. "Promise ye won't tell Ma an' Pa?"

"Course we won't. We'd be getting in trouble morn'n ye, on account that ye don' have to go home."

"Still that's hardly any good, fer now it's a lie."

"Oh, hardly."

"I do think so."

"Well, I s'pose we can tell them if ye really wish it."

"Oh, do as ye please." I turned back to my horse in defeat.

"What a pretty horse," Suzie said. I didn't answer.

"That the one yer ridin'?" Tim asked.

"Aye."

"Whose is it?"

"Mine."

"How'd ye come to own a horse?"

That, I didn't want to disclose, so I kept quiet. I was in a sulky enough mood that I don't think Suzie nor Tim thought much of it, and they let the subject drop.

Suzie fiddled with the stall door and let herself inside.

"Now yer goin' to get yer dress all dusty," I said.

"Oh, it could never be clean after riding in a cart all day," she responded. She walked up to Fisheye. "My, he looks wild, doesn't he?"

"Only from that side," I responded. "That's why they call him Fisheye. Look in his other eye and he's docile as a plow horse."

Suzie bent sideways to look at the other side of Fisheye's face, and she laughed outright, which made me laugh a little, too. "What an amusing horse! I don't believe I've ever seen such a thing."

I chortled in spite of myself. "Let's hope he's a fast horse today."

"Oh yes, I'm sure he's fast. I reckon we should find a spot to watch this race."

"I reckon ye shouldn't stay that long."

"Oh but of course we will. We must see you and your horse run."

"Ma and Pa will surely expect you soon."

"Oh, quit goin' on 'bout Ma and Pa, will ye?" Tim asked. "They expect us to be dwaddling about town all day, on account that Suzie said she wanted to look at the ribbons, and ye know how Suzie is when she gets looking at ribbons."

"Quick as a lick, that is," Suzie said.

"Well today, I s'pose," Tim agreed. "I told her we could come here if she'd only hurry up and choose a roll, and I've learned she's capable of making timely decisions, after all."

"I don't like this. Sounds like yer lying to Ma and Pa."

"Sounds like ye haven't been emptying yer conscience to them, either," Tim said, and he was right, which was maddening. Horses were clopping down the aisles, now, gleaming and prancing and led by shabbily dressed grooms, scrawny boys, and weathered men.

"I would like to go see the grounds. Shall we, Suzie?" Tim asked.

"Aye," Suzie answered, leaving Fisheye's stall and taking Tim's arm.

"Oh, please don't," I said. "It's no place for good lads and young ladies. Even the barns are better than the trackside."

"I do think ye forget yer not even two years my senior. I hardly think ye can tell me what to do in such a way," Tim responded. "Besides, I don't have a mind to miss the first race."

Tim was one year and eleven months my junior, and I was the one who'd been living away from home for going on a year. I felt a world of wisdom and experience open to me which Tim surely couldn't understand. But he and Suzie had already begun parading away, and I was in no mood to chase after them, so I let them go and hoped their own decisions would be on their own shoulders, though I felt a most dreadful responsibility for them being there at'all.

Somehow, dust had settled on Fisheye again. I brushed him down and finished with a damp rag, and he looked a masterpiece. I saddled him in his stall, for I had no intention of paying a groom to saddle him at the paddock, and then I waited as I heard the bugle calls and the cheering crowds and watched horses lathered with sweat return to the barn.

My stomach was up in knots. The horses from the third race began returning. I stuffed the helmet on my head, tied up the chinstrap, took Fisheye's reins in hand and led him out of his stall.

He knew there was excitement. He jogged behind me, even as I walked, jogging and jigging sideways and getting in three steps where one would do the trick.

We reached the paddock, and I started leading Fisheye in circles, with the other horses.

"Jock, groom, owner, and trainer, eh?" Ronnie said. He was leading another horse in the race. I might've laughed, but I was too nervous.

I glimpsed Berton standing with his father, hearing a lecture, I suspect. He was doused in mud, and I wondered if he'd won anything. Then I saw Tim and Suzie, and my disquietude doubled over again.

"Eh! Tim!" I called. He turned toward me and walked over. "I'll need ye to give me a leg up before the race."

"Fine," he said. "Happy I'm here, aren't ye?"

I still was not. But I peered sideways at Tim. "Ye haven't been bettin' on the races, have ye?"

"Only one. I won it. Should I bet on you?"

"Nay. Ye shouldn't bet at'all. Bet no more, please."

"Don' ye think yer goin' to win?"

"I'll try. But I've never seen this horse run before, nor most of the others. I don't know who's liable to win."

Tim shrugged. Willy the bugler began the call to the starting line.

"Right, now watch how they do it, eh?" I said, pointing out as one by one, the jockeys jumped and the grooms added a lift, and then the riders were in the saddles.

"Sure," Tim said, nodding.

"Ready? On three." I held onto the reins and Fisheye's mane with my left hand and placed my right just behind the saddle on Fisheye's back. I bent my left leg at the knee and bounced on my right leg. "One, two, three." I jumped on three, and Tim clumsily caught my leg around the ankle and mostly pushed me into Fisheye's side as he began walking away. I scrambled and somehow ended up on top of the horse with as little grace as you could imagine, about five yards away from where we started. I clamped my legs tight around Fisheye's middle and pulled back on the reins.

An old man waved at me from the ground. "Hold it, hold it. Yer my horse." He caught hold of the reins and began walking us toward the starting line. I didn't see where Tim or Suzie went, so concerned I was with gathering up the reins and getting my feet in the stirrups. Fisheye pranced around excitedly, and the old man jerked hard on the reins every few steps, growling for Fisheye to settle down.

We reached the starting line with the rest of the horses. I looked to my right and saw Berton, adjusting his cap, on the horse beside me. I checked my foothold in the stirrups one last time and grabbed two fistfuls of mane. The white flag went up, and then it went down as the gun went off.

Fisheye took off like a puppy at a fox hunt. He bounded after the rest as I rose in the stirrups and the grooms waved their hands bloody murder behind us. I took a face-full of dirt right at the beginning from the horse that veered in front of us. I squinted and ducked my face away from a direct assault, and then worried that Fisheye, too, was attempting to avoid catching the stinging clods of dirt straight in the face, and I laid the whip on his hide.

The little horse could run, I knew it, he just wasn't running now. I hit him again, and he shot forward, except now I had to steer him around the other horses in the pack. We took a wide turn as the group of running horses strung out ahead of us. We were nearing the far turn, with the lead horse still ten or fifteen lengths ahead of us. The crowd was roaring along the outer rail, a blurred mass in the semidarkness, waving handkerchiefs and jumping up and down. Fisheye's ears perked up and he bounded forward with renewed strength, though his breath was ragged, and I could feel the fatigue in his stride. He wanted to run, though, and we outstripped three other horses and swept under the wire a nose behind the third-place horse.

I pulled Fisheye up, and he was happy to settle into an easy walk, his sides heaving. I turned him back towards the barns.

I had no thought in my head of my siblings until Tim ran out and caught Fisheye's reins and patted his lathered neck.

"Glad I took yer word an' didn't bet on yer horse," he said. I slid down from the horse, my knees nearly buckling when my feet hit the ground, and my whole body shaking from the exertion as I stood there.

"Respectable fourth," I said.

"Oh sure. Ye passed up some o' the others. Not bad at'all," Tim said. "Wasn't saying ye' did a bad job, only glad I didn' bet on yer horse."

"Right," I said. "Well, I'll take him back and wash him, now, and you and Suzie best be getting home."

Tim spun around as if looking for Suzie. He looked quite ridiculous, but all the same, my stomach dropped out as I wondered in horror if Tim really had lost Suzie.

"Tim," I said. "You haven't left Suzie alone in this of all places?"

"Course not," Tim said. "She's just hangin' back 'round there." He gestured generally behind him in a maddeningly offhand manner. Something about it gave me misgivings.

"Tim," I said. "You haven't been drinking, have ye?"

Tim didn't answer.

"You've been drinking when you ought to have been chaperoning your little sister in this of all places?"

"'Tis only a drop or two. Hardly a drink, an' I think me sister can handle her own, thank ye."

I stuffed the reins back into Tim's hands and pushed him towards the barns. "Take my horse back and wash him off. I need to find Suzie."

I waded into the boisterous crowd, terrified lest my sister should be jostled among the cursing, half-drunk men and jumping, gesticulating women who could hardly be called ladies. Some of the crowd parted ways for me, dripping with mud as I was, but I brushed against a fair few too distracted to make way, for I was in too great a hurry to give any heed to their clothes.

There she was, amid all these strangers and rough folks, talking exuberantly. I caught sight of her and was there in an instant, taking her by the arm before I even realized with whom she talked.

"Chester! How glad I am to have happened upon Corrine!"

There was Corrine, looking sweet and earnest, smiling broadly. In the gathering dusk, her dress was no more faded than any other; the hem might only be in shadow, and not soiled with mud as I knew it was.

"Oh," I said. "How'de'ye'do, Corrine?"

"Very well. 'Tis such a pleasure to meet your sister. You must bring her over for tea sometime."

I thought it would be very bad indeed for Suzie to become friendly with the Drinks, and I found it unbelievable that the Drinks partook in tea.

"Oh yes, and you must visit the farm," Suzie said. I cringed and hoped Corrine would not make good on the offer.

"My, how I'd love to!"

"Suzie, ye really ought to be heading home. Ma will be worried sick with ye out past dark."

"Oh, nay, she's expecting us to be late."

"Don't test your luck. You know how these things go. Come along. Good day, Corrine."

I pulled Suzie away. "Pleasure to meet ye, Corrine," she called, and then she traipsed willingly enough along with me.

"My, ye didn't tell me there was a new girl in your life! And what a pretty little thing she is. And such a sweetheart."

"Suzie, please don't be spreading that nonsense around."

"Oh don't say 'tisn't true. This makes me feel much better about Alida. Perhaps your heart wasn't really so cold if 'twas meant to be elsewhere."

"Fiddle de. I don't know what she told you, but ye musn't jump to conclusions."

"Oh she's such a nice girl, though. And she has a brother."

"You stay away from that brother. He's been in and out of jail any number of times."

"Really? Whatever for?"

"Oh come, let's change the subject. I'm in no mood for gossip. You let Tim drink and gamble, and now I'm liable to get in trouble for it."

"I let him do no such thing. If he did it, and I'm not saying he did, 'twasn't my fault."

"I'm saying he did, and 'twas your fault."

We were nearing the barn. Fisheye was in the wash stall, and Ronnie was lathering the horse up. Tim was standing nearby.

"What're ye doing, letting Ronnie wash the horse?" I asked.

"Well he said I was doin' it wrong."

"An' he was, too," Ronnie said.

"How on earth would ye manage to wash a horse wrong?"

"He was jus' throwin' water, no soap, missin' half o' the horse."

"Sounds like laziness to me," I said. "Thank ye, Ronnie, I'll finish up."

"Yous welcome." He handed me the bucket.

I tipped the bucket over Fisheye's back and watched the sudsy water stream down his legs and pool beneath his feet.

"Tim, fill another bucket, would you?" I handed him the bucket and he meandered off as I squelched some of the water out of Fisheye's coat. Tim returned with only half a bucketful of water, but it was enough to finish up the bathing, and then I put Fisheye back into his stall.

"I reckon I've got to drive ye back home, then," I said. "Where's the cart?"

"Ye don' have ta drive us nowhere," Tim said.

"I'm not sure how much ye were drinkin, but I'm sure it's too much to be driving Suzie around."

"I could drive," Suzie said.

"It's dark. I don't reckon ye ought to."

"I'm perfectly capable of drivin.' 'Twas only a drop, like I told ye."

"Come along," I said. They'd hitched the cart under a tree, where the poor horse, Alfie, had been waiting the better part of the day.

"Did ye give 'im any water? Oats?"

"We stopped by a trough in town."

"What was that, five hours ago?"

"I don' reckon 'twas that much time."

"Ye both know better than to treat a horse like that." I ought to have taken the horse back to the stable for a drink and some food, but my siblings getting home and my frantic ma were at the forefront of my mind. "You give him a good grooming and a good drink and a good meal as soon as ye get home, ye hear? Well, right after ye tell Ma you're back, but before ye get yer comeuppance."

We climbed into the cart, and I took the reins and turned the horse back up the hill. He was slow at first, but as he recognized the path towards home, his pace quickened and his ears perked.

I drove them most of the way home. We were all tired, and the ride was very quiet. I pulled the horse up half a mile up the lane from home. He didn't want to stop, now that we were so close to home, the poor fellow. I handed the reins to Tim.

"Right, ye drive on home, announce your return to Ma, and treat that horse right. Suzie, if Tim ain't fit to drive ye take the reins, ye hear?"

Suzie nodded, and Tim didn't even argue at my ordering. "Alright, so long." I stepped away from the cart and Tim flicked the reins. The horse moved forward, the cart squeaking and rumbling behind him. I turned to begin the long walk back to the barn.

I was too tired to be angry by the time I returned. I simply found my stall after a bit of shuffling through the dark aisle and banging my shins on buckets and pitchforks and the like, and then I collapsed on the cot and was out in an instant.

Chapter Fourteen

It hardly felt like I'd slept at all by the next morning. Yet I was no longer too tired to be angry, so I was in a foul mood. I wasn't even hardly feeling any better after galloping six horses, one after the other, of course, around the track. They all vexed me by prancing and spooking and snorting and the like. When I jumped to the ground after my last ride, I must've forgotten how high up I was, and I sent a great shock up my ankles. I might've mumbled something foul under my breath, and when I looked up, there was Corrine at my shoulder.

That gave me a fright and sent the depths of my foul mood deeper at being caught in a foul mood, and at swearing, by a lady. Never mind no one else seemed to mind swearing around Corrine. She didn't bat an eye at it, and I reckon I'd even heard something of the sort pass her lips.

"Pardon me, Corrine. I didn't see ye there."

"Hallu, Chester. Did I startle ye?"

"Nay."

"I'm that glad. Ye haven't seen Berton around, have ye?"

"Nay. Not since last night, that is."

"Nor I. We reckon he's off for a few days again."

"Off where?"

"Oh, who knows."

"In jail, do ye mean?"

"Nay. Goodness me nay."

"Pardon me. I didn't mean offense, only I know he's been held up there before."

"Oh, it's true enough, 'tis. But this is different. He claims he will be away only for a few days or so, an I don't reckon he tells anyone where he's going, I only thought I might ask ye on the chance."

"Hm."

"Ye had a nice race last night," Corrine said. She looked up at me, her eyes brown and soft, her hair soft in the gentle morning light filtering into the barn through the dust hanging in the surrounding air.

I shrugged. "I don't reckon 'twas too nice."

"Oh, 'twas. I was hoping for ye."

"Thank ye," I said, grinning in spite of myself, though she still hadn't won over my foul attitude.

"Can I help ye with anything?"

"Thank ye, nay," I said. "I'd better get to cleaning, now."

Still, Corrine hung around, sometimes drifting about the aisle, and sometimes speaking to the grooms and stroking the horses' noses.

***

Later, how surprised was I when twice in two days did a brother of mine show up at the track? Very surprised, I was, and afeared, too. 'Twas Duncan, led in by Ronnie, who had found Duncan poking 'round asking after me.

Now Duncan is not at'all the vengeful type, nor the angry type, nor the yelling type. He has that quiet anger that does the most in making a body feel perfectly terrible 'bout himself. This is what I was expecting, a real dressing down for leading my younger siblings astray, introducing them to a racing track and letting them spend the entire evening there, gambling and drinking and rubbing elbows with the folks who frequent such establishments.

But Duncan appeared in a perfectly sunny mood.

"How'd'ye'do, Chester?" he asked me, clapping me on the shoulder. He's a good head taller than me, and broader, already a man.

"Mighty fine, how'd'ye'do?" I asked, confused and nervous at his grin.

"Oh, things are looking up. Ye remember that adjacent property I've been trying to buy off of Mrs. Castleman?"

"The widow next door?"

"That's right. Well she really is going to go and live with her daughter in Maryland, so she's finally ready to think seriously about selling. We've worked out a deal, I think, only I need to get things hammered down with a loan. So I was hoping for your help, you see?"

"My help? Duncan, ye know I don't have any money."

Duncan laughed. "Well what've ye been doing down here, if not making money?" he said, still laughing. I laughed too. "Nay, I'm going to the bank. You worked in the bank a while. I figured ye might help me, if nothing else, ye might vouch fer my character."

"I can hardly be much help with anything regarding banking. I was useless at it. And if yer going to Tate's, I doubt I'd be much help for yer character."

"Humbug. Won't ye go with me?"

"Well surely I'll go. I'm only warning you I can't be much help."

"Are ye busy now?"

"Nay."

"Let's go, then."

I followed him out and was distressed to see poor, poor little Alfie back between the cart shafts. He looked fine, if a little sleepy, his head drooping towards the ground, his lower lip dangling, and one hind hoof resting cocked. He hardly even twitched his ears when Duncan untethered him.

"He sure looks sleepy," I ventured.

"Tim and Suzie had him out all day yesterday. I would've given him a rest, but I want this deal on paper before Mrs. Castleman has time to change her mind again. She's really better off moving to Maryland, but she doesn't like the thought of a change."

"Hmm. Does he need a drink, do ye think?"

"I don't reckon that'd hurt. Ye got some buckets round here?"

"Sure, right near the barn," I said. Duncan and I climbed into the cart and Duncan twitched the reins. Alfie sauntered towards the barns.

Alfie took a long pull from the water trough, not concerned at all by the racket of whinnying that came from inside the barn at seeing another horse out front. We turned away and took the road into town.

"How's the harvest going?"

"Looks like a good year. Plenty dry, plenty of sun. Tim's actually a bit of a help this year. When he's not driving Suzie into town, that is. That girl would stay out all day if ye let her, and Tim will let her. I reckon he doesn't wish to rush back to half a day's work."

I left it at that and enjoyed the sun. It felt nice and warm, and I might've slept but for the jolting and rumbling of the cart.

'Twas less and less pleasant the nearer we drew to town. My stomach was doing turns on account of my nerves. I hadn't been back to the bank since I'd quit it, and I wasn't all too keen to return.

"Do ye have an appointment?" I asked Duncan.

"Nay. Do I need one?"

"Hardly likely. I don't reckon Mr. Tate can be too busy to see you, though he might act like it."

We jumbled on forward.

"Do ye have yer price worked out?"

"Course. The real trick is getting Mrs. Castleman to move. Once that's settled, she's moren' reasonable on the price. She's agreed to sell it for a song, to be truthful."

"Well good for you. And ye've got quite a bit saved up, haven't ye?"

"A fair start. And Pa has put forth some too, in exchange for a percent of yields for the first five years. We've got the whole thing worked out so long as I can get the last quarter from the bank. And so long as Mrs. Castleman doesn't change her mind before we can get a signature."

"Oh come, you can't be saying ye'd turn Mrs. Castleman out of her house if she changed her mind after ye got a signature?"

"Nay, not what I'm saying. Though I don't know what we'd do. But what I reckon is that Mrs. Castleman wouldn't dare change her mind after signing a document. It wouldn't be the thing fer a lady to do, you see. She could never reconcile it with the strictures of Mr. Castleman."

We were parading in front of the town houses, now, the front gardens growing closer together till there were scarcely gardens at all, just houses lined up together. Then we turned on to Market Street and clopped along the dusty road in front of the shopfronts with their bells tinkling as people processed in and out.

Duncan pulled Alfie up in front of Tate's Banking and Loans. We hopped down and Duncan tethered Alfie to the hitching post out front.

"Right, then, onward ho," Duncan said, wiping his hands on his trousers.

I followed Duncan into the bank. It took a second for my eyes to adjust to the dim light, and only then did I see Casey gazing cooly at me from behind the teller's counter.

"Good day. Welcome to Tate's Bank," Casey said. "To what do we owe the pleasure?"

"I'm looking for a loan, sir," Duncan said.

"You have come upon Tate's Banking and Loans," Casey said. "We may be able to help you."

"Well of course we can—" Mr. Tate said, blustering from the backroom to the counter area. He stopped short upon seeing me. "Chester! I'll be. *You* want a loan?"

"Nay, sir, 'tis my brother here. He's looking to buy a piece of property to expand the farm, you see."

"Well then, I'll let your brother explain his own enterprise. Ye remember what I said about banks and society, don't ye?"

"Of course," I said. "Banks are good for society."

Mr. Tate looked at me sharply. "There's a bit more to it than that. Come along to my office, Mr. Carter."

Mr. Tate held the swinging partition back for Duncan to walk behind the counter, and I followed closely behind. "Just through that door, there, and take a seat."

Duncan took the seat in front of Mr. Tate's heavy oak desk, and I pulled up a wooden stool from the corner of the room as Duncan rose again to shake Mr. Tate's hand and make a proper introduction.

"So, Duncan," Mr. Tate said, settling himself impressively behind his desk and tapping his quill upon a blank sheet of parchment there. "Do tell about this land venture."

"Aye, sir," Duncan said. "Ye may be familiar with my family's farm down in Glen Mills. We grow barley and wheat. This fall we should harvest 120 bushels. Last year we did 112 bushels. The adjacent property is owned by Mrs. Castleman. Her husband died some five years back, and she's done little with the property ever since. The fields have been mostly fallow. Not grown over yet, and good, fertile soil. Perfect timing to bring it back into the rotation and expect a good crop. She's been considering moving to Maryland to live with her daughter for the past few years, and this would really be best for her, for she's not so young and doesn't have any family nearby. She's finally agreed to sell me the land for ten dollars an acre. 'Tis a great deal for everyone, I'm assured. A song for the quality of property, and an excellent way for Mrs. Castleman to make good on her move. I've got a hundred saved up myself, and my pa is putting in two hundred for five percent yield for five years. I'm seeking a loan for the other seven hundred dollars, you see."

I saw beautifully, and I knew that Mr. Tate saw too. Duncan had a way with his stories. He surely didn't need me there. He'd have his loan no problem, though Mr. Tate would be inclined to make Duncan worry.

"How much land?" Mr. Tate asked.

"One hundred acres."

"Has it a house?"

"Aye, a neat little house."

"What're ye goin' to do with that?"

"Keep it up and maybe live there in a few years. May eventually become the hired hand quarters."

"And how do ye intend to farm an extra hundred acres of land?"

"We'll switch out fifty acres of it fer fifty of ours next year. Ours are needing a break, and this way we won't have to sacrifice any of the planting area. We can handle that extra area. We've farmed that much in any given year before."

"Are ye planning on inheriting the farm?"

I could tell Duncan felt that unreasonably invasive, but he answered. "Aye, in truth I am. But the Castleman plot could be farmed independently of my family's farm all the same."

"What about yer other brothers?"

"Well surely I've no designs to turn them out! But they've by an' large left the farm after other pursuits, anyhow."

I kept my eyes down, but I felt Mr. Tate looking at me. "Ye really think ten dollars an acre is a song? I financed a ninety-acre parcel that sold for under five hundred only a few months ago."

"I'm not familiar. Which parcel was that, pray?"

"Ah, well, we'll leave it at that."

"I reckon there might've been some differences. The Castleman farm is a fully functioning farm ye see, with a house and a barn and the drainage and water all settled. It only needs to be maintained and brought into work again."

"Well, sir, ye talk a good talk an' it seems like ye've thought this out. I'll tell ye what I see a lot of. I see lots of young men like you, full of ambition, ready to make their ways into the world, talking a big talk 'bout all their options. They've got an answer fer everything, a plan fer everything. But when it comes down to it, there's always something unexpected that goes wrong, and once it really happens, there's no more answer. The plan folds."

"Shucks. Ye say this happens often?"

"What I'm saying is, why can I afford to bet on ye when young men so often fall short after promising me there's only upside?"

"I reckon because I've been farming me whole life. I know mostly 'bout what can go wrong, and I mostly know how to handle it. I only look on this as an expansion of what I've already been doing, not a new exploit."

Mr. Tate nodded. "I'm prepared to advance those seven hundred dollars, which ye need, at ten percent."

Duncan looked at me. "Thank ye, sir. Might I converse with Chester?"

Mr. Tate gestured largely that we might but made no efforts to facilitate the move.

"We can step out to the street if ye like," I said. It'd have to be the street, and preferably across the street from the bank where we could hope for privacy.

"I reckon we can discuss this with Mr. Tate," Duncan said, glancing back at Mr. Tate, "If you'll oblige us, sir. I reckon it's best we're all in accord."

"Right," I said. "Well, as I see it, you're a safe bet. And the loan isn't hardly much at all. How soon do ye think ye can pay back the principal?"

"I reckon within five years of good years, ten for poor years."

"'Tis a safe bet and a short time frame, then," I said. "Mr. Tate usually only charges ten percent on the risky bets, or the thirty-year horizons."

"Now, now, I don't judge the risk of a bet by what a brother says 'bout his brother," Mr. Tate interjected.

"What do ye think about the risk, please?"

"Farming is always risky. Ye have to wait fer the sun to shine and pray for just the right amount of rain."

"Yet every year since I've been alive, we've had crops enough to feed the towns and some, good years and bad," I said.

"Praise God," Mr. Tate added.

"I reckon Duncan's a pretty good bet as they go."

"I reckon ye can't be so hoity toity about the bankin' industry with ye not being in it and so."

I said nothing more.

"I've heard tell that six percent is reasonable. I only need five years."

"Five years at seven and any subsequent will be ten."

Duncan glanced at me. I shrugged. "Deal," Duncan said, and offered his hand across Mr. Tate's heavy desk. Mr. Tate shook it.

"Pleasure doing business with ye, young man. And now fer the paperwork."

Mr. Tate drew up the arrangement, Duncan read it back, and they both signed.

"Might I take with me a promissory note to show to Mrs. Castleman?" Duncan asked.

"Right ye are. I'd hate fer Mrs. Castleman to have to take a gentleman on his word," Mr. Tate said, laughing.

"Business is frightening for a widow."

Duncan had his promissory note, and Mr. Tate shook his hand again and opened the door for us to leave. He shook my hand on the way out, and then he led us through the office and opened the door to the street for us.

"Best of luck with your business, now," Mr. Tate said.

"Thank you, and same to you," Duncan said.

We hadn't gotten a pace from the front door when Alida TenEyke appeared directly in front of us, as if she'd fallen from the sky into our path. She must've been minding her business in town and happened upon us, but I was taken aback at seeing her so suddenly.

"Good day, Miss TenEyke," Duncan said. He bowed, and only then did I remember to dip my head as well.

"Good day in turn," Alida said. She curtsied to us, and she smiled warmly at me.

I was too surprised to smile back, though I wanted to. She was a winsome girl, and even more so when smiling.

"And here ye are, again at the bank," Alida said.

I didn't understand her meaning. All I could think to say was, "Aye." We were, in fact, at the bank.

"Chester obliged me by accompanying me to ask for a loan, you see," Duncan said. I wondered at him for spreading his own business. And it wouldn't interest a fair young lady at'all.

"Oh? An exciting business venture, I trust? Simeon does, too, appreciate a good venture."

Never in my life would I have expected Alida to encourage Duncan's too-personal extemporization, especially when it regarded banking and loans.

"Oh, I hardly consider it a venture. I'm only expanding the same old practice with an adjacent parcel," Duncan responded.

"How come ye by this, pray tell?"

"Perhaps ye know Mrs. Castleman?"

"Of course, the dear woman."

This, at least, was turning towards acceptable conversation.

"She's finally all but decided to move to Maryland to live with her daughter."

"Well that's surely a fine turn for all involved."

"Aye," Duncan agreed.

"Well all the best of luck and more to you. And your family," Alida added, without looking at me. "I must take my leave and see about this post."

"Pleasure seeing you, Miss TenEyke," Duncan said, bowing again. I hardly bothered to bow, and 'twas unnecessary, for Alida didn't look my way after nodding to Duncan and walking off briskly.

"My, ye sure did bore her 'bout yer business plans," I said, when Alida was a safe distance away and Duncan and I were approaching the horse and cart.

"She hardly looked bored. And she did ask. I couldn't let ye lead her to believe ye were working there again."

"There's no reason she would've believed I was working there."

"I had the distinct impression that's exactly what she assumed."

"Well, ye've got yer loan. I 'spect that's all that matters."

"Hardly. I 'spect it might be almost too late to call on Mrs. Castleman by the time I get home. I may have to wait until the morning."

"I can walk back to my...er...place," I said. "Ye run straight on home and see if ye can't speak with Mrs. Castleman directly."

"Nay, I'll drop ye off first. It really is better manners to call in the morning, anyhow. And she ought to be more pleasant in the morning, if I had to guess."

I accepted the offer for transportation back to the track without further argument, and we rode the rest of the way in silence. I was droopy-eyed exhausted, and Duncan was pensive, surely thinking over his plans for plowing and the order of next year's harvest.

I bade Duncan goodbye and good luck and disembarked in front of the K barn. Duncan turned Alfie around and flicked the reins, and the old boy trotted off again.

'Twas the midafternoon, and the broad daylight was soft and dim inside the barn, the air warm and still. The horses were mostly dozing or chewing on hay, and there was scarcely a person around. Only a cat moved in the aisle. I let myself into my stall, climbed into my bunk, and fell asleep.

Chapter Fifteen

I awoke to the commotion of the evening feed. I let myself out of the stall and wandered over to Fisheye's stall. He was chewing on the stall door, making big sucking sounds as he did it. I swatted at his nose, and he backed away, only to return and bob his head at me.

I picked up notes of the grooms' conversation. They were discussing the old bank robbery again. It'd been going on a month hence. Mr. Tate had recovered, apparently, but it still made good conversing, and grooms had precious little news to discuss.

"Did ye hear 'bout it?" Ronny asked, walking up behind me.

"Bout what?"

"The bank robbery."

"Sure, I saw it happen."

"Now I know that 'ain't true."

"'Tis true. I was just across the street."

"I done saw ye snoozing in the stall."

"Mhmm—what's that got to do with it?"

"Ye didn't see it if ye was snoozing.'"

"But this was weeks ago."

"Nay, there's been another one. Jus' this afternoon. In Kensington."

"To be sure, this is true?"

"Well tha's what I done heard from Green Gene. And it's been goin' around."

"Well I'll be. Which bank was robbed?"

"Oh, More Man Field was what it sounded like. Now I'm none too sure."

"Moore's and Manfield, ye mean?"

"Yep, tha's the one. Tha's what they done said."

"Did they catch the robbers?

"Nay. Done runned away too fast. Dressed like a pair o' Injuns."

"Same as last time."

"Reckon 'twas the same people."

"I bet."

"Anywho, I got ta be gettin' ta work. See ye."

Ronny sauntered off, but as far as I could tell, not to get to work. He fell in with another group and started on about the robbers again. 'Twas all the whole barn could talk about for the rest of the evening and the next morning. Even a topic like that, though, grew dull on account that no one had any new information. Really, no one knew anything at'all.

Mr. Drink wandered around.

"Ye want to ride my horse in the third tomorrow?" he asked.

"Well sure I *do*," I said. "But do ye want me to ride yer horse?"

"I surely want someone to do it."

"What about Berton?"

"Haven't seen 'im in a few days."

"Here's the thing, Mr. Drink," I said. "I'm up to ride yer horses any day. But I'm surely not up to clear my schedule to ride yer horses and then get kicked off 'em at the last minute."

"Oh, don't take it personal," Mr. Drink said. "'Tis only the way things go 'round here. Plans change. Everyone's got ta deal with it."

"It's surely no way to conduct business. I would like assurances I will ride yer horse in the race, even if Berton shows up this next moment."

"Tha's not the way we do it. A trainer's got the right to switch his rider up until the starting line."

"I find that unacceptable."

"Here I was, tryin' ta give a youn' rider a good opportunity, an' yer too offended ta take it. 'Tain't smart, lad. I reckon there are plenty other folk 'round here willin' ta take whatever shot they got to ride me horse."

I said nothing.

"An I reckon I'll go find one o' 'em."

"Wait—" I said.

Mr. Drink stopped and turned to look at me, a sideways grin forming on his face.

My pride got the better of me. "Oh, never mind. Do as ye will."

Mr. Drink shrugged and turned away again. I sourly regretted my principled stance, for any chance at riding a horse was better than none.

I exercised the horses the next morning, including Mr. Drink's horses. He paid for each ride, as was custom. We spoke not at all about our conversation the previous day, though I was burning to know if he'd found a man to ride his horse.

Corrine flounced into the barn around noon as we were finishing up for the day. She brought her father a lunch basket. I settled down on a hay bale, and she approached me.

I rose. "Good day, Corrine."

"Good day." Slyly, she reached into her pocket and produced a biscuit wrapped in a handkerchief. "A bite for ye from me an' me mum."

"Why thank you," I said, truly pleased at the gift. Those biscuits were toothsome. I bit into it immediately.

"Now me pa says ye won't ride his horse. Whyever not, ye mean thing?"

"I don't at all wish to be mean. I'd ride his horse any day if only he assured me he wouldn't renege the last minute for Berton to ride."

"Oh come, now, don't be silly. How could Pa let you ride if Berton is willing to do the job?"

"So what, must I just refuse to ride any other horse in that race on the chance that Berton *doesn't* return and I'm needed for the job?"

"Do ye have other horses ye might ride in that race?"

"Well...nay, not yet anyway."

"Oh, come then. What's the harm?"

"I reckon it's the principle of it."

"The principle?"

"Aye. An' last time, ye see, I did have to give up some other rides to take yer pa's horses, an' then I didn't get to ride 'em at'all."

"Oh I knew it came down to this. Always ye men feeling slighted an turning yer pride into a principle."

"Can't ye see 'twas unfair?"

"But hasn't he treated ye well mostly?"

"Course he has. I mean nothing against a friendly relationship. 'Tis only business."

"I'd say 'tis a poor way to repay that."

"So what, ye want me to ride yer father's horses now, do ye?"

"Aye, so what if I do, an' it'd be good fer you, too."

"Well fine, then, ye can go tell him I'll ride, if he still wants me."

"Now there's a sensible man." She patted me on the shoulder and skipped off to talk to her father. I stuffed the last of the biscuit into my mouth and scowled. In spite of myself, I wasn't unhappy at Corrine's insistence, for I had no other riding prospects. Still, I hated to renounce my principled stance.

Corrine flounced back to me in short order. "He'll have ye ride. An' ye might join us fer dinner tomorrow night. I thought tonight would be nice, but Pa says he doesn't want ye eating before the race. Course, ye still must eat. Don' let that get to ye. He goes on 'bout how he never ate and won all the races, but I don' reckon he really remembers, fer how could he not eat?"

She paused. "I do not know," I said.

"Well anyhow, how's yer horse?"

"Oh, he's fine."

"May I see him?"

"Of course. He's right over there." Where he always was, in his stall and chewing on the stall door. He stopped and poked his head forward long enough to let Corrine pat him, and then he pinned his ears, shook his head, and went back to chewing on the door.

"Oh dear. You musn't eat that. What a bad lad ye are," Corrine mumbled. "So many of Pa's horses do that. He says they even give up their hay sometimes to chew the door. 'Tain't right, and it does no good fer their running. They're liable to lose a hundred pounds that way."

"What's there to be done?"

"Oh, I haven't a clue. Pa hasn't figured out how to stop it, though I reckon the horses always give up chewing wood for grass when we send 'em out to pasture. I reckon they're liable to be bored here."

I nodded that indeed they were, and I watched Corrine scratch behind Fisheye's ears. She finally turned to me, wiping her hands on the skirt of her dress. "I reckon I'd better be off. Ma will want me. I'll put in a few cents fer ye to win it tomorrow."

I chuckled. "Surely not."

Corrine smiled and skipped away. I worried she wasn't making light about placing a bet.

***

The next morning, a nip in the breeze portended the end of summer. Berton didn't appear for the morning exercises, nor the afternoon feed, nor the pre-race grooming. Berton wasn't there when I walked the track with the other riders, looking for soft spots, rocks, and mud. Corrine brought no word of him when she skipped down the barn aisle, her skirt dragging in the dust.

Nervously, I loitered in front of the stall of the big mare I would soon ride in the race, scuffing the sole of my boots in the dust and flicking my riding crop against the palm of my hand. The grooms brushed the mare and wrapped up her legs. They put a bridle on and led her out toward the track.

"Still no Berton?" I asked.

"I ain' seen him in days."

"Right, well I'll go with ye, then."

I followed behind the mare a pace or so to the right, just offset enough to be out of the dust. We approached the paddock. A valet came bobbling out with a saddle, and he and Mr. Drink tightened the girth from either side of the horse as the groom held the horse's bridle and twitched her ear and the horse trembled.

"She don' like dirt in 'er face. Break early an' git 'er out front," Mr. Drink said to me, slightly winded from saddling the horse.

"Aye, sir."

"Riders up!"

I grabbed the reins and put my hands on the horse's withers and back and bent my left leg. Mr. Drink lifted me straight up and I swung my leg over the horse's back as she pranced forward. The groom jerked the reins, and she twisted around him, bringing me back to face the paddock. And there was Berton, jogging towards us. Mr. Drink saw him too, and his gaze turned to me. I averted my eyes and put all my focus on the horse. I squeezed the mare with my legs and twitched her nose towards the track, though the groom still had control of her head. The groom led us towards the track.

"Hold up," Mr. Drink called from behind us, but I gave no indication I'd heard, and I don't reckon the groom heard. The bugler was playing, and the other horses were being led out to the track. I squeezed the horse again, and she pranced forward, dragging the groom along. I busied myself with putting my feet into the stirrups. The mare's hooves were sinking into the sand of the track now. Far too late to switch riders, surely. And we were still marching along to the starting line.

The white flag was up and down, the crops were flying, and the grooms were waving and yelling as we doused them in dirt and left them far behind. The mare broke slow, and I got a clod of mud to the face almost immediately. I reckon the mare did, too, for she hadn't any power, no matter how I chased her with my crop.

We finished last. A valet ran out to the track to catch the mare's reins as we jogged around the corner from the finish line. I jumped down and took the reins myself to lead the mare back to the paddock.

"I told ye she didn' like dirt in 'er face. An' what de ye do but break last an' chase the lot o' 'em down the track?" Mr. Drink said.

"She had a bad break, and we couldn't recover," I said.

"*She* had a bad break?"

"Aye."

"Now yer blamin' it on me horse?"

"Is it my fault?"

"O' course it's yer fault. 'Tis always the rider's fault when they break bad."

I looked past Mr. Drink to Berton and Corrine hovering behind him. Berton shook his head slightly, and I grinned a small grin.

"I'm sorry," I said. "I hope you'll let me try again another time."

Mr. Drink grunted and turned away. "Git that horse walkin.' No good to have her standin' there after runnin,' even if she didn't hardly try."

I started walking the mare toward the barn.

"Hold up, now." The groom hustled up behind us. "Ye jus gotta give me a minute ta git from the startin' line back here. Oughtta have two men on the job, really."

"Aye, sir," I said. I handed the groom the reins, and he led the horse away.

Corrine and Berton were still standing around in the paddock, and I didn't see Mr. Drink around, so I returned to say hello.

"Sorry fer takin' yer ride," I said to Berton.

"'Tain't no trouble. I reckon ye hardly made a thing on it, anyhow."

"Nay. Ye might've made something of it, though."

Berton shrugged. "Rider can't hardly do a thing. It's all in the horse, no matter what they say. Trainers jus don' like ta hear it."

"I think ye rode a great race," Corrine said. "I saw ye tryin' ta get her goin.' Tain't yer fault if she didn't respond."

"Well thank ye," I said, my eyes dropping to the ground. I suddenly felt every bit of mud and dust that was caked onto my face and coating my clothing. "So where were ye, anyhow, Berton?"

"I've been trying ta get him to tell me!" Corrine said.

"Go on, then," I said.

"Oh, I've been around an about. Same ol,' same ol.' Nothin' worth tellin' 'bout."

"I hardly know what the same old same old is," I said. "Won't ye go on an' tell us anyhow?"

"Nay. Leave it fer another night."

That was a final answer, and the finality of it surprised me, for I hardly knew Berton to be a decisive character. I glanced at Corrine, and she pursed her lips but said nothing.

"I am gonna buy me a horse, but though. Ye lookin' ta sell Fisheye?" Berton asked.

I'd never much considered selling Fisheye before, though, to be sure, he'd hardly been earning his keep.

"Nay, don' sell him yer horse," Corrine said.

"Why not?" I asked.

"Aye, why not?" Berton agreed.

"Well he's the only horse ye got, isn't he?"

"So what?" Berton asked.

"I reckon he's also my sole asset," I said, though I immediately wished I hadn't made such an unflattering statement in front of Corrine. I don't reckon she understood it, though.

"But what's that got to do with anything?" Berton asked.

"Well I don't know, I reckon I was planning on running him a few more times, maybe standing him fer stud."

"If ye don' want to sell him, ye can jus' say so."

"I'll consider it, how's that?"

"Fine, only I might not still be lookin' by the time yer done considerin' it."

"I understand," I said. "How much are you offering?"

"Fifty-five, and he's worth no more'n that. Less than that to most folks."

"I'll take it under advisement." I excused myself and walked back to the barn, where I cleaned myself as best I could and then crawled into bed.

Chapter Sixteen

Duncan showed up the next morning, just after I'd finished my morning exercise rides, and I was hardly even surprised to see him.

"How'de'do?" I asked.

"No good. No good at'all."

He didn't look good. His hair was disheveled, and his beard was untrimmed.

"Whatever's the matter? Is everyone alright?"

Duncan caught my wild eye and his face softened. "Oh, it's nothing like that. It's all fine, really, it's only about Mrs. Castleman's parcel."

"Oh." I couldn't help but feel relief. "Has she lost her nerve again?"

Duncan nodded.

"Decided against moving, did she?"

"Nay. She wouldn't have me in for the past several days, and then she stops by round teatime to tell Ma that she's selling to Mr. TenEyke."

"Mr. TenEyke? What's he want with Castleman's farm?"

"I surely don't know. But believe me, Mrs. Castleman got sharper words from Ma than Ma would care to have ye know. Still, Ma couldn't get the price out o' her, and she still won't hear me whenever I stop by. I reckon I could get a larger loan if need be. That plot's worth it, I think."

"Sure, I reckon ye could," I said.

Duncan nodded, resting his chin on his fist and frowning at his boots.

"Is that the plan, then, to ask for a bigger loan?"

"I at least want to speak with Mr. Tate. I need to keep him advised of the situation, of course. He might have some advice."

"Almost certainly he will."

"Well, would ye like to come?"

"Aye," I said. I climbed into the cart and Duncan flicked the reins.

Duncan was sharp with the reins and Alfie shook his head and stepped on hurriedly. We made it to Mr. Tate's in short order.

Duncan was on the ground and had the reins around the hitching post before the horse had really stopped moving. I followed a few paces behind as he bounded up the stoop and walked through the door to Mr. Tate's bank.

Casey was slumped behind the counter, but he straightened up when we walked inside. Mr. Tate poked his head through the door from his office.

"We make good on our deal?" he asked.

"Nay. We've been overbid."

"Nay!"

"Aye. 'Tis true. She's got an offer from Mr. TenEyke, an' it must be pretty good for she's off talking to me, that's for sure."

"So ye don' know the offer?"

"Nay."

"Well, I doubt ye wan' ta spend any more'n what we talked about anyhow. What're ye thinkin'?"

"I'm just seeking advice. 'Twas a darn'd good deal, this I know. I'd sure be glad to hear of a way to salvage it."

Mr. Tate perked up at "advice." "Come along, young man, let's have a discussion in my office, shall we?"

I followed Duncan behind the counter and back to Mr. Tate's office.

Mr. Tate shut the door softly behind us. "Have a seat."

Duncan sat across from Mr. Tate's desk and I pulled up my stool.

"Had ye heard anything about Mr. TenEyke gettin' into the mix?"

"Nay. An' I can't hardly understand it, for he's got nothin' ta do with farmin.'"

"Na, he's looking fer an investment. If I had a gander, I'd say he was lookin' at turnin' round and selling it."

"To me?"

"I don' reckon he really minds who he sells it to, so long as he gets something for his trouble."

"Do you reckon he was really tryin' ta undercut me?"

"Oh, to be sure, he'd object to that language."

"I can't believe it!"

"Nay, I suppose you're right. No way he'd know ye were fixin' ta buy the property. Must be an unlucky coincidence. Really not too clean of the widow Castleman, though."

I found Duncan's eyes turned to mine.

"I reckon he might've known 'bout me lookin' into the property. That is, if Alida told him," Duncan said.

"Oh, now yer goin' on an' tellin' the ladies all 'bout yer brother's business? I taught ye better than that. That's no way ta treat yer brother any moren' a way ta treat a lady."

"Nay," I said. "We only just ran into her on our way out the other day."

"'Tis no business etiquette to bring discussions out of the office."

I frowned.

"Nay, 'twas I who mentioned it," Duncan said.

Mr. Tate clucked. "Well, I don't reckon there's naught ta be done 'bout that now. Now, here's what I suggest. Take it to him as a gentleman that ye were engaged in talks with Mrs. Castleman 'bout this property an' ye'd appreciate his help. Mr. TenEyke is a gentleman, an' I'm sure he'd be happy to do ye a favor knowing it'd stay in the family."

Duncan frowned. "I don' quite understand. Stay in the family?"

"Well sure. Yer brother ought ta marry his daughter one of these days, eh?"

"Uh. Actually, I don't reckon we'll be gettin' married ever. She doesn't want too much to do with me these days," I said.

Mr. Tate sighed. "Now that was quite the match. What'd I tell ye 'bout keepin' her happy?"

"To keep her happy," I said.

"Well ye must not've done it."

"I don't reckon there's any use in this," Duncan said. "We can still speak with Mr. TenEyke. He is still a gentleman, an' he's got plenty of money and no use for farming. I don't reckon it'd be too much heartbreak fer him to let this deal get away."

"Well, ye sure can't go into it with that attitude. Ye want him to know you know how much of a sacrifice yer asking from him, and how much ye would appreciate his help. Stick to the young man wanting the help of a wise one, that's what I'd do."

"Well thank ye, sir," Duncan said. "I appreciate yer advice. An' I hope I can return with some good news."

"That's right, young man. Ye stop by anytime yer needin' a thing. Ye'll make out ta be a good businessman, one o' these days."

Duncan rose and shook Mr. Tate's hand. I followed suit.

"As fer ye," Mr. Tate said to me. "Ye can start listenin' ta me anytime."

"Yessir," I said. "Speaking of that, I would like some business advice. I have this horse, ye see. I was planning on racin' him, maybe standing him fer stud, but I've jus' got an offer ta sell. What'de'ye think?"

"Who wants ta buy yer horse?"

"Berton Drink."

"Berton! How's he got money fer a horse?"

"How de ye know Berton?"

"Oh, everyone knows Berton. In an out of trouble, that lad."

That didn't satisfy my curiosity of how Mr. Tate knew Berton, but Duncan was fidgeting near the door, so I didn't press the issue.

"I don't reckon I know where he gets his money. Does it matter?"

"It does if it's stolen."

"Surely it's not stolen."

"If it's honest money, there can't be much of it. How much did he offer?"

"Fifty-five dollars."

"Good lack! That can't be honest money."

"Well, thank ye, sir," I said. I followed Duncan to the door.

I wondered if I'd really be morally accountable for taking dishonest money. It surely wasn't stolen, for I wouldn't put Berton up to real stealing. But I wouldn't be surprised to learn it was from mule racing or illegal wagers.

"Ye don't want anything to do with dishonest money," Duncan said. He must've been reading my hesitation. "But if ye think it's a good price, fair chance someone else would be willin' ta buy."

I nodded. "Problem is, I don't reckon I'd know a good price if it walked at me."

"Well ye need to do the math. What did ye do at the bank if not fer calculations like that?"

"Scribing. Cleaning. I hardly did calculations at'all. Wish he would've taught me something useful."

"Sounds like he tried."

At this, we were both cross enough to climb into the cart and set a good pace towards the TenEyke house. We both seemed to take for granted that I'd be going, though I surely couldn't hope to make the situation any better, and I reckon I might've made it worse.

Rosie answered the door. "Hello, dears. It sure has been a while, Mr. Chester. Who are you all comin' ta see?"

"We're calling on Mr. TenEyke," Duncan said.

"He's out right now. Would ye like me to tell him ye were here?"

"Do you know when he'll return?"

"Oh, I reckon in the space of two hours. I wouldn't counsel ye to wait, though. Ye could set up an appointment or call on him at the law office."

"It's a matter of some urgency," Duncan said. "Do ye think he'd talk to us at his office?"

"Well now, ye'd better go on an' tell me what this is all about or I can't hope to help ye properly."

"It's about a farmin' property."

"Oh, the widow Castleman's farm?"

"Aye, that's the one. Do ye know why he wants it?"

"Oh sure, he's settin' Mr. Simeon up fer expansion. He's in the seed business, you know."

"Oh." Duncan looked deflated.

"What makes ye look so sad at that?"

"I was thinking he weren't about to use it, only that he wanted an investment property. Now I don't reckon he's planning to sell ever."

"Well, to be truthful," Rosie lowered her voice and leaned out of the doorframe, "I don't reckon Mr. Simeon will have much use fer it, neither. He does too well for himself with his *other* business."

"The seed company?"

"That one does fair. 'Twas the *other* I was referring to." Rosie straightened up and resumed her former volume. "I reckon Mr. TenEyke would welcome the business talks more in his office than his parlor."

"Yessum, thank ye very much," Duncan said. I parroted his words, and we both bowed and hurried back to the cart before Rosie had shut the door.

I'd never been to Mr. TenEyke's place of work, but we both knew where it was, just off the main street, catty corner and behind Mr. Tate's bank. Alfie trotted along with his head in the air, anxious for our hurry.

We parked the cart and tied up the horse and jumped down in time to see Mr. TenEyke striding past us, apparently heading for home.

"Mr. TenEyke! Mr. TenEyke, sir," Duncan called. He ran over and was at Mr. TenEyke's shoulder as the latter turned around.

"Goodness. Mr. Carter."

"Do excuse me, sir. I was hoping we might discuss some business."

"Business? Dear me, I was only just heading home for the evening. To be with my family."

"Aye, sir, dreadful sorry. We can walk with ye, if only ye can spare a moment."

Mr. TenEyke only then noticed me. His reserve deepened. "I surely don't know what business we might possibly discuss. But ye might walk with me *toward* my home."

Duncan and I fell into step with Mr. TenEyke, who seemed to want to walk unnaturally briskly. I walked on the other side of Duncan, who walked at Mr. TenEyke's arm.

"It's about Mrs. Castleman's farm."

"Oh? What about it?"

"Well, I hear now she's going to sell to you. But, ye see, I was in talks with her to buy the property for months before I heard of this deal."

"Oh?"

"Yessir. I don't suppose she told ye of that."

"No, she surely did not."

"Well, I reckon I've a mind to ask fer some sort of a deal. Ye see, it's next to our family farm, and I'd a mind to expand the operation. I reckoned ye wouldn't want to farm it yerself, ye see, an' might be amenable to helpin' a young man out."

"Oh? Well, Mr. Carter, I regret that you are mistaken. The property is a gift to my son, who does intend to farm it."

"Yessir, understood, sir. I suppose I'd only like to say, I'd be a willin' buyer if ye or your son ever gets a mind to sell."

"Well then say it. Goodness, what's with the *I've a mind to ask* and *I'd like to say*. Just say the thing and be done with it, will ye. Now, if ye don't mind, I shall attend to supper with my family."

We had indeed reached the walkway to the TenEyke front stoop. I caught Rosie watching us through the parlor window.

"Yessir, good day sir," Duncan said. He extended his hand.

"Good day, sir," Mr. TenEyke responded, shaking Duncan's hand. He nodded to me, and I mumbled good day.

Duncan and I watched Mr. TenEyke climb the steps. Rosie took his hat and let him inside, and then waved at us as she closed the door.

Duncan abruptly spun and strode off. I tailed him to the cart.

I couldn't think of anything to say, so I kept my mouth shut. We rode in silence to the track, where I jumped out and raised a hand in farewell to Duncan as he turned the horse around and trotted off again.

I turned and walked, slowly and head down, to the barn. I heard trotting hooves ring behind me. I looked up. 'Twas Sheriff Hoogkirk. He passed me by, and then nearly fell off his horse from looking around to see me. He righted himself and spun Champlain around.

"Chester, eh?" he said, returning to me and passing me up again. I stopped and he turned his horse to talk to me.

"Good to see ye, sir."

"I just saw yer brother on the road. He looked in no mood for a chat."

"Nay, sir," I said. There was a pause. Mr. Hoogkirk wanted the details, I knew, but I was in no position to give them. "What brings ye to the area?"

"Oh, it's those darned robberies again. Ye heard of the second one, I trust? Much the same as the first, a couple o' ruffians dressed as Injuns and taking notes in broad daylight."

"Aye. Terrible shame."

"So, of course, Mr. Tate's back on my case, for he still hasn't gotten his money back, and he wants me investigatin' here an' there, lookin' at this an' that, hittin' all the bettin' houses and gamblin' shops and the little bakeries. Anywhere a man might make stolen money look honest."

"Hmm." I nodded along.

"What's more, he's even got a suspect in mind. I'm not so sure about it, but I told 'em I'd have a look. Ye said one of the Injuns was short, didn't ye? I'd have it in me notes, for sure, but I haven't had a chance to look through 'em."

"Sure he was," I said. "And both thin."

Sheriff Hoogkirk nodded gravely. "I best be on, then."

"Who's your suspect?" I asked.

"I don't like to tell at such a stage."

"Yessir."

"But ye've been involved in the investigation since the beginning, I know, so I reckon I can tell ye. Mr. Tate thinks 'twas Berton Drink."

"Berton Drink? Surely not!"

"Why not?"

"Well, he's a nice fellow, I reckon. Sure, a little loose with the law, but he wouldn't rob a bank."

"Ye know him well?"

"Well. Nay, perchance not all that well. I've talked with him a fair piece. But why do ye think he did it?"

"Me, I haven't formed no opinions on the matter yet, though I have arrested the lad a fair few times. He is a right decent man, never gets violent when he gets caught. Mr. Tate thinks he happened upon money no one can account for, and he's known fer disappearing on folks."

"That's no evidence! I don't reckon it'd hurt to talk to him, though. He can tell ye he didn't do it."

"Was he around the Thursday of last?"

"That was a few days ago?"

"Yes."

"I don't reckon I'd remember."

"Ye don't see him when he's around?"

"Well sometimes I do. I 'spect I know better when he's not around, as that's when I might get to ride his pa's horses."

"An' ye don't remember from that Thursday?"

"Oh hold on. I do reckon Berton was gone, for I rode his pa's horse on Friday. He came back that Friday just as the race was starting."

Sheriff Hoogkirk nodded with his eyes closed. "Do ye know where he was?"

"Well, nay. But I don't reckon that means a thing. His sister, she thinks. Well, I don't know if this is true and I hope ye won't get him in trouble fer this, but his sister says he's off to see some mules run on those days."

"Well, I'll have to ask the man himself," Sheriff Hoogkirk said. "Let's hope he'll be around."

He turned his horse around me, awfully close to my toes, and trotted off to the barn. I followed more slowly, hoping I hadn't caused a mostly innocent man's arrest.

I walked back to my stall and sat down on the bed, keeping my eyes down, not wanting to see what was happening outside. I waited for moments on moments. And then there was shouting in the barn. I tried to keep myself away, but the shouting continued, and I was drawn to the door, then down the aisle and out into the twilight.

"Now this is too much! Ye jus' find 'im easy to arrest, so now ye have ta do it when ye can't do yer job, ye just arrest who's convenient. Too much!" Mr. Drink shouted.

"No one here can tell me where he was the day in question. Not even Berton, and he's been given chances," Sheriff Hoogkirk said.

"Where he wasn't don't prove nothin.' Anyway, he probably was here. I just forgot."

"I have on good authority he wasn't here. Berton is under arrest, but he'll get his trial."

"You know he wouldn't do no burglary. No armed robbery. He ain't even got no gun."

"Berton can tell us all that, if it's true," Sheriff Hoogkirk said. Berton was remarkably quiet, suffering his hands to be bound amid the crowd of onlookers who'd come pouring out of the barns to witness the commotion.

"He done told ye it weren't him!"

"Then where were you that day?"

Berton gave no answer. Sheriff Hoogkirk mounted his horse. "I don't want no troubles nor shenanigans, now. Berton will come along, then." He rode out slowly, with Berton traipsing along beside him. We all watched as they climbed the hill.

Mr. Drink swore and kicked the dirt with the toe of his boot. "What am I gonna tell his ma?"

I meandered back to the barn as the rest of the onlookers cleared out. No one wanted to answer Mr. Drink, and they all wanted some space from Mr. Drink to gossip.

Ronnie and Green Gene slipped into our stall.

"What'de'ye make of that?" Ronnie asked.

I shook my head.

"Do ye reckon he might've done it?"

"I reckon he did. He's always sneaking off fer somethin' slippery," Green Gene said.

"But surely he'd stop at bank robbery?"

"Why should he?"

"On account that it's a capital felony."

"All the more exciting with death on the line."

"Who was the other man, then? There were two together."

"Ye don't have to have every little piece worked out to think a man's guilty. I ain't got no idea who the other was."

"I don't think he did it," I said.

"Why not?"

"He's an agreeable fellow."

"That's hardly proof."

"I don't need any proof to think he didn't do it. An' as far as I've seen, there's no proof that he did it."

"What about him not being here? An' no one knows where he was?"

"That's no proof that he was robbing a bank."

"Then why don't he say what he was doin?"

"Probably because he was racing mules on the street or the like."

"It'd be better fer him ta just say where he was, even if it were racing mules."

"I reckon he doesn't want to drag anyone else into trouble."

"There ye are again, thinking he's an agreeable fellow."

"Well I do think he's an agreeable fellow. Don't ye?"

"Oh, I hardly know him, only I do reckon he stole a biscuit from me once."

"Ye can't truly hold a grudge from that, can ye?"

"Don't tell me I can't. Course I can. An' it shows proof he'd do such a thing."

"No it does not."

"Sure it do, too. Proves he's willing ta steal."

"Willing to steal a biscuit is hardly willing to steal from a bank."

"What's so different about it? Stealing's stealing."

"Come now, I don't think he did it."

There was a tapping at the stall door. It opened as we stared at it, and Corrine peered under the top partition.

"Berton's been arrested!" she said. She was breathless and had a windswept, tousled look, more so than usual, her jumbled curls loose, the hem of her dress muddy, and still wearing her kitchen apron.

"Aye," I said. "We know."

"Then surely do something about it!"

"I beg your pardon, ma'am," I said. I rose, and wished I had something to offer her, at the very least an inoffensive place to sit. "I hardly know what can be done."

"Go talk to the Sheriff, will ye?"

"Again begging your pardon, but there's nothing to say."

"Drop it with the 'ma'am' and 'begging pardon' and talk to me like you know me," Corrine said. I blushed at the implication. "Now come saddle your horse and go straight away to the Sheriff."

"I truly tell you there's nothing I could say that will release him. I've yet vouched for his character, and 'twasn't enough."

"Come with me this instant," Corrine said. She took me by the hand, and I suffered myself to be led forcibly out of the stall. She took me a few doors down, and then we ducked into the stall Mr. Drink used as his office. The wood board floor sank and squealed with each step. A wobbly iron desk stood pushed against the back wall. Corrine shut the door behind us so only light and no breeze came in through the window. 'Twas stuffy and close, and I felt uneasy being shut in a room with Corrine, as pleasant as I found her.

"Ye must tell the Sheriff it couldn't've been Berton. Don't ye know it?"

"How would I know it?"

"Ye know he couldn't do something like that!"

"Then why won't he go on and say where he was?"

"Probably on account that he was racing mules or skipping seeds. Nothin' bad, but nothin' good, neither."

"Ye can tell the Sheriff if ye know as much."

"I've yet been there and told 'em, but he won't believe me on account that I'm his sister and he knows I wasn't there."

"I wasn't there neither."

"Oh, does it really matter so? Ye can keep 'im out of trouble, and it's hardly a lie, fer we all know he didn't do it."

"But Corrine, I can't see it that way."

"Oh, if ye had any loyalty ye would."

"Come, now, that's not right."

"Oh, but it is. Ye never really liked me, anyhow, if you won't do this for me."

"Corrine! I like ye very much and I'm very grateful to your family."

"Please, Chester?"

I couldn't say anything, for I couldn't bring myself to say no, but I knew I couldn't do what she asked, either.

Corrine looked at me, her big brown eyes hopeful, then accusatory. "Fine then, you hateful boy!" She spun on her heel and jerked open the stall doors, the bottom and then the top, and stormed out.

I peered out after her. She was hurrying away, now trotting down the aisle, as onlookers watched. They all turned to me, and I turned deep red. They must've known what we were speaking of. I hoped they did, for that would at least put me as an innocent, honorable party. 'Twas loads better than whatever else they might think when a girl storms out of a locked room with a boy.

I was muddled about the head. I felt ill-used, as I gathered Corrine did. But I reckon I couldn't lie even if I'd wanted to, for I'd made it clear to the Sheriff that I didn't know where Berton had been during the robberies. I returned to my barn, tended to my horse, and tried to stay out of the way. I didn't happen upon Mr. Drink for the rest of the day, and that was fine by me. I heard he was in the city, calling on Berton and delivering some of his wife's biscuits.

Chapter Seventeen

Counselor Worthingham called on me the very next day. Not personally, of course. He sent a messenger, a young bloke who reminded me of me from a few months ago: timid, uninspired, and utterly unhelpful, going about official business and attaching whatever purpose he had to the title of his superior. The title of his superior was Counselor, so this lad felt himself rather important.

He came wandering around the barns, asking after a Mr. Chester Carter. I heard Green Gene point him towards the track. I don't reckon the poor lad understood a word of Gene's toothless garble, but he understood the gesture and turned to the track. I stood up from behind the horse whose legs I was wrapping and called out to the poor soul.

"I am he," I said.

"You are, sir?"

"Yes. I'm Chester, that is, if that's who you're looking for."

"I am. Chester Carter."

"Then I am he."

The lad walked towards me, and I came from around the horse and shook his hand.

"I'm here on behalf of Counselor Worthingham," he said. "He's the prosecutor of the city, ye see, and he'll need ye to answer a few questions."

"About that robbery, then?"

"Aye. And he needs ye straight away."

"Straight away, does he? I've got races to ride."

"Aye, but this is mighty important. We need ye right away fer lives and liberties are at stake."

"How do ye mean?"

"A man is in jail. That's his liberty we're taking away."

"How 'bout the lives?"

"If he's guilty, he'll swing."

"I surely don't want that. Let him go, why don't ye? It sounds like ye don't have half a case against him."

"Pray excuse my pointing out that you may not be privy to all the evidence we've accumulated. And letting him go is the other half of the lives at stake, for what if he goes on and kills someone next?"

"And what if that man goes and kills someone?" I returned, gesturing at Green Gene. "It's about as likely as Berton killing someone. Berton's never hurt a body."

"And neither may ye be privy to the entire history of this man."

"It sounds like I can't tell ye anything, then. Good day to you."

"Nay, ye are a witness to a crime, and ye must come and speak with the Counselor. Please, sir, he really did tell me I couldn't take no for an answer."

"Truly, though, can't I just tell ye the same thing I told the Sheriff and every other bloke who asked? I was across the street from the bank, and I saw two men dressed—"

"Nay, I can't be the one to take your statement. You must tell this to the Counselor. Please, sir, I brought a cart, and I'll give you a drive there and a drive back, and ye may even get a nickel for your trouble, though you've got to keep quiet about that bit. Please do come."

"Oh, alright, but I've got to put this horse away and feed another one besides."

"That's quite alright. Might I give you a hand?"

I directed him to fill the water pail, and the lad scampered off immediately.

We finished up in the barn, and I followed the lad to his horse and cart. I struggled to keep up, the boy was walking so fast, though he was a hand shorter than I.

We climbed aboard and the lad had the horse trotting up the hill in short order.

"Say, I didn't catch your name," I said.

"Simon," he said.

"Good to meet ye, Simon."

"Good to meet you likewise," Simon said. "I'm sorry about drawing you away from your work and such. But it really is important. I'm sure you want justice as much as the rest of us."

"Oh sure." That was quite a lot of purpose for one lad. He no longer reminded me of me at'all. "Are ye training up to be a counselor yourself?"

"Aye."

"Good fer you. I hope ye get there some day."

"Me too."

We listened to the hoofbeats and the wheels creaking for a while.

"So ye don't reckon he did it, then?" Simon asked.

"Oh I haven't the faintest. Well—no, that's not true. I don't reckon he did it. He might get into trouble sometimes, but not like that. He hasn't any reason to rob a bank."

"That's right—on account that he's got plenty of money, eh?"

"Oh come now, I don't know what kind of money he's got nor where he gets it, so if you're trying to trick me into saying something that'll get ye some evidence, ye really ought to leave off."

"Don't be mad, I'm truly not trying anything, just curious. You don't think he did it, I gather because you're friendly with the lad. And you saw the first robbery, too. Anything about that made ye think 'twasn't Berton?"

"Nay, I hardly saw anything clearly. Just two men in war paint. The horses didn't look like racing horses, though. They were big, broad horses." I thought a while more. "And now that I think of it, the men seemed bigger than Berton, too. Berton's rather small, ye know."

Simon nodded along. "We're only accusing Berton of being one of those men, though. I do think we have a statement from Sheriff Hoogkirk saying one was short and the other was tall."

"Maybe," I said. "One was certainly shorter than the other, but I don't reckon he was short, or at least not quite so short as Berton. Really I can't even remember how big they were, only I reckon I would've noticed had one been short like Berton. But anyhow, it still doesn't hardly make sense, for who would've Berton robbed a bank with? I don't reckon he's mixed in with a robber crowd. I can't think of anyone I've seen him with who might do such a thing."

Simon looked sideways at me.

"Come now, ye can't be ready to accuse me, are ye? I was beside the Sheriff the entire time."

Simon nodded. "Yes, yes, that's true. We only want to know what you know, that's all. But methinks you're trying to absolve him in your own head. Might ye try to come at it with a more open perspective?"

"Sounds to me like you've got someone in prison ye want to pin it on and be done with," I retorted.

"We're only looking for justice."

"Justice my eye," I grumbled under my breath. Simon drew the cart up to the courthouse.

"Counselor Worthingham has an office in the courthouse," Simon said. "He's the prosecutor. Ask for the prosecutor and tell them your name. I'll be in shortly, but ye can get started first."

I jumped down from the cart and walked up the courthouse steps. They were stone, and the door was imposing oak. It looked heavy but swung lightly. Inside was dim and cool. The floor was stone, and the desks were polished and shiny. A Sheriff's Deputy—I didn't know the town had need of a Sheriff's Deputy, but his badge said it, stood leaning on a desk.

"Can I help ye?"

"Yes please," I said. "I'm here to speak with Counselor Worthingham."

"I'll take you to his office," the Deputy said. I followed him across the shiny floors into a wing of the building with short door frames and a narrow hallway. The walls were all beige and the light was very dim. There were no windows.

We made it to a little room with a few cushioned armchairs. "Ye can have a seat," the Deputy said. He rang a little bell on the table. "I reckon the Counselor is busy at this moment, but he'll see to you shortly. You can wait here."

I thanked him, and the Deputy left the little room. Nothing stirred there, and it was stuffy. There was nothing on the walls, only a worn rug on the floor. I was still waiting there when Simon hustled in.

"Has he seen ye yet?"

"Nay."

"Did ye ring the bell?"

"Aye. The Deputy did, anyway."

"Then I reckon he's busy."

"I reckon we didn't need to have such haste after all," I said.

"Well—" Simon said. "'Tis just the way things are sometimes. You know how 'tis. He'll be here shortly. I reckon he might need me to scribe. You wait here."

I had no intention of leaving, so I nodded curtly and leaned back in my chair as Simon carefully and quietly let himself into the Counselor's office. He was back out in a second. I opened my eyes and raised a brow.

"He must be in court, then," Simon said. "I'll go check on him."

Off he went without waiting for my approval, and I sat back to await his return.

It was long enough before he returned that I was feeling rather ill-used at being dragged from my work in supposed urgency to speak to someone who would not speak with me. I had nothing to do, moreover, no words in front of me to study, no art on the walls to ponder, no one to speak with. I might've gotten up to wander around, but the imposing courthouse did a fine job of intimidating me into staying where I'd been placed. So I dozed off instead, lulled into a stupor that became sleep in that still and silent, empty room.

It did me no disservice to get a rest in a quiet room. The barns were never really quiet, and my work was laborious, and I was usually hankering for sleep. All the same, it's no good for a young man to be roused from a catnap in the middle of the day, so it put me in a surly disposition when the Counselor barged into his own parlor, followed closely by Simon.

"Good day to you," the Counselor said. He was an elder, but not old, distinguished, with a neatly kept gray mustache and a shiny leather briefcase.

"You must be Mr. Carter. Thank you ever so much for making the trip to speak with me today. I appreciate you, as does your county."

I nodded to it, perturbed by being caught sleeping yet not so discombobulated to know that I shouldn't be thanked as if I were making a gratuitous sacrifice, for I felt nearly as compelled as if I'd been brought to court in shackles myself.

"Do come into my office and we'll discuss what you saw."

I rose and walked through the door Mr. Worthingham held open for me. I took a seat in an oak chair across the desk from Mr. Worthingham, and Simon sat on a stool behind me.

"Sheriff Hoogkirk described his remembering, but we'd like to hear it afresh from your perspective," Mr. Worthingham said.

"Right, well, I was across the street from the bank, making light with the Sheriff and Pete, and we looked over and—"

"Stop there. Let's return to something you said. You were with the Sheriff and Pete?"

"Aye."

"We hadn't heard about Pete before."

"Surely I've mentioned it before. 'Twas I, the Sheriff, and Pete standing across the street."

"Note that, Simon, we'll have to speak with this Pete. What is his surname?"

"Pete's surname?"

"Aye."

"Hmm. I always called him Mr. Pete, even when I was younger. Might be—oh—O'Lander. Nay, that's not it. O'Malley? McPherson?"

"What does he do?"

"Ye mean his work?"

"Aye."

"He drives the pie cart. And the lumber cart sometimes. He's always around town."

"Do you know this Pete, Simon?"

"Aye. Well, never spoken to 'im meself, but I reckon I know who Chester's talkin' 'bout."

"Good. Do excuse my interruption, Mr. Carter. Please continue."

"Well we looked across the street and saw two men on horses ride up to the bank. I noticed them on account that they had painted their faces to look like Injuns. Injun war paint, you know, and they had feathers in their caps, too, but ye could tell they were white men, and they were wearing white men's clothes, otherwise. So they got down from their horses and just let the reins drop to the ground, didn't tie up their horses or nothin, and the horses just stood there with their heads sort of droopy, like they'd sooner go to sleep than wander off. The men walked into the bank, and then they walked out of the bank again not too much later. They got on their horses and then Casey ran out of the bank yelling and shouting, and then everyone was running and shouting."

"What did they look like?"

"I couldn't tell ye on account of the war paint."

"Tall or short?"

"One was taller than the other, but I don't rightly know whether either was particularly tall or short."

"What did their hair look like?"

"They were both wearing caps."

"So their hair was short enough you couldn't see it from under the cap?"

"I reckon. Or I just didn't notice it."

"How could you tell they were white men?"

"I don't know. I 'spose I don't know for sure they were white. It'd never occurred to me that they weren't white, for they just seemed white."

"Could you see their hands or their necks?"

"Oh sure, that's probably it."

"And you said they were wearing white men's clothes?"

"Aye."

"How so."

"Well they weren't dressed up as Injuns, that is."

"What clothes were they wearing?"

"Oh, a shirt, trousers. I don't reckon anything special, for I didn't notice anything special about it."

"And they just walked out of the bank."

"'Twas a fast walk, mind ye. And 'twasn't more'n a few steps to their horses."

"And then they galloped out of there?"

"Aye. We were all runnin' after that."

"And the horses?"

"Oh, that's right. They surely weren't racehorses. Bigger bodied, they were. And docile as goats, at least whilst they were waiting outside the bank. But they sure could raise dust in a hurry. They were gone quick, and none of us could catch them."

"What color horses?"

"Oh, bay, sorrel. Not too flashy. Big, good-lookin' horses, but none too flashy."

"And the saddles?"

"Nothin' I noticed. Mayhaps they had a few rolls or a few bags aboard, but nothin' too special."

"Anything, Simon?"

"No sir."

"Is there anything else you can think to tell us, Mr. Carter?"

"Well *I* don't think Berton did it."

"That may be, and if it is so, he'll be acquitted in a court of law. Speaking of which, you may be called upon to testify as an eyewitness. I trust we can count on you to show up to court if so ordered."

"I'd surely rather not."

"We appreciate the difficulty of such a task, but it is your civic duty, and obligation, mind you. The Court does have the power to order the arrest of a witness who refuses to testify. I'm confident you would not drive us to such extremes. I was only impressing you with the importance of your role in our justice system."

"Aye sir, I wouldn't refuse a court order. I only hope you'll leave me out if ye can spare me."

"Duly noted, sir. We will only call upon you if necessary. We appreciate your help very much. Thank you for coming in today. If you think of anything else, please do stop by and let us know."

"Aye, sir."

Mr. Worthingham rose and shook my hand. "Good day to you, Mr. Carter, and thank you again. Simon will drive you back, yes?"

"Aye sir," Simon said.

I thanked Mr. Worthingham and followed Simon out through the parlor and over the shiny stone floors and down the courthouse steps. 'Twas a cloudy day, but even so, the daylight shocked my eyes after being so long in the dim courthouse.

Simon drove me back to the barns and dropped me off there, chatting about the bankruptcy proceeding he was "handling" the entire way.

As soon as I walked into the barn, Ronnie informed me I'd been summoned to town again, this time by a lad on behalf of Mr. TenEyke.

"What on earth does he want with me?" I asked.

"He wants to hear 'bout the robbery, same as everyone else."

"Well I daresay everyone's good and heard 'bout it by now, for I've retold it enough times."

"I'd hear 'bout it again, eh. What kind 'o war paint would ye say?"

"I haven't the faintest. But what's Mr. TenEyke got to do with the robbery?"

"Well he's a lawyer, ain't he?"

"Not criminal."

"Course I know not all lawyers are criminal. In theory, that is."

"I mean he doesn't do criminal cases."

"The lad said he was working for Berton."

"Working for Berton? How's Berton going to pay for the likes of Mr. TenEyke?"

"Berton don't do none too shabby fer himself. He wins races."

"So what does he want from me? Why does he want me back in town?"

"That's what the lad said."

"I don't understand why they can't just come here. Why must I be summoned here and there and back again?"

"They're the important ones."

"Does he want me to go now?"

"Aye. The lad said to go as soon as ye might. They're not holdin' off long fer the trial."

"Ye think I can take the pony?"

"It ain't doin' nothin.' I'll tell Mr. Bean that's where he gone."

"Thanks, Ronnie," I said. I bumped around for the tack and saddled the pony, in no sort of hurry, but not wasting time on brushing, either.

Chapter Eighteen

I swung into the saddle and rode the pony out of the barn, down the path I'd just returned over, wondering how I'd missed Mr. TenEyke's lad on the street. My mind was too tired from talking over the robbery day and night to do any more thinking on it, and I reckon I didn't think of anything the entire ride. The clopping hoofbeats filled my head, and there was nothing more to think on.

I rode right up to Mr. TenEyke's office, tied my pony to the post out front, and walked into the office.

Mr. TenEyke was standing just inside, briefcase and hat in hand, as if he were about to leave.

"Ah, Chester. Good of you to come. And so soon."

"Aye, sir, I was told you were expecting me."

"Yes, of course, of course," Mr. TenEyke looked around with his belongings in hand, as if weighing whether I might wait for another day.

"I've come five miles, sir."

"That's right, that's right, and good of you to do it, too. Do come back to my office, now, and we'll have our discussion right quick."

Mr. TenEyke passed his belongings off to the lad who appeared and invited me to sit in a chair facing his desk.

"Please do tell me what you saw of the robbery," Mr. TenEyke said. He took out a sheaf of paper and a pen and set these on the desk in front of him.

I launched into my tale, which I knew backwards and forwards, having repeated it so many times.

Mr. TenEyke didn't take notes, and he didn't ask questions. I finished my story, and he nodded solemnly.

"Thank you very much, Chester. I may have to call you as a witness at trial. You will willingly testify, I trust."

"Mr. Worthingham said the same thing," I said. "Would you both call me?"

"I may, or I may stick to cross-examination. Nothing to be worried about, of course. That's a good lad."

"You are defending Berton, then?"

"Aye. All persons deserve a defense."

"I didn't know you did criminal work at all."

"Oh, normally I don't, but I offered to pick up this case *pro bono* to be sure young Berton would get a proper crack at a defense."

"When do you expect the trial?"

"It's set for next Monday. So long as no new evidence comes to light, it should start on Monday. We'll need you waiting outside the courtroom in case we need your testimony. We can't have you *inside* the courtroom if you testify, though, you see."

"Aye. Yessir."

"Well if you'll excuse me, Chester, I must be getting home to my family."

"Of course, sir," I said, rising.

"Thank you again for coming to town. 'Twas most helpful."

That I doubted, but I inclined my head and passed out the door ahead of Mr. TenEyke. We parted on the steps to his office, and I returned to my pony to ride home once more.

***

I returned to the barns frightfully weary. 'Twas no easy time to speak to a girl, but there was Corrine, sitting on an overturned bucket with her back leaned against the wall. She'd been waiting on me, for as soon as I dismounted, she walked to me, without her usual flouncing way and smiles.

She walked cooly and quietly, and I thought how very serious she looked, almost like a lady.

"Hello, Corrine," I said.

"Where have ye been?"

"I've been speaking with Mr. TenEyke. He's the counsel representing Berton."

"I know that—good. Ye must go back there and tell him how ye know Berton was racing mules."

"But I don't know Berton was racing mules."

"I'm about to tell ye how you know Berton was racing mules."

I waited.

"He always quits eating at least a day before the races and he takes a string of mules from the farms around the area when he's going off to the races. Ye know, the secret ones."

I nodded.

"So ye tell Mr. TenEyke that this was going on, and that's evidence that Berton was racing that day."

"Sure, but I didn't see any of that happening. I certainly didn't see a string of mules leaving the area."

"Please, Chester?"

"Corrine, I cannot testify about something I didn't see. That's not the right way. You'd have to testify about this if ye saw it."

"I plan to. But it will mean more coming from you."

"*Is* it even true?"

"Of course it is!" Corrine said, but her brown eyes drifted from mine. "I can't abide that you'll do nothing to help us."

"Pray give me an honest task, Corrine, something I can do for you, and I will do it at once and gladly."

"You loathsome—how many times will you call me dishonest? I won't stand for it—ye all high and mighty refuse to help me and disparage my name to boot. If you won't help me, I hope I'll never speak to you again."

"Corrine—" but she had turned and was walking away. I didn't call after her. I was too tired, and if she wanted to never speak to me again, I couldn't help but notice I wasn't heartsick for her loss.

All the same, the next morning I was back on the pony, riding into town, as soon as I finished my morning chores. I worried Mr. TenEyke was not doing his utmost on Berton's behalf, despite his grand statements of his own generosity.

I'd never been to the county jail before, but I heard 'twas one of the gentler ones. A good Quaker influence keeps a town civil towards its prisoners. They'd done away with the shackles and were feeding the prisoners enough so they mostly waited to be hanged to die, and only half the county was happy for it.

Still, the stench of prison in the late summer met me long before I met the guard. I dismounted and he took the pony by the reins and looked me over.

"How'd'ye'do. Ye visitin'?"

"Aye sir."

"On Christian duty o' do ye know the fella?"

"I know him. Can't that still be a Christian duty?"

"Aye, reckon can be both. Wasn't what I meant, though. We get lots o' those Quakers 'round here."

"Ah," I said, nodding. "I'm here to see Mr. Berton Drink."

"Ye just missed his pa, then."

I surely was glad of that, though I only inclined my head at the statement.

"Come right along this way." He tied the pony to a hitching rod and unlocked the great iron door with an impressive key on a ring filled of keys, all smaller than the one now turning the lock.

I followed the guard inside, and he fastened the lock behind us. It was very dark. Only small shafts of light shone through narrow windows high in the walls. The stone walls and floors were damp, and each footstep echoed through the hallway. I heard coughing and murmuring and men calling out, perhaps for some food. I sorely wished I had brought food. I hoped Mr. Drink had filled Berton up with his ma's home cooking. And I hoped he'd at least accept my visit.

"Here we are," the guard said, stopping at a cell. "Mr. Drink, ye've another visitor, ye lucky lad."

"Pray tell how lucky ye feel next time yer wrongly imprisoned," Berton said from inside. I heard rustling in the darkness, and he moved near the bars. The guard pulled a stool across the floor and set it in front of the cell.

"Oh quit yer moanin' an' say hello to yer guest."

"Howde do, Chester. 'Twasn't expecting ye."

"How'de'ye'do," I said.

"I'll leave ye to it," the guard said. "Hollar if ye need anything."

"Thank ye, sir," I said. The guard tipped his hat and stomped off, his footsteps growing quieter as his form dissolved into the darkness of the hallway.

"What brings ye here?"

"You, of course. I was hoping ye'd have something good to say on your behalf. Ye see I spoke with Mr. TenEyke yesterday—"

"Say on my behalf? Haven't ye ever heard of the presumption of innocence?"

"Sounds familiar."

"All prisoners are presumed innocent until proven guilty. I don't have to say nothin' on my behalf an' they've got to let me go regardless, on account that they've got nothing to prove me guilty."

"What if they have just enough to convince the Jury? It'd sure be better if ye had something to say fer yourself. They've got enough to throw ye in jail in the first place, after all."

"Are ye tryin' ta be me lawyer?"

"Nay. Only I did speak with Mr. TenEyke and it didn't sound so—"

"Haven't ye heard of attorney-client privilege?"

"Sounds familiar."

"Me attorney ain't allowed to tell ye nothing I tell him in secret."

"All right, well he didn't reveal any secrets. It only seemed like he wasn't ready to come up with an alibi. How come ye won't just tell 'em where ye were? Ye might get a slap on the wrist fer illegal racin,' but we're talking 'bout capital punishment fer robbery here."

"Ye sound like me lawyer an' me mum talkin' through me dad all in one. I may have to take it from them, but I'm not so bored that I'll have to listen to it from ye."

"Oh, please, I mean no offense."

"None taken, an' don't mind what I just said. I'm rightly bored out o' me wits, and I'll take any verbal abuse from anyone, fer it's better than quiet and loneliness. I do appreciate yer making the trip for me sake."

"Well here 'tis, I feel I owe it on account that the prosecutor said he may have me testify—"

"Testify? You?"

"Aye. Course, only 'bout what I saw of that first robbery. It's got nothin' ta do with ye."

"Nothin' ta do with me? I'm the defendant. Haven't ye heard of witness tampering?"

"Uh. That I have not."

"I can't be talkin' with a state's witness! They'll have me strung up fer witness tamperin' faster'n they could string me up fer robbery!"

"But yer not tamperin.'"

"It ain't about what I'm doin,' 'tis 'bout what it looks like. Leave this instant, do, and don't go gloatin' on yer good deed o' visitin' the prisoners."

"I'm sorry. I am. I didn't mean nothin.'"

"I know, but get gone," Berton said, retreating to the interior of his cell again. I was out like a flushed hen, dragging the stool to the wall, hustling down the hallway, almost running, my footsteps echoing as fast as my heart pounded.

"Quick visit," the guard said pleasantly when he opened the door for me, drenching me in a stream of dazzling sunlight. I'd been pounding on the door like I were being chased from the inside.

"Aye, sir," I said.

"That's quite alright. It does try one's spirits to be in there, even if only for a little while."

I supposed he thought me a terrible coward, and that only bothered me a little until I looked up and saw a beautiful creature walking towards us.

"Ah, Rebecca. Me daughter," the guard said, turning around with the door locked behind us. "She'll be bringin' me dinner."

She was indeed carrying a basket.

"Howdedo, Rebecca," the guard said.

Rebecca smiled and curtsied. "Howdedo."

"Howdedo," I said, bowing.

"This lad's just been visitin,'" the guard said.

"Pleased to make acquaintance. I'm Rebecca." She extended a gloved hand, and I took it.

"The pleasure's mine, Miss—"

"Ernet," her father filled in.

"Pleased to meet you, Mr. and Miss Ernet," I said.

"And your name?"

"Chester," I said.

"Good to meet you, Mr. Chester." Rebecca handed her father the basket and I recognized my superfluousness.

"Pleased to meet you," I said again, and I bowed again, and then I untethered my pony, mounted rather awkwardly as the nag did a pirouette, and tipped my hat in farewell. It wasn't until we were trotting down the road that I realized with a pang I really ought'n't to have given my name like that, for now they'd known who'd been visiting Berton, and they'd have their evidence for witness tampering. I'd dealt him a bad card nearly every turn, but I was determined to stick in the game until our luck changed. For shame.

***

Mr. TenEyke must've been home for dinner when I arrived at his office. I agreed to wait in the parlor, and I thought of all the avenues he ought to explore, noting them in my head, and reviewing them until I could come up with another.

Mr. TenEyke walked in and stared when he saw me. "Well hello there, Mr. Carter. Good to see you again."

"Likewise, Mr. TenEyke."

"What can I do for you?"

"I'm here about the robbery. I've thought of a few things, ye see, and I'd like to discuss them."

"You remembered more of what ye saw?"

"Perhaps. Also some ideas for clearing Berton's name."

"That's hardly an eye-witness's job. You're just there to tell what you saw."

"Do ye mean to call it witness tampering?"

"Good heavens, no. Where'd you hear of witness tampering?"

"Nowhere, I just—heard of it."

Mr. TenEyke peered over his spectacles at me. "Care to speak in my office?"

"Yes please," I said.

I followed Mr. TenEyke into his office, and he shut the door behind us. He sat down heavily and threw his briefcase on the desk. He leaned back in his chair and stared at me. "Go on with your ideas."

"Well, I know Berton's got the presumption of innocence, but I still think it'd be good if he presented his own side of the story. A defense, you see."

"Chester, if I did not see, I'd be no lawyer."

"Aye, sir, well if I were on the Jury, I'd like to know where Berton was at the time of the robberies. Either would do. I wouldn't even care if I couldn't know both times."

"Alibi," Mr. TenEyke said dryly with a curt nod, letting me know I was wasting his time.

"Right, well has he told ye?"

"Chester, lad, if he had told me, there'd be no reason for me to reveal it to you."

"Attorney-client privilege?"

"May apply, but even if not, there's no real upside to spreading our case around the town before trial. It might even be jury tampering if we were unlucky enough to tell a venireman."

"Right, well even if Berton won't tell, what if you just found out if there were any mule or draft races in the area on either of those days? His sister thinks that's where he was."

"And I have spoken to his sister. But if ye think it's a lawyer's province to scour the country looking for illegal races that happened in the past— Chester, I appreciate your involvement. I will see you in trial." Mr. TenEyke stood up, and I felt compelled to do the same. There were more things I had wanted to say, but I couldn't think of them. I wished I'd written them down, but Mr. TenEyke was out of patience with me, and I was too flustered to come up with another trial strategy.

"Yessir. Forgive me for intruding on your job."

"That's no trouble, Chester. Perchance you should consider a career in the law. Seeing as you found banking unsatisfactory."

I squirmed under the comment. I bowed and took my leave without meeting his gaze again, and I found the door myself and got out of it.

I felt discouraged enough that I only wanted to go home and see no one for the rest of the day, and I was trotting the pony towards the pleasure gardens when who else but Sheriff Hoogkirk went trotting by me in the other direction.

"Ahoy there! Mr. Chester Carter!" he called. I reined in the pony and turned him around. The Sheriff had also spun his horse, and we retraced our steps until we were side-by-side.

"Good to see ye in town again, young man."

"Yessir. It's good to see ye as well."

"I'm sure ye heard—Berton's trial is set to begin Monday."

"Aye. Ye don't think Berton did it, do ye?"

"Well I arrested the lad, didn't I? I wouldn't've arrested him without probable cause."

"Oh. I can't bring myself to believe he did it."

"Then where was he those days, and why won't he tell us?"

"His sister thinks he was at an illegal race and doesn't want to get in trouble."

"Pah. No one cares 'bout the illegal race when we've got a bank robbery on our hands. He's risking a hanging ta try to save himself a night in prison, ye think? Now *that's* what *I* have a hard time bringing myself to believe."

"He believes in the presumption of innocence. He wants to get himself off scot-free."

The Sheriff shook his head. "We'll leave it to the Jury to decide. There's evidence against him."

"Have ye tried looking for illegal races on the days of the robberies?" I asked.

"Well there's an idea. I hadn't thought of that. My—what'd'ye think, might ye be the next county sheriff one day? It's not nearly so stuffy as banking."

I squirmed, for Sheriff Hoogkirk actually meant it, the good sir. "So ye'll try lookin' for races that happened on those days?"

"I'll look into it. Problem is, most of these illegal races don't go on advertising themselves, nor inviting the sheriff, to be sure. But I know some folks. I know the usual suspects, and they ought to cooperate if I promise it won't cause 'em trouble."

"Thank you, sir."

"That's just fine, Chester. How's your ma?"

"Well, I think."

"You visited recently?"

"Nay."

"Oh, do. Go on home and see your ma."

"Yessir."

"That's a good lad. Good day, now. Until Monday!"

"Yessir."

Sheriff Hoogkirk spun his horse around and took off, and the pony was happy to be heading for home once more.

Chapter Nineteen

I went home to the farm on Sunday. I took Fisheye with me, as a riding horse, for the pony was about spent and looked very sour at me when I approached. Fisheye wasn't much better for being fresh. He pranced and jogged the first several miles, no matter how hard I pulled on the reins. I daren't say he'd been away from the pleasure garden grounds since he was a colt, and I'd hazard a bet that he'd never been ridden anywhere but the track and the path to the track. He mostly settled down three miles into the trip, only scooting forward a few bounds every time the grass or a twig rustled just so, and he'd quit whinnying for his barn mates by that time, too.

Mr. Bean saw me leaving and warned me I was ruining my horse by taking him out like that. A racehorse has got no business riding to the farm and back, he told me. I kept my course, for what good was it having a horse if you couldn't use him to get you home? And I wanted to get home, first on account that I hadn't been home in nigh on a month, and more pressingly that I wanted to get away from all the folks wondering about Berton robbing the bank and Corrine asking me to perjure myself in court.

Yet what was the first thing out of Suzie's mouth when she ran up to greet me on the chestnut-lined road?

Her animation was such that Fisheye shied off the path and ran me through the branches, which put me into a churlish state. I hoped Pa wouldn't notice the twigs I'd bent and broken with my face, and the immature chestnuts I'd shaken to the ground. Suzie hadn't even apologized for startling my horse before she was telling me that Berton couldn't've done it.

"What makes ye so sure?" I asked.

"He's no burglar. He's a fine man."

"Would ye know a burglar when ye see one?"

"I know one who isn't when I see one."

"I don't reckon ye hardly know Berton at'all. An' that's a good thing, for he's not the type fer a young lady to be hanging around."

"What a high-and-mighty scoundrel you've become! What makes you any better than Berton?"

"I reckon we are friends, and I reckon he's innocent, but does that mean I should perjure myself?"

"Wouldn't ye do that for a friend? Wouldn't ye do it for me if I might be hanged if ye didn't?"

"But ought I, even in those instances?"

"Yes! What a foolish question! Of course."

"Let me get off this horse before ye spook him across town again," I grumbled. I wanted heartily to be done with the topic once and for all, though even my mind couldn't leave it alone.

***

Suzie had me reconsidering my previously firm resolve, but Ma weighed in. "Nay, of course ye must tell only the most truth."

"I don't know that it'd be dishonest to help him get off on account that I don't think he did it."

"Anything that's not strictly the truth must be dishonest."

"But what if it were Suzie who might be hanged?"

"What a terrible thing to say! How could ye say such a thing? An' to compare your sister to Berton. Terrible thing."

"'Tis but a hypothetical. What would I do then?"

"There's no good in considering such an evil idea. I've told ye the answer."

"I think there's every good in considering a hypothetical. It tests the principle. 'Tis no good to stand by principle if the principle falls in some situations."

"Aye, 'tis good, and it would do to thank the good Lord for not testing your principles in such a way. Ye've been given an easy cup, as I see it, and it's no good to make a moral quandary where none ought to lie."

***

As much as I'd've preferred to avoid the subject all together, I sought counsel from Duncan and Pa. "I'd do my best to stay out of it," Duncan said. "Seeing as ye don't rightly know one way or the other."

"I can't stay out of it, for both sides want to call me to testify."

"Then testify to the truth, the whole truth, and nothing but the truth, so help you God. That's what they say, ain't it?"

"And what if Berton is hanged because of me?"

"Wouldn't be because of ye. If ye try some sort of trickery and get caught, or if ye get him off an' it turns out he did it—now that'd be something on your conscience. But if ye stick to the truth, you're only letting justice play out as it may. Nothing to attribute to you, one way or t'other."

"Aye," grunted Pa from under the cart he was working on. "No use givin' yerself airs an' addin' to yer importance. Only causes problems. 'Tain't about ye, and 'tain't because of ye."

Somehow, I couldn't feel confident my advisors would feel so sure if they wore my shoes. I wouldn't've minded an acknowledgment that the decision was a tough one.

"I know ye don't never care to take my advice anymore, but ye'd do well to stay clear of the Drinks. They're mixed up in nothing good all too often," Pa said. I was too cross to answer, but I thought to myself that it was good I'd stopped listening to Pa's advice.

***

On Sunday I was served with a witness summons. The law waits for no man and makes no allowances for days of rest. An old man waited for me in the barns when I returned from the farm. He couldn't've handed off the witness summons, for he himself was tasked with delivering it. No one else could be trusted. 'Twas that important.

"Can ye read, lad?"

"Aye."

"Well read that aloud, then."

"Philadelphia County, Commonwealth of Pennsylvania. Greetings: We command you, Chester Carter, that lying aside all business and excuses whatsoever, that you be and appear in your proper person before the Honorable Judge Mason at the Philadelphia County Courthouse on the 18th of August, AD 1818, at 9 o'clock, to give evidence of what you know regarding the matter of the robbery of Tate's Bank and Loans and Moore's and Mansfield Bank."

"Do you understand this?"

"So long as it means what it says, I think I must."

"I need a verbal confirmation that ye have read and do understand the summons."

"Aye, sir, I've read and understood it."

"Right then, have a good day. Ye get to keep yer summons so ye don't go on fergettin.' Don't ye ferget now, mind ye."

"Yessir. Good day to ye."

"Because if ye ferget, yer liable to be thrown in jail yerself, don't ye know?"

"Yessir."

The old man stared hard at me, decided I was impressed enough to obey the court order, and walked away.

***

Monday came, and by that time, everyone knew the prosecutor had summoned me. I don't know how they knew it, for there'd been nothing said on the summons regarding which side had summoned me. I reckon it was the service man who'd asked everyone and his brother at the barn where he could find me and when I might return. Naturally, they all seemed to think that meant I was planning to incriminate Berton, and I got no end of embittered stares. Every glimpse I caught of Corrine or Mr. Drink was cut short when they hurried away, and I was glad, for I wanted no more confrontations. I got back on Fisheye, who was substantially calmer after his long ride the day before, and trotted into town as the sun rose.

The lad who worked for Mr. TenEyke must've been waiting for me at the courthouse, for he began walking towards me as soon as I arrived. Fisheye didn't like that—he started backing away and tossing his head like he hadn't just jogged five miles.

"Sorry, Mr. Carter. Didn't mean to scare the horse. Mr. TenEyke would like to see you straight away and as soon as possible, please."

"Alright," I said. I jumped down so I could walk Fisheye along beside the lad.

"If ye don't mind, wouldn't ye ride your horse?" the lad asked. "Mr. TenEyke says it's a real urgency."

I agreed, but Fisheye didn't want to stand still long enough for me to get my foot in the stirrup, so the lad had to hold his reins for me whilst I mounted. Then I kicked him into the bounciest, fastest trot I'd ever ridden to make up time.

I pulled up Fisheye at Mr. TenEyke's office, but he ran right by it, evading the bit, and I had to circle him about and bring him back to the office. Then I realized I couldn't go right in, for I was wary about tying Fisheye to the hitching post. I thought it most likely he'd start and snap his reins and run off before I'd return, for he'd been looking for things to spook at all day. I waited by the front steps for the lad to catch up to us, panting and gesticulating wildly for me to go on in and speak with Mr. TenEyke. But I wasn't much harried, for I'd been fooled about Mr. TenEyke's great hurry before.

"I don't want to tether my horse," I shouted to the poor lad as soon as he was within earshot. "Would ye hold him for me?"

The lad ran on faster, and poor Fisheye felt he was being run out of town and did his best to bolt away. But the lad made it to the stoop without Fisheye dragging me more than a few paces, and I handed the reins to the heaving lad with the admonition that he should keep his eye out for things to spook at, for Fisheye surely would. Sure enough, the tinkling of the bell as I opened Mr. TenEyke's door gave them both quite a start, one after the other.

Mr. TenEyke beckoned for me to enter his office as soon as I stepped into the parlor. I complied.

"Thank you for coming on such short notice," Mr. TenEyke said, closing the door behind us. "Where is Peter?"

"The lad you sent for me?"

"Aye."

"He's holding my horse. I don't think I can safely tether him, you see."

"That's fine. Chester, we have some very important matters to discuss."

I settled myself in the chair and waited for Mr. TenEyke to continue.

"I know for a fact that Berton is not guilty of bank robbery."

I was most taken aback. "How do ye know?"

"Why sound thee so surprised?" Mr. TenEyke asked. "Weren't you saying yourself that Berton didn't do it?"

"Well, at least, I don't *think* he did it. But how do you *know*?"

"It's a very delicate matter, and I cannot disclose it."

I frowned a little, but I didn't press the issue. I knew how lawyers were with their secrets, and I had no goal of causing problems in that regard.

"But now that I know he didn't do it, I need your help."

"Oh?"

"Aye. Don't ye think ye can make a bit of a stronger statement on Berton's behalf? I'll cross examine you on the robbers' heights. They were taller than Berton, yes?"

"Taller? I—Mr. TenEyke, you're not asking me to lie, are you?"

"Lie? Good heavens, no. I know Berton didn't do it, and I'm sure the robbers were taller than Berton, and didn't you mention you didn't notice either robber to be especially short?"

"Well, that's what I think, on account that I didn't notice their heights."

"Right, well ye can say that on the stand."

"Sure, I can say *that* on the stand. I *can't* say for certain that they *were* both taller than Berton."

"Chester, please understand the importance of the situation. Juries do not take kindly to such word games."

"I understand the importance. I don't understand why I need to perjure myself when you're the one who knows he's innocent. Just tell the Jury how you know it, why don't you?"

"Chester, it's a very delicate situation, one that you would not understand, and I cannot introduce that evidence. We need to find some other way."

"Mr. TenEyke, I believe *this* must be witness tampering."

"I know not where you heard such a term, but I won't have you breathing word of it surrounding my practice. I've been building the credibility of the TenEyke name since before you were born. There is nothing nefarious at play here."

I said nothing, I only continued to sit stonily across the desk from Mr. TenEyke.

"I have no more to say on the matter. I had thought you would be more willing to cooperate, but no matter. I'll see you in court."

It sounded like a threat, though the words were light. I rose and bowed to Mr. TenEyke and left without another word.

Peter was out front, standing at Fisheye's shoulder and scratching him behind his ears. Fisheye's head was lower than I'd ever seen it before, but it jerked up with a start as the door swung shut behind me.

"Thank ye, Peter," I said. "Good lad for holding him for me."

"Not a problem. 'Tis a good-lookin' horse ye've got there."

"Thank ye. He's a racin' horse."

"Is he now? He sure do look fast."

"He doesn't act it, though," I chuckled. "He hasn't won me any money since I've owned him. Might as well be a riding horse."

"He'd be a good ridin' horse. Pretty enough fer just about anyone, I reckon."

"That's the truth. And did ye notice his eye? The left one. Like a person's eye with the white on the edges."

Peter took a look and gasped. "My! He do look at me just like a person. I reckon I'll stay here on his right side."

The door opened. "Peter. Please," Mr. TenEyke called. "Good day, Mr. Carter." Then he disappeared and the door swung shut again.

"I reckon I'd best get going," Peter said. "Good to meet ye."

"Same to you," I said, and I swung up on Fisheye as the horse turned circles and meandered slowly away from me.

We clip-clopped over to the livery and I rented a stall for Fisheye for the day. Then I walked to the courthouse, and I was still early.

Chapter Twenty

I lingered on the courthouse steps, waiting to be called. I sat down, watched people traipsing along the street, and tried to clear my mind, for I didn't want to think of Berton and robbers and lawyers again until I had to.

A shadow fell over my shoulder, and I looked up to see Counselor Worthingham.

"Hello, Mr. Wothingham."

"Hello, Mr. Carter. I heard tell you were idling out here, so I thought I'd see for myself."

"I'm sorry. I was only waiting to testify."

"Very good. We haven't yet picked a Jury, but when we do, you'll be our first witness after opening statements."

"Yessir."

"You can wait just outside the courtroom. Come along."

I followed Mr. Worthingham into the dim, stone building. We took a turn into a wing, and Mr. Worthingham stopped outside a set of double doors.

"You can wait here," Mr. Worthingham said, pointing to a bench along the wall, facing the doors. "The Bailiff will retrieve you when it's your turn."

I sat, and Mr. Worthingham went through the double doors. They were thick, wooden doors, hung on great iron hinges so they swung lightly. I glimpsed the same dark stone floors inside the room, and more rows and rows of benches before the door swung softly shut.

I had ages to wait, and the ages dragged on all the more for my not knowing when I could expect to go, and feeling compelled to stay there on that bench until I was called upon, for far be it from me to be absent at the crucial time.

I memorized everything about those doors. A plaque hung to their right, claiming the courtroom as the honorable Judge Mason's, the handles were smooth and inviting, and there was a large gash on the left door around the midline. There was a locking mechanism, too, which looked near as good as that of the prison, but I knew it wasn't locked for how often and easily the doors swung open and shut and people walked in and out, Mr. TenEyke and Mr. Worthingham among those who did so most frequently, with only Simon and Peter passing through with greater frequency. Sometimes they gave me a nod as they walked through, other times they simply breezed on by. As far as I could see, which was not far, I couldn't tell that anything was happening inside. It always looked still, quiet, and solemn.

The bench gained people beside me. Witnesses, I suspect, some who I knew and some who I didn't. I didn't speak to them, for I wasn't sure I could without earning a trial for myself and getting thrown into jail in the meantime.

I saw Mr. and Mrs. Drink and Corrine walk into the room, though I wished I hadn't. They avoided looking at me.

I was growing hungry, but even more, I needed to relieve myself. The latter reached such dire straits that I called out to Simon as he hurried out of the courtroom for the fifth or sixth time that morning.

"Simon, sir,"

"Eh Chester?" he said, turning but still taking small steps backwards, away from me.

"Might I relieve myself?"

"Of course," he chuckled. "Outhouse is just behind the courthouse. Don't talk to anyone, for ye never know who's a venireman. We might be ready for ye in an hour or so."

I thanked him and was out the door and behind the courthouse in a flash. I found the outhouse, which had quite the line, and I neither spoke nor looked anyone in the face for fear he'd speak to me.

I returned to find my spot on the pew taken, so I stood, leaning against the cool stone wall for a while until my legs tired of that, and then I took a seat on the floor with my back against the wall.

I was glad when Sheriff Hoogkirk showed up, for it'd surely been another hour at least since I'd spoken to Simon, and I still had no word of testifying.

"Ahoy there, Chester," he said.

"Hello," I returned. I wondered if the Sheriff were a person I shouldn't speak with.

"Still haven't gone, have ye?" he asked.

"Nay."

"Have they taken any witnesses?"

"Nay. I'm the first."

"And I'm likely one of the last for the state, so I reckon I've got a good piece left to wait. Listen. I'll be close by. Let 'em know I was here if they ask for me."

"Ye mean yer just leaving?"

"Well sure. What good is it fer me to sit and wait here? I've testified at Lord knows how many trials, and I've never witnessed a trial that starts on time, much less one that calls me within three hours of when they tell me to be in court. Now I've taken to showing up two–and-a-half hours late."

"But aren't ye worried of contempt?"

"Nay, I'm not. Judge Mason don't want to hold the sheriff in contempt, for then he'd have to call in a sheriff from the next town over to arrest me. And Mason's late too often himself to hold it against anyone else, in me opinion."

"When do ye think they'll take me?" I asked.

"Have they got their Jury yet?"

"I don't know."

"Well they need their twelve men picked, then they'll do opening statements, and then it's your turn. Opening statements only take an hour. But the Jury is another question. Might take an hour, might take six."

"Hours?"

"Aye. Got to be just-so. Procedure, procedure. Well ye take care. I'll pop in every so often," the Sheriff said, and he walked away from the envious stares of his fellow witnesses.

I waited there for at least another two hours, watching people go in and out through those swinging oak doors, before the Bailiff finally came to get me. He wore beige and had a shiny badge, and he opened the door and called, "Mr. Chester Carter," without leaving the courtroom.

I jumped up at once.

"Aye sir."

"Come along."

I followed the Bailiff into the courtroom. 'Twas impressive, with rows of pews, mostly filled with unfamiliar faces, though I saw a few racetrackers. The floors echoed with my steps and the windows were covered with green velvet curtains that reached the floor. At the front was the Judge, seated up high behind a massive wooden desk that took up the entire back wall. A mousy reporter sat, quill in hand, at a little desk in front of the Judge, and the Jury filled out a flight of hard-backed wooden chairs on the left side of the room.

I was directed to step up to the clerk, who directed me to raise my right hand and swear to tell the truth, the whole truth, and nothing but the truth, which I did, and then the deputy directed me to sit in a little chair between the Judge and the Jury. I was enclosed in a sort of box, and now I was facing the gallery. I could look to my right at the Jury and to my left, and upward, and see the Judge glaring back down at me.

"Speak loudly, son," the Judge said to me. I nodded.

Mr. Worthingham stood up from the table in front of me. Mr. TenEyke and Berton sat at the other table in the center of the room, in front of the pews.

"What is your name, sir?" Mr. Worthingham asked.

"Chester Carter."

"Speak up, lad," Judge Mason said.

"Chester Carter."

"And what was your occupation on July 3rd, 1818?"

"Was that the date of the robbery?"

"Yes."

"Objection!" Mr. TenEyke called. "Mr. Worthingham is testifying."

"Overruled," Judge Mason said. "We all know there was a robbery."

"Where were you employed on that date?"

"I was working for Mr. Tate at Tate's Bank and Loans. I was an apprentice for him."

"And what were you doing three hours past noon?"

"I was walking back to the bank after having delivered a document to one of Mr. Tate's clients."

"Did anything attract your notice during that trip?"

"Yes. I ran into Sheriff Hoogkirk and Mr. Pete, and we three talked a bit."

"Then did anything further attract your notice?"

"Yes. Across the street, a couple of men dressed as Indians rode on horseback to the bank, and then they got off and went inside and—"

"Let's take it slowly: a couple of men dressed as Indians, you said. In what way were they dressed as Indians?"

"They were wearing war paint on their faces—red and blue and white painted over their entire faces. They were wearing normal clothes, though."

"What do you mean by normal clothes?"

"Oh, just breaches and shirts. Nothing special about them."

"And then you said they went into the bank."

"Yes."

"What happened next?"

"Not long after, they walked back out of the bank."

"They walked?"

"Yes. At first. Then Casey Tucker, who's an apprentice for Mr. Tate, he came running out of the bank yelling about a robbery, and then the men got on their horses in a hurry and galloped off."

"Were the men carrying anything with them when they left the bank?"

"Aye. 'Twas a bag."

"Were they carrying the bag on their way into the bank?"

"I don't rightly know. That wasn't what I noticed."

"So the men galloped off. What happened next?"

"Sheriff Hoogkirk tried to fire on them, but his gun wasn't loaded, so he handed me his gun and got on his horse and galloped after them."

"And what happened next?"

"I didn't have any powder, so I couldn't load the gun, but I kept it and started running after the Sheriff. And then nigh on the whole town was running after those men, but I didn't see 'em after that."

"Did you eventually stop running?"

"Oh yes, I finally caught up with the Sheriff, and he'd stopped at the bridge out of town. He said he'd lost sight of 'em there and wanted to regroup before going into the woods."

"And then what happened?"

"I gave the Sheriff the gun and he loaded it, and then we agreed I could join his party to go after the robbers in the woods."

"Did anyone else join the party?"

"No."

"So 'twas just you and the Sheriff?"

"Aye."

"Did you set off at once?"

"Nay, first I went and borrowed a horse from the closest farm, and then we set off."

"How long was it before you set off?"

"Oh, about an hour or so."

"So that might put it around four-and-a-half hours past noon that you started through the woods, looking for the robbers?"

"That's probably about right."

"Did you find them?"

"No."

"Did you find a trail to follow?"

"I didn't see one. The Sheriff thought he might've found one, and I think that's what we were following."

"Objection! Hearsay," Mr. TenEyke said.

"To explain subsequent conduct," Mr. Worthingham said.

"The Jury is not instructed to disregard the witness's most recent statement," Judge Mason said.

"When did you stop looking?"

"Around dusk."

"Why was that?"

"We weren't making any progress, and it was getting dark."

"What happened next?"

"We went back into town, and I returned the horse."

"Were you involved in any of the investigations following that day?"

"Yes. I went with the Sheriff to the racetrack, and I went with Mr. Tate around to lots of other banks looking for the stolen notes."

"Let's start with the racetrack. Why did you go to the racetrack?"

"Mr. Tate said the robbers might try to pawn off the notes in a gambling house to make it seem like the money was honest."

"Objection! Hearsay."

"Sustained. The Jury will disregard the witness's most recent answer."

"Subsequent conduct, your honor."

"Overruled. The Jury may consider the witness's answer to the extent that it explains his subsequent conduct."

"Could you explain that more for the Jury? How would taking stolen notes to the racetrack help disguise their stolen character?"

"Ah—well, you see, lots of money changes hands with the gambling, and lots happens in little amounts, and—I don't reckon all of it gets accounted for on account that there may be some side bets going on, and if ye simply exchange the stolen notes for the other money changing hands and write in some of the gains as if it's from gamblin, and then ye don't even have the Tate's notes anymore, mayhaps ye've got notes from another bank, or better still, mayhaps ye've got silver. I reckon that's sorta how it works, but it's been a while since I thought of banking matters, and I can't explain it any better than that. Mr. Tate would explain it much better."

"Thank you, that's a start. Did you find any evidence of this going on at the track?"

"I didn't. I don't think Sheriff Hoogkirk did either, though he asked to look in the books."

"Are you familiar with the defendant?"

"Yes."

"How do you know him?"

"We went to school together. Well, he was a bit older than me. And then we met up again."

"Where was that?"

"The racetrack."

"Objection."

"Why?"

"Argumentative."

"When is the defendant's place of work ever kept from the Jury?"

"Objection! Now Mr. Worthingham is testifying and assuming facts not in evidence."

"Your honor. Your honor—"

The court reporter turned toward the desk that towered above him and tapped his quill on the oiled oak top. Judge Mason jolted awake.

"Sustained, sustained."

"Your honor, perhaps the court reporter could read back the last line of question and answer?"

"And have the Jury hear again what has just been ruled prejudicial and misleading?" Mr. TenEyke asked.

"I've made my ruling. Move on, council."

"You also mentioned you went around with Mr. Tate to other banks to look for stolen notes."

"Aye, we looked for the stolen notes and we were also just putting out word and asking for the other banks to look for the notes for us, you know, if someone came in looking to exchange a large amount of Mr. Tate's notes for money or for other notes."

"Did you find any of the notes in that way?"

"I don't think so. But you'd have to ask Mr. Tate that. I don't know that we'd know for sure, on account that a lot of the notes weren't marked, so they were like any other note that was bought honestly."

"Please explain the marking process for the Jury."

"Lots of the notes have a sort of number or such so that Mr. Tate can write in the ledger where it's going and keep track of his liabilities like that—

well, I don't know what more I should say, on account that it might be a trade secret."

"The Court will remind the witness that the witness is under oath and must testify to the whole truth," Judge Mason said.

"I think the Jury has heard enough about the markings, thank you Mr. Carter," Mr. Worthingham said.

"The Court will return the question to the witness: tell us about the markings, please."

"Ah, well, I've really said it all, I think. Mr. Tate just marks the notes so he can tell 'em apart and notes 'em in the ledger so he has a sense of where his liabilities are. Course, they change hands. That's the beauty of 'em, but he's still got to know the total liabilities out so he can cover 'em when they come back."

Mr. Worthingham looked at the Judge, who nodded.

"The State has no further questions for Mr. Carter at this time."

"Cross examination?"

"Yes, your honor," Mr. TenEyke said. He rose and Mr. Worthingham sat.

"Mr. Carter, you said you are acquainted with Mr. Drink?"

"Yes sir."

"Would you recognize him when you saw him?"

"Yes."

"Do you see him in the room today?"

"Yes."

"Please point him out."

"He's sitting at your table," I said, pointing to Berton while trying not to look at him.

"Did you recognize either of the men you saw robbing the bank?"

"No."

"Did you notice anything unusual about the robbers' heights?"

"No. One was taller than the other, perhaps."

"Was the shorter one particularly short?"

"I can't say that he was."

"Is that a no?"

"I didn't notice that he was particularly short."

"Is Mr. Drink particularly short?"

"Objection. Foundation."

"The witness has testified that he is acquainted with and would recognize Mr. Drink."

"Overruled."

"Well?"

"He's rather short."

"Would you have noticed if a man as short as Mr. Drink had robbed the bank?"

"It's possible."

"You said you didn't notice anything particular about the robbers' heights. Doesn't that imply that you would have noticed had one been particularly tall or short?"

"Ahhh—I suppose."

"So neither was particularly short?"

"I don't reckon."

"So no?"

"Objection. Asked and answered."

"Move on."

"No further questions," returned Mr. Worthingham.

"Re-cross?"

"Yes, your honor. Mr. Carter, on the day you witnessed the robbery, were you well acquainted with Mr. Drink."

"No."

"On the day of the robbery, when was the last time you had seen Mr. Drink?"

"I reckon it would've been five or six years hence, when he was still in school."

"Would you have recognized Mr. Drink, covered in face paint, on the day of the robbery?"

"Speculation."

"Sustained."

"When were you reacquainted with Mr. Drink?"

"It would've been shortly after the robbery, at the pleasure gardens."

"Did you recognize him instantly?"

"I didn't. He recognized me, actually."

"Thank you, no further questions."

"Briefly, your honor," Mr. TenEyke said. Judge Mason made no movement. "If a dwarf had been one of the robbers, and if he were wearing face paint, would you have noticed his height?"

"Speculation!"

There was no motion from the Judge's bench.

"Objection, your honor."

"Sustained."

"No further questions."

"May the witness be excused?" Judge Mason asked.

"Yes."

"The witness is excused."

I stood. The Bailiff retrieved me from the witness box and led me out of the courtroom.

"The Court will adjourn for dinner," the Judge said, banging his gavel. "To recommence in one hour. The Jury is admonished to form no opinions and make no discussions among themselves or among anyone else regarding the case or any facts of it." The Judge stood and left through a door behind his desk.

"All rise for the honorable Judge and the Jury," the Bailiff yelled from behind me. "I wish he'd give me a chance to dismiss the Jury first," the Bailiff grumbled. The folks were filing out of the pews, and I followed them outside.

Mr. Worthingham caught up with me by the door. I wished he wouldn't, for I felt the eyes of the Drinks upon me, and I resented how he'd used me to implicate Berton.

"Thank you kindly again, Mr. Carter," he said. "That's all we needed from you. You're free to go, or you can watch the rest of the trial, if you'd like."

"Thank ye, sir. I think I will watch the trial."

"Very good. Do excuse me."

I did, and I exited the courthouse to a bright, warm day.

Chapter Twenty-One

I had a mind to get myself a bite of dinner from the alehouse, for I'd been hungry an hour earlier, but it seemed everyone else concerning themselves with the case had gone to the alehouse for sustenance, and I didn't fancy running into the Drinks. Most of my hunger had dissipated, anyway, during my testimony, and I didn't mind saving a few pennies and being a tad lighter for my horses, so I ate no dinner.

Instead, I wandered around for a spell and returned to the courtroom well before the hour was through to await the recommencement of trial.

The courtroom was empty, save for the Bailiff, snacking on some biscuits. He waved me in when he saw me lurking by the door, and he allowed me to sit in silence in a pew as he finished his dinner. The town trickled into the gallery until the pews filled up. I kept to myself as best I could. Then the lawyers appeared, and then the Bailiff went to retrieve Berton from wherever they'd put him for dinner, and it must've been an hour and a half before the honorable Judge Mason reappeared. The Judge asked the Bailiff for the Jury, which the Bailiff produced and seated and declared all in attendance and seated, and court was again in session.

The State next called Sheriff Hoogkirk to the stand. I reckon someone had given him a warning during dinner, for he trooped right in when the deputy stuck his head out the door. He swore his oath and took his seat in the witness box like he'd done it a million times before, and I reckon he had.

"Please introduce yourself to the Jury," Mr. Worthingham said.

"I'm Sheriff Ralph Hoogkirk."

"Is Sheriff your title?"

"That it is."

"Were you the Sheriff on July 3rd, 1818?"

"That I was."

"What were you doing that day, three hours past noon?"

"I was having a conversation with Pete when young Mr. Carter walked up, and then I was having a conversation with Pete and Chester, and then we looked across the street and saw two men dressed as Injuns get off their horses and walk into the bank."

"Could you describe the way these men looked in any more detail?"

"Red and blue face paint and wearing normal hats."

"Could you make a positive identification of either?"

"Nay."

"Is that because you don't know the robbers or because of the face paint?"

"I reckon I wouldn't've been able to pick out a lad I knew if he were one of the robbers on account of the face paint and that they were far away."

"Is it possible the defendant was one of those robbers?"

"Objection! Foundation! Speculation!"

"Sustained."

"Is Berton's appearance consistent with the appearance of the robbers?"

"Objection."

"Overruled."

"Aye."

"What happened after the men dressed as Indians walked into the bank?"

"Well, I was mentioning how strange it was to Pete and Chester, and then we watched 'em walk back out. Then Mr. Tate's helper lad came running out yelling about a robbery and they galloped off and I galloped on after them."

"Did you ever lose sight of them?"

"Aye, they dashed through town and made it across the bridge, and then they disappeared into the woods."

"What did you do then?"

"I recouped and tried to gather a search party to go into the woods."

"Did you go into the woods?"

"Aye, Chester and I struck out and followed their trail until 'twas too dark to see."

"Did you do any further investigation?"

"Yes. I went to the pleasure gardens looking for those lost bills."

"Why did you look there?"

"Lots of notes changing hands, and not all of it gets into the bookkeeper's records, so it's just the place to exchange stolen notes for something that's not stolen. At least, that was Mr. Tate's theory. He suggested I investigate there. Thought it made sense, meself, but nothing came of it."

"What do you mean, nothing came of it?"

"Well, lots of money changing hands and not all of it gets recorded, so 'twas impossible to look for these notes so far as I could tell. I couldn't ask the goers to turn out their pockets so I could inspect. I did find the bookkeeper, though, and asked her to make especial notes of any transactions involving Mr. Tate's notes."

"Did you find evidence in that manner?"

"Nay. She never had any notes to share when I followed up."

"Did you ever find any evidence regarding who perpetrated the robbery?"

"Well sure, eventually."

"What was that, and how did it come about?"

"That was mostly thanks to Mr. Tate. He knows his bank best and he sure do like to say he knows where his bills are. He thought he had found something for us at some point."

"And what was that?"

"He found a lad who had some money he wasn't supposed to have."

"Is that lad in the courtroom today?"

"Aye, that he is."

"Please identify him for the Jury and the court."

"Berton, right there."

"May the record reflect the witness has identified the defendant."

"The record will so state."

"What did you do when Mr. Tate had pointed out Mr. Drink as a possible suspect?"

"I went to go have a chat with 'im. Asked him what he was about and such."

"And what was he about?"

"He never could tell me where he'd been the days of the robberies."

"Did you, however, investigate any potential alibis?"

"Sure. We'd gotten information that mayhaps he'd been out racing horses or mules on the streets, on account that he wasn't around the garden area where he lives and works, but 'tain't too uncommon for him to disappear for a bit at a time.

"Objection. Hearsay."

"Overruled."

"Did you look into that possibility?"

"Sure did."

"What did you find?"

"Nothing."

"What do you mean by nothing?"

"I asked around, tried to find if there'd been illegal racing that day, and I couldn't find a thing."

"Is that something you could find if it had happened?"

"Well yes. I talked to a load of people, and they all ought to have been willin' to speak to me, seeing as it could've exonerated a friend."

"Speculation."

"I'll move on. No further questions for this witness."

"Mr. TenEyke?"

"Aye. Mr. Hoogkirk, you were looking for races that had gone on in the past and which were purposefully concealed from the law, yes?"

"How do ye mean?"

"Berton's mule races were unlawful, and they were certainly scorned by polite society. They would have been kept secret, don't you agree?"

"Before the fact, yes, after the fact, less so."

"You're a sheriff."

"Yessir."

"You represent the law. Why would someone who had participated in something that may be illegal reveal this to a law enforcement officer?"

"On account that I asked for the information, and I made it clear I meant no prosecutorial action on account of it. I was simply trying to exonerate a man for a severe crime should it turn out that he has an alibi."

"But those who you talked to—they wouldn't have known this."

"I told 'em so."

"Do you think they believed you?"

"Speculation!"

"Is it your impression that these interviewees believed you?"

"Aye."

"How can you be sure?"

"You only asked about my impression."

"So you're not sure?"

"I reckon I'm fairly sure."

"Fairly sure?"

"I'm sure."

"How can you be sure?"

"I talk to a lot of people in my day."

"And you always know if they're being forthright with you?"

"I've gathered a sense for it, mayhaps."

"How many people did you interview relative to this, anyway?"

"Oh, eight or ten."

"You interviewed eight or ten people and you didn't bother to put it in your report of the investigation?"

"I only did it recently. Just the other day."

"Why did you wait so long to do this investigation?"

"That's when I got the idea for it, on account that there were folks who were sure that's what he was doing and wanted me to look into it."

"So you didn't even try to look for an alibi before the other day?"

"Nay, that was only this particular alibi. I asked him about where he was, and I asked his family and those who worked with him if they knew. I was always on the lookout."

"You were casually on the lookout for an alibi when you had put a boy in jail? You'd taken away his liberty, and you were just keeping a lookout for exculpatory evidence?"

"Objection. Argumentative."

"Nay, 'twas more'n casual. I was doing a serious job, to be sure."

"No further questions."

"Redirect?"

"None."

"Good. The Court will recess for half an hour. The witness will be excused."

I had a mind to find a bite to eat, for my appetite had revived during Sheriff Hoogkirk's testimony. I stepped outside and couldn't help noticing what a beautiful day it was, not too hot for mid-afternoon. And then I saw Suzie.

"Suzie! What a surprise!"

"There ye are! I had a wonderin' if I could see ye in court."

"I've been watching."

"Then I can yet see ye speak?"

"Nay, I've already testified."

"Oh. I'd hoped to catch you in advance, for I wish to recant my bad advice."

"What makes ye change your mind? Ma's argument? Or Pa? Or Duncan?"

"Truthfully, 'twas Rebecca's."

"Rebecca? I don't know Rebecca."

"An old schoolfellow. Her father's the guard at the jail, so she must be well acquainted with these sorts of things."

"Rebecca! Oh! I do know Rebecca. I only just met her the other day. I didn't know you were schoolfellows. My, pray tell you didn't tell her about this."

"Well I had to tell her something. Else, how would I have gotten her advice?"

"Oh Suzie. You must not be so free with such things. My, she must think me a horrible, unprincipled soul."

"Nay, she doesn't think things like that. Don't you worry, she's too good to judge us for our folly."

That I could readily believe, but I was still mortified at the thought of Rebecca knowing my moral struggles.

"I do trust that you didn't follow my prior poor advice, though?"

"Nay, don't worry. I didn't follow your advice."

"That's right good of ye."

"And I trust you didn't come all the way to town simply to change your advice, did you? And certainly not alone, I trust."

"Nay. Duncan was taking a trip for some seeds, so here I am on that account."

"Then let's off to the seed store for some dinner, shall we?"

"Yes, let's."

We walked over to Simion's seed store. Duncan was walking out and nearly collided with Suzie as I opened the door for her.

Duncan put his hands on Suzie's shoulders and looked over her head at me. "Good," he said. "I was just going to find you. Come along."

"We thought we'd join you for supper at the seed store," I said. "We're hungry. At least I am."

"Not here and not now. I need to speak with you," Duncan said. Duncan never lacked resolve, not in matters of import, but he did not often speak so finally on matters of convenience or comfort.

I was quiet at once and followed him back down the street, the way we'd come.

"I need to speak with Mr. TenEyke."

"He's been in court all day and will remain all week. He's surely got other matters to attend to."

"I think he'll see us for this."

"Is it about the widow's place?"

"Nay."

"What, then?"

"In truth, I don't know. I reckon Simeon thinks I know more than I do, for I haven't the faintest what he was talking about with the lads. I was looking over the seeds, I was, and I wasn't listening, and I don't reckon they knew I was there, for all of a sudden Simeon was asking me to leave and saying I hadn't heard a thing, neither."

"A thing about what?"

"I don't know. All I know is I think he's up to no good, and it's upon me to tell his poor father about it."

"Why is that upon you?"

"Because his father can set him straight if he wants to. You know, before he really gets into trouble."

"But ye didn't hear a thing, as I understand. I think Simeon's just an unfriendly one as they go."

"'Twas more'n just unfriendly. That man was hiding something."

"Well, what then?"

"He was hiding it."

"Tell me exactly what he said."

"He was talking about money."

"Sure, he owns a store."

"He was talking about money he can't spend."

"He's saving up," I offered.

"Until it's been cleaned."

"He dropped some notes in a puddle, mayhaps."

"No, it sounded more like he had to disguise money."

"Counterfeit?" Suzie asked. But I was thinking of Mr. Tate's theory on the stolen notes.

"I don't know. Mayhaps. Or mayhaps nothing. I reckon Mr. TenEyke ought to know either way."

"I don't know about that," I said. "Simeon is a man. I don't reckon ye need to be tattling to his pa about everything ye hear him saying."

"'Tain't about everything I hear him saying. This one thing in particular. And if Mr. TenEyke is buying an investment property for his son, I do think he deserves to hear the particulars."

"Are you sure it's not about the widow's farm, after all?" Suzie asked.

Duncan scowled. "Do you really think that of me?"

"Well here we are again, discussing that property you want. And we all know he wronged you to get it. I'd not hold it against you for wanting something to do about the matter."

"Never mind, then, let's go back to the seed store and get some supper."

"What? It's not like you to be so easily persuaded."

Duncan stopped walking and suffered the rest of us to stop as well.

"I'd hold it against me if I brought a man under suspicion because he'd wronged me before."

"Well mayhaps that's not in your mind at'all," Suzie said. "I'm sorry I said it. I'm sure you were only thinking of your duty."

"Nay, I can't pretend I don't harbor some resentment against Simeon. I'm ashamed. Please do entirely disregard what I said about him."

"Have ye watched any of the trial?" I asked.

"Nay."

"What ye've described sounds quite a lot like how Mr. Tate describes washing money."

"So it's not a problem?"

"Nay, 'tis illegal and how Mr. Tate would expect a bank robber to hide the origin of stolen notes."

"Well ye must know I'm not accusing Simeon of bank robbery. I'm taking it all back. He must've just been talking about the trial."

"It's worth bringing up. Come on, Duncan, let's catch Mr. TenEyke before he gets back to trial."

Now Duncan was hesitant, but I was so set on an audience with Mr. TenEyke that he assented, and we marched to his office.

Mr. TenEyke wasn't seeing anyone in his office, we were told by Peter, the clerk. He was a little too pleased to tell us so, I thought, but I couldn't hold it against him when he surely didn't get to say anything of import to anyone, ever.

"Pray tell him we have information of utmost importance, and if we cannot speak to Mr. TenEyke about it, our only hope is to go to Sheriff Hoogkirk with the information," I said.

"If it's that type of information, I reckon the Sheriff is exactly who you ought to tell," Peter said.

"Oh, let them in," Mr. TenEyke called through the closed door to his office. Peter sank a bit in his boots and opened the door to the office without saying another word.

"I don't believe I've had the pleasure of meeting this young lady," Mr. TenEyke said.

"Suzie Carter, sir," she responded.

"Very well. Do forgive Peter," Mr. TenEyke continued, "I tell him I can't be distracted during trial, and he takes it a mite too seriously. What can I do for you?"

"My brother, Duncan," I said, after a pause where I'd hoped Duncan would speak, "overheard something concerning at the seed store."

Mr. TenEyke inclined his head to Duncan, who was now obliged to speak.

"'Tis true. We—well I heard Simeon speaking on disguising some money when I was in his store. He became very defensive over it. I fear this is something nefarious, but I know you can help him."

"Well, lad, I think you have let your imagination quite run wild with you. Surely you didn't hear anything nefarious."

"It gives me great relief to hear you say that."

Mr. TenEyke frowned at him. "It does, eh? Well, sir, I seem to remember you having a certain interest in the widow's property a while back."

"You musn't think I harbor any ill will regarding that."

"Well, it might settle you completely if I were to offer you the farm for a song. We can draw up the documents as soon as the trial's over. I need to get back to work now, though."

"Sir, I don't understand your meaning."

"You could pay fifty dollars for the farm, couldn't you?"

"I was prepared to pay twenty-fold that amount for it."

"Then fifty should do you quite well and leave you feeling most settled and happy."

"Settled and happy? I'll tell you the truth, it leaves me feeling most unsettled to have you connecting the farm to my fears of Simeon's conduct in such a way."

"Don't be unreasonable. You can forget all about that."

"Maybe before you attempted to bribe me to do the same."

"You accuse me, now?"

"It gives me no pleasure. But what else could this be?"

"I will not accept a lecture in my own office."

"Very well. Good day." Duncan rose and left the office with Suzie and me hastening to follow him out.

Chapter Twenty-Two

"We're going to the Sheriff," Duncan said when we had left. I trotted a few steps to catch up with him. Poor Suzie was dragging her feet behind us.

"Are ye sure? Ye couldn't ask fer a better deal on a parcel."

"Which sure points to wrongdoing. My, what a scoundrel. And to think we thought him honest as the day is long."

"Just a moment—we don't know he did anything."

Duncan just shook his head and walked on like his coattails were aflame. We reached the courthouse.

"Where is the Sheriff?" Duncan asked the Bailiff.

"I don't know. I reckon back at home for supper."

Duncan cut back onto a side street and we hustled down it. Then we turned back onto the road out of town. 'Twas our good luck that Sheriff Hoogkirk was walking down the same road towards us.

Duncan hailed him, and I joined in.

"By golly, it's the Carters. More of 'em than I've seen together in a moment."

"Sheriff, we need yer help," Duncan said. 'Twas the best thing a body could ever say to the Sheriff, and he swelled and smiled.

"At your service, one and all."

Duncan relayed the story in a hurry.

"Hold it—what is it you're accusing?" the Sheriff asked.

"I'm not accusing anything. Except mayhaps that something is going on. What, I can't say. But Chester thinks—"

"I only think it sounds similar to the sort of thing Mr. Tate was talking about robbers doing with the money. I'm not accusing, neither."

"Well if no one's accusing, what do ye expect for me to do?" Sheriff Hoogkirk asked.

"An investigation."

"And before the trial ends. It might be exculpatory evidence after all."

"We need more time. We need to speak to the Judge right away. They sometimes do this, you know. Can't remember what they called it. Wish we had a lawyer," the Sheriff said.

"That's the other thing. Berton's not done right by if his lawyer is an interested party," I said. "Well right away. To the courthouse!"

We trotted that way down the road, I feeling most weary for all the hustling and the want of dinner, and Suzie looking as I felt. We bounded up the steps to the courthouse and hastened through the cool entryway. The Sheriff led us past the courtroom door to a door that read, "Judges Chambers." He pounded on the door.

Of course, 'twas a young man who opened the door, the court's clerk, clearly.

"'Tis the Sheriff and a witness and some other folk," he shouted upon opening the door.

"Highly improper!" the Judge's voice responded.

"We request—we move—some motion. The trial cannot continue!" the Sheriff shouted.

"Let the lawyers make the motions!" the Judge shouted back.

"Shall I let them in?" the clerk shouted.

"No! Highly improper!"

Sheriff Hoogkirk persisted with, "We can't let the lawyers make the motion on account that—" I nudged the Sheriff.

"Might be best kept quiet," I said. That, I think, was enough to stir the Judge's curiosity.

"On account that what?" he shouted.

"May we speak in quiet?"

"Bring them in."

The clerk stood aside, and we filed into the Judge's chambers. We meandered behind a low, swinging door and took seats in front of the Judge's massive wooden desk. He wasn't wearing his black robe anymore, and he frowned at us over spectacles.

"Hardly secretive if ye bring in half the town and a witness to hear about it."

"Your Honor," the Sheriff said, his inflection at the words causing me to doubt their sincerity, "These are witnesses to some potential wrongdoing which I would like to call to the attention of the Court."

"Very well. Call it to my attention."

Duncan retold his story regarding what had happened in the seed store and the ensuing encounter with Mr. TenEyke.

"We need more time to investigate," the Sheriff concluded, "And Berton needs a new lawyer."

"You don't come into my chambers and tell me what needs to be done."

"Pardon me, Judge, let me rephrase it as a request."

"Motion?" Suzie suggested.

"Lawyers make the motions."

"Request," Sheriff Hoogkirk said again.

"Which will be denied," the Judge said.

"Please, in the interest of justice. I must investigate this evidence. It could be we've got an innocent man on trial," the Sheriff said.

"I see no evidence of any misconduct, and I refuse to end a trial midway for a shadow of an allegation which in no way implies that Berton is innocent. We already knew Berton didn't act alone."

"You mean we already knew the robbers didn't act alone. We still don't know anything about what Berton did or didn't do," I said.

The Judge scowled.

"I've seen you stop trials before. What do ye call it? Misfire?" the Sheriff asked.

"Mistrial," the clerk said.

"That's it! We move for a mistrial."

"The lawyers make the motions."

"Well Mr. TenEyke sure ain't gon' ta make that motion. We've done explained that," Sheriff Hoogkirk said.

"If counsel elects not to make the motion, 'tis of no interest to you."

"I'm interested in justice, please, sir."

"That's enough. Vacate the chambers. I'm already late for court."

"We just ask for some more time to look into the new evidence," the Sheriff said.

"I'm not wasting a Jury and risking double jeopardy for this nonsense. If new evidence comes out, he can have a new trial at that time."

"Not if he's already been hung."

"Clerk, get the Jury in. Let's recommence trial."

"How about a new attorney for Mr. Drink? Mr. TenEyke won't try to put on this kind of evidence on account that it don't look none too good fer his son."

"Where's Mr. Berton going to find a new lawyer ready to proceed in the next five minutes?"

"Just a little extra time should do it."

"I've already denied the continuance."

"The Jury is seated," the Clerk said.

"Why didn't you tell me? Where's my robe?"

The Clerk returned with the robe and put it over the Judge's head. He knocked twice on the door.

"All rise for the honorable Judge Mason. Court is now back in session pursuant to adjournment," the Bailiff said in the courtroom. The Judge left his chambers with us feeling most disheartened.

"Pardon me, but please ye to vacate the chambers," the Clerk said.

"Hardly does please me," I mumbled, and Suzie chortled. But we allowed the lad to lead us out the back door of the Judge's chambers.

"I'll commence to interviewing. I'm looking into this Simeon fellow," Sheriff Hoogkirk promised. "I might need to refer back to you at some point. Be easy to find, eh?"

Duncan promised to comply, and we watched the Sheriff walk away.

"I'd best be getting home with Suzie," Duncan said, finally, when the Sheriff had disappeared from view. We had meandered to the courthouse steps, devoid of purpose, and we stood staring off under the gray sky.

"Right then," I said. "I'll watch the trial, I reckon."

"Write me how it goes," Duncan said.

"Say hello to Corrine and Rebecca for me," Suzie requested.

I mumbled that I didn't reckon I'd have occasion for speaking to either of the ladies. I shook Duncan's hand and hugged Suzie and let them on their way. Then I returned to the door of the courtroom and snuck in as inconspicuously as I might.

The trial dragged on another day and a half. Mr. Tate testified regarding his banknotes and how racing and gambling would've been a good way to pass them off for honest money. Casey Tucker testified about the two men robbing the bank, guns drawn, demanding money. I hadn't seen a gun on either, neither when they walked in nor when they walked out, but Casey was adamant they both carried pistols.

"Mr. Tucker," Mr. Worthingham said, "is one of the men who you saw robbing the bank that day in the room today?"

"I—" Casey looked at Berton. "I don't know. I couldn't tell ye on account of all the face paint."

"Is the Defendant's size and appearance consistent with him being one of the men who robbed the bank?"

"Objection! Foundation! Speculation!"

"Overruled."

"I suppose."

"Yes or no?"

"Well yes, I reckon consistent with."

"No further questions."

"Mr. TenEyke?"

"Yes, your Honor. Casey, you don't know what the robbers look like under the face paint, do you?"

"Nay."

"Any number of people could've been under that face paint, right?"

"Yes."

"Would you recognize the person without the face paint?"

"Nay."

"No further questions."

The witness was excused.

Mr. TenEyke put on a witness or two testifying to Berton's mostly good character.

"Would your opinion on Mr. Drink change if ye knew about his propensity to partake in illegal mule racing and off-the-books gambling?" Counselor Worthingham asked of one such witness.

"Oh, come now, no one really minds such things."

"So you know him to partake in such things?"

"Well—I don't know if it's true or not true. I only know 'tain't too uncommon, and it don't harm no one."

"Would your opinion on that change if you knew five people have been killed in illegal horse and mule racing in the past three years?"

"Come now, far more than five people die in farming accidents each year."

"Is it your opinion that illegal racing and gambling are the same as farming?"

"Argumentative!"

"Only asking a question, your Honor."

"Denied."

"In your opinion, are illegal racing and gambling the same as farming?"

"Nay."

Mr. TenEyke had no more witnesses and nothing that portended an alibi for his client. Mr. Worthingham began his closing statements with a description of the robberies, and then he spoke on the events leading to Berton's arrest and the evidence they had against him, which I'd never believed was much, but when Mr. Worthingham laid it out, it seemed encyclopedic as a textbook. He had unaccounted for money, he had friends in illegal activities, he had a history of law breaking, he was short and slight, he had access to horses. Mr. Worthingham ticked each fact off on his fingers, and I wish I'd been paying better attention, for it surely seemed to me he repeated a few.

Mr. TenEyke went next. He argued the "evidence" was entirely circumstantial, and that there were so many other explanations for every bit of evidence, which created abundant reasonable doubt.

Mr. Worthingham responded that any individual piece of evidence may be insufficient to convict, but with it all intersecting as it did, it compounded and became a corpus delicti which required a conviction in the interests of justice and in accordance with the law.

The Jury received its instructions and retired to deliberate. I waited around. I don't know if the Drinks felt any more consternation than I, for I felt a guilty verdict for Berton would be a guilty verdict on mine own conscience.

Then after just a fairly brief time they had a verdict, or so said the Bailiff, and I was back in the courtroom, sweating, sitting behind the Drinks who were sitting behind Berton, who looked so small and young in his chair next to the stiff-necked Mr. TenEyke, in the imposing shadow of the Judge behind his raised and enormous desk.

We stood as ordered and the Jury filed into the jury box. They kept their eyes to themselves. They were quiet. We were all quiet. The Judge ordered silence anyway.

"Foreperson, please stand," Judge Mason said.

A little man in the front of the box stood.

"Have you reached a verdict?" the Judge asked.

"We have."

"How do you find the Defendant?"

"We, the Jury, find the Defendant, Berton Drink, guilty of two counts of robbery."

A collective gasp swept the court. Corrine slumped into her mother's arms. Mr. Worthingham nodded grimly. Mr. TenEyke put his hand on Berton's back and whispered something into his ear. I wanted to shake the man, I did! Whatever he'd done on Berton's behalf hadn't been enough, he who'd told me he knew of Berton's innocence. And he must've really known, embroiled as his son was in nefarious business dealings.

"Very well. The Court accepts the Jury's verdict. The sentence imposed by law is death by hanging which will be carried out—" the Judge consulted his desk, "the thirty-first day of October, year of our Lord eighteen hundred and eighteen. That's in ten days."

I was shocked and appalled, and I would've remained there in the courtroom, sitting shocked and appalled and gathering dust, had not the onlookers risen en masse. I was obliged to move out of their way, and the slow, shuffling crowd herded me out of the courthouse.

Fragments of conversations about supper and the weather and the harvest drifted to me. How they could speak of such things when a young man had been sentenced to hanging, I could not fathom. I wanted to go straight home. Not to the pleasure gardens, where I was Berton's accuser. I wanted to go to my home. To my parents' farm where I'd done as advised and where I could fall in with the plows and feel like I'd been gone not more than a week. Where they'd need me as any farm needed extra hands those days.

But I wasn't expected at home, and I had commitments to ride in the next day's races. I scrawled a letter home with the trial outcome and started for the barns. Fisheye knew the path and kept it well, wanting no guidance from me, which suited my preoccupied mind just fine.

"Ye goin' ta the gov'nor's?" Ron asked, catching Fisheye's reins as I rode him towards the barn.

"The gov'nor's? Where's that?"

"The capital."

"Why?"

"I reckon you're not. I'm supposed to give this bundle of bills to the convoy heading to the gov'nor's."

"Why?"

"On account they might need it for lodging and meals and such."

"Nay, why is there a convoy to the gov'nor's?"

"Oh, to ask for a pardon."

"Are they in good spirits?"

"They will once they've this here sack with 'em."

"Does the gov'nor oft' give pardons?"

"I surely don' keep track. I reckon he must, seeing as he's the only one who can do it."

"Ye think I can join the convoy?"

"'Tis yet set. If ye ain't party, ye ain't party and that's just fine. Cain't afford to support another lad on it. But I've got to find that convoy before they get goin.' 'Scuse me."

Ron wandered off, and I could hear him repeating the conversation midway down the barn aisle, and then again at the back of the barn as I doused Fisheye with water and put him back in his stall with a few forks full of hay.

I went to bed early, exhausted from the days of travel into town and the emotional strain of the trial, but I slept like a guilty monk. I heard every grumbling snore from Green Gene, every rustle in the bed from Ronny, every snort and swish from each of the horses in their own separate rooms.

I was up before the sun, when the morning was still dim and gray, and I had my chores done in short order. With racing in the evening, there wasn't much exercising to do.

"There goes the convoy," Ron said. "They're well provisioned, at least."

I followed Ron's gaze out the open end of the barn. I was just in time to see three riders on trotting horses disappear over the crest of the hill.

I wanted motion, I wanted answers, and the races wanted eight hours before beginning, so I saddled Fisheye for the umpteenth time to take him back to town.

"Good-lookin' pony ye got there," Green Gene said.

"He's got some races in him yet," I responded.

"Not the way yer ridin' him. Yer cornfusin' him, an' that ain' the way to condition a horse for the track, besides."

"Right, well, good thing I'm not training him for you."

"Nay, 'tis a pity ye ain't training 'im fer me, otherwise ye might actually win sommin."

I scowled. "Give me a leg up, would ye?"

Green Gene obliged, keeping one hand on his breakfast pipe and allowing Fisheye to walk away as he threw me into the saddle. I let him continue on as I put my feet in the stirrups, and he picked up a trot pointed up the hill as soon as we left the stuffy shade of the barn.

We made it to the jail in record time, I think. Pity there weren't three or four-mile races, for I'd have Fisheye in tiptop condition for such a race.

I cringed with guilt as Fisheye slowed to a halt in front of the low stone building, but my mind wouldn't let me stay away.

Mr. Ernet was in his guardroom, and he recognized me immediately.

"Young man. Back for your Christian duty, and to see your friend?"

"Aye, sir."

"Shame to hear the sentence. Though I suppose we ought to hope and seek justice, bitter though it may be."

"I do hope for justice, but first I hope my friend is not guilty."

"Come along then, shall we?"

The guard unlocked the huge iron door, and it squeaked eerily as it swung open. We stepped into the cool, moist, and dark hall. My stomach fell through the floor and my arms went clammy all at once. But it wasn't the dankness of the hall. 'Twas the thought that I'd gone to visit a man with not much more than a week to live. I'd never thought a hanging to be barbarous before, but then I'd never known the convict.

We walked down the hall between cells, the only sound our footfalls echoing off the stone walls. Some of the other convicts peered through their bars at us as we walked by, but none called out to us today.

Berton was back in his old cell. Not much smaller than my stall at the barns, but chill and damp and without a way out.

"You've another guest, Mr. Drink," Mr. Ernet said.

There was some shuffling within the cell. I peered inside and found Berton sitting on his hard little stool, peering back out at me. He recoiled just a smidge when he saw me, and his brows went up.

"Here we are and pardon me, sir, let me get this door," Mr. Ernet said. I kept silent as the huge iron door grated open. I stepped into the cell, as indicated by the guard, and he shut me inside.

It didn't smell all too nice in there. Berton kept to his stool, so I stood.

"Well?" Berton asked. The guard's echoing footsteps receded. Now there was only the coughing and rustling of the other inmates to listen to.

"I came to visit."

"Why?"

"I reckon we're friends."

"I reckon we're not."

"Would ye not like me to visit you?"

"Nay."

"Very well, then, I shan't."

"You didn't come to visit me anyhow."

"How do you mean?"

"I reckon you have a real reason for being here."

"You're doubting the Christian duty in my heart?"

"Aye."

"Well, then, I did want to know if you did it or not. For the life of me, I'd only believe ye did it if ye told me."

"What do I care if ye believe I did it or not?"

"I reckon it'd be nice to have a few people on your side."

"'Twou'd've been nice back during trial. Don't reckon it matters now."

"That's another thing. I don't believe Mr. TenEyke gave his full ability to your case."

"And why is that?"

"Are you friends with Simeon?"

"Friendly."

"I reckon Simeon had something to do with it."

"I sure never liked TenEyke, but he took my case at no charge. It's the most anyone's done for me in this matter."

I looked to the ground. "Do you know if Simeon had anything to do with it?" I asked, finally.

"Oh, just be gone with ye, ye hateful lad. Ye feel like a little detective, do ye, and ye go on and pretend to be friendly, no respect for the dead, none at'all. Here I am locked up and set for hanging and ye force yerself upon me. Be off with ye, do, an' don't be back!"

I reckon the whole jail heard that frightful parley, for I heard a few snickers from the adjoining hall, and then Mr. Ernet's footsteps came echoing towards us. He unlocked and opened the cell door, and I nearly fell out into the hall, so quick was my retreat. I didn't take leave of Berton, I just hurried down the hall after the guard. I might've thought I'd feel better out in the sun, but the light only illuminated my shame. Berton had seen through my noble facade in the dark. He'd known at once I'd visited to benefit my own tormented soul, and he'd been proud enough to tell it truthfully.

I hardly even took leave of the guard, though he was surely being especially friendly toward me, probably assuming that Berton had taken the stress of his situation out on me, an innocent party. But I couldn't endure such charitable company at that moment.

Fisheye was willing, and he took off like a bird dog. I'd fallen into a bad habit of not fighting his explosive energy at the beginning of a trip, I simply allowed him to gallop off until he tired himself out sufficiently to be content to continue at a jog.

Thus, we tore down the path from the jail. But there was Rebecca, just walking sweetly down the path towards us! I jerked on the reins, and Fisheye, more on his own account to avoid hitting the girl than at my command, leapt off the path and took a few strides on the grassy knoll before dropping back to the worn path.

We hadn't bowled Rebecca over, I was quite sure, but I felt even worse than I had a minute earlier. I lugged backwards on the reins, trying to slow Fisheye. He kept the bit in his teeth and ran on. I pulled now only on the right rein, bending his neck until his nose was near my foot, and he was forced to slow to a lurchy canter. I got him spun around and trotted him back to Rebecca.

Upon reaching her, I jumped to the ground. Fisheye fidgeted and tugged on the reins as I bowed to Rebecca.

"Do forgive me, Rebecca," I said. "I'm ashamed at having gone by you so fast."

"Oh, there was no harm to me from it," Rebecca said. "Though I do hope you note all the carts traveling along this path. It must be quite dangerous to take such a speed on such a busy road."

"Aye, you are right, of course. I really ought to train my horse to mind me better, and to mind the traffic better."

Rebecca inclined her head. "He is a lovely thing, though."

"Why thank ye kindly. He's a racing horse, really, by training and blood." As soon as I said it, I wished I'd kept it to myself, for such a dear and virtuous girl could have no good feelings about horse racing.

"Oh? Well that explains the pace, I suppose."

"You are going to see your father?" I asked to change the subject.

"Aye."

"May I escort you?"

"Thank you, no. I'm almost just there. There's really no need."

I would have loved to insist, but for the few problems I saw. First, that I was unworthy to walk beside her, after having nearly run her over only minutes earlier. Second, that I was resigned to take Fisheye, who was liable to tread on someone's foot, or at the least to make the pace uncomfortably fast. And third, I could not offer to place Rebecca in the saddle, for I didn't trust Fisheye to be gentle with a lady. So I did not insist, and I only bade farewell to Rebecca and watched her continue on her way.

When she disappeared behind a hill, I mounted Fisheye and set him towards the barn. He must've been similarly subdued by Rebecca's gentle admonishment as I, for he maintained a calm canter at my request and kept the pace the entire way to the barn.

Chapter Twenty-Three

The races that evening were quick. I only rode two and lost them both. I felt a frenzied excitement jumping down from the horses, so covered in mud that I couldn't blink without dislodging dust into my eyes or speak without tasting dirt, but the exhilaration passed quickly, and my dismal feeling at Berton's predicament settled heavily on my shoulders once more.

I walked back to the barns in the dark, my shoulders sagging, dragging my weary feet through the dust, feeling every bit as dirty as I looked. I hadn't the energy to look over my shoulder at the pattering feet I heard running up behind me.

"Chester. I need to speak with ye."

'Twas Corrine. Her face was so pale it nearly shone in the dark. Her soft brown eyes looked deep and shadowed. Her dark ringlets were loose and free about her face, but colorless without the light.

"Corrine," I said. I hadn't the presence of mind to think of anything else to say.

Corrine glanced around, then she took my arm and tugged me off the path.

"Come, sit, and speak with me."

I allowed her to lead me off the path, behind a little stand of trees. Had I wanted to resist, I wouldn't've had the strength, but I was too guilty before her to deny her a conversation. There was nowhere good to sit, so we stood. Corrine glanced around again.

"I need your help," she said in a low voice, speaking very close to me and catching me with her deep eyes.

"Please let me help you."

"I hope ye will," Corrine said meaningfully. "I beg ye."

"What can I do for you?"

"Ye must go to the jail and speak with the guard there at one o'clock this morning. You must take him back to his house, if you can."

"What on earth? Never in my life have I made a call at such an hour as that. What would occasion such an untimely call?"

"Never mind that. Ye will?"

"I–I can't, not without an occasion. 'Tis unseemly."

"No, it's not unseemly. He's up at all hours and enjoys friendly calls. You will do it for me?"

"Why on earth?"

"As a favor to me. Ye did say ye would help me."

"How would that help you at'all?"

"Don't you know Rebecca?"

"I do."

"Rebecca has told me he gets ever so tired and lonesome keeping watch so late at night. It would do well for ye to speak with him."

"So me speaking with Rebecca's father in the middle of the night on account that he gets lonesome is how I can help you?"

"That's it. Rebecca is such a lovely girl. She's my dear friend, and this would help me out marvelously."

I looked at Corrine closely. I couldn't see into her eyes in the darkness, but she tipped her head down anyway. I worried for her.

"Corrine, please don't do what I think you want to do."

"I don't know what ye mean."

"Surely ye do. Please don't do it."

"Chester. Will ye do this for me? Please."

I resented Corrine for asking that of me. Yet I still wanted to tell her yes, but I could not take part in a jailbreak. I was too tired to be principled, and I was held hostage by her gaze.

"Aye. I will do this for ye," I said, knowing it was a lie as it passed my lips. I couldn't be a party to a criminal enterprise, no matter how guilty I felt before Berton and Corrine. But as soon as I'd said it, the weight on my shoulders grew. Corrine stepped towards me and tried to clasp my hands and kiss my cheek. I backed away from her as quickly as I could.

"I must get going," I said.

"Thank you, Chester. I'll be forever indebted to you," Corrine said.

I hurried away, only my inner turmoil fueling my retreat. I burst into my stall. Ronnie and Green Gene were out, probably playing cards, and I rejoiced in the silence. I shut the door behind me and sank onto my bed, holding my head in my hands.

I really did want to help Corrine, and lying to her was no way to do it. I sprang up and ran back out of my stall, out of the barn, and back down the path towards where I'd left Corrine. It was dark, and long shadows lay over the path. The small clumps of trees growing here and there were patches of blackness.

I slowed to a walk, straining my eyes. I saw no one on the path. I continued on, back towards the track, no longer lit up and empty of spectators.

I saw a pale dress bobbing in front of me.

"Corrine?" I called. She turned and stopped. I ran to her.

"Corrine. I cannot. I will not aid in a jailbreak. It will only cause more problems, more suffering. People get killed in those sorts of ways. If you will not give me your word to stop this idea, I will be forced to alert the guard of your plans."

Corrine looked up at me, her large eyes narrowed, shaking from fury or fear, I don't know which. "You. You're all wrong! You don't know a thing. You mustn't say such hateful lies."

"Understand me—"

"No! I don't and I shan't!" She shook free from me and ran down the path. I watched her go, and then I turned myself and ran back to the barns. I had no trust that Corrine would stop her plot, and I needed to warn the guard, though I had misgivings about that, too. I had no solutions, but I couldn't be idle.

Fisheye was dozing when I appeared at his stall door, but his head was up in an instant and his eyes widened, especially the fish eye, when he sensed my excitement. I had him saddled in a moment, despite his restless fidgeting, and then we were out of the barn, and I swung into the saddle as Fisheye turned circles around me.

Fisheye galloped off down the path we knew so well, and I urged him on over the shadowy, uneven ground, against my better judgment. I kept him galloping until I felt him tire, and then, fearing he would stumble in the darkness, I slowed him to a rolling canter. At the first wood, I slowed him to a trot, for sticks often littered the path, which was narrow and winding through the trees.

Fisheye stopped so suddenly and swerved so sharply I nearly toppled off headfirst. As it was, I fell onto his neck and wrapped my hands around him. I righted myself to see a man standing there, holding Fisheye by the reins.

"Pardon me," I said, "what is the meaning of this? You have upset my horse."

"Pardon me, sir," was the reply. "We only need to speak with ye a moment."

I raised my eyes and saw another man, on a horse, farther back in the woods. A second horse waited nearby.

"Pardon me, sir, but I cannot spare the time. I'm in a hurry."

"Pardon me, sir, but we will speak with ye," the man said. I looked him up and down. He kept a firm grasp on Fisheye's reins, and Fisheye was standing more quietly than I'd ever seen him stand.

"Well speak, then, if you please."

"We can't have ye goin' to warn the guard about nothin' tonight," the man on the ground said. I glanced up at the other man. He was astride a big horse, but he did look rather short. The horses were sorrel, I could tell, despite the darkness.

"Warn the guard about what?"

"I haven't the faintest what ye were planning on warnin' the guard 'bout. But there will be no disruptions of his peace on any account."

"It is moving how concerned so many people are for Mr. Ernet's peace of mind," I said. "And here I was, not knowing anyone even knew him."

The man bowed, as if to accept responsibility for his noble actions with some semblance of modesty.

"Oh come now," I said, becoming vexed all at once. "Why are we playing at gentlemen? I'm no gentleman, and I know you aren't either. I witnessed the first robbery, and I saw you two do it."

The two men glanced at each other. I wasn't sure about my conclusion before I said it, for I recognized not the faces of the men in the slightest, but their looks confirmed it.

"Then you know why we must do this," the man on the ground said.

"Why you must attempt a jailbreak? Nay, I cannot understand it."

"It's to prevent the murder of an innocent man."

"Oh. Now I understand." I looked at the men with some newfound appreciation. I wouldn't've thought robbers to have such decency at such great personal risk. "I believe you're right, but going about it in all the wrong way," I said. "The correct thing is to admit to your own guilt and Berton will be released."

"Surely ye can understand why that is out of the question."

"Yes, I understand why you would not find that an attractive option. But it really is the correct way to go about it. Ye did what ye did knowing ye could be hung for it. This lawlessness you try instead only takes you further from the realm of good standing. This is the sort of thing that gets good men killed."

"Not if ye keep your mouth shut and let us handle it. We're saving a life, not out to hurt anyone."

"What's Berton got to do with it, anyway?"

"He's in jail."

"Why is he in jail?"

"They thought he robbed a couple of banks."

"Yes, but why did they think that?"

"On account that he was social with us. An' he didn't turn us over, even to save his own neck. He's a good man, Berton."

"All the more reason to turn yourself in for him."

"We're not going to keep talking in circles here. I can see ye get the point, and I'll thank ye for your discretion."

"You're robbers, not murderers, right?"

"Aye."

"And you're not out to hurt anyone?"

"We're out to save a life."

I jerked the reins to the left and clapped Fisheye's sides with both heels. He responded like a muzzle blast, just like I knew he would. The man stumbled and lost his grasp on the reins, and we were free. I gave Fisheye his head and let him find his way over the rutted, root-lined path, far too fast to be safe. I clung to his mane and pressed myself against his bobbing neck as twigs pulled at my hair and snagged at my clothes. I heard pounding hooves behind me and shouting for me to stop, but I didn't turn around. I was too concerned with anticipating Fisheye's sharp jukes and awkward leaps over some of the bigger ruts.

We were out of the woods in a moment. I urged Fisheye on over the widening path, standing over his withers and squinting between his ears at the dark path ahead, the wind making my eyes water. I prayed he wouldn't stumble, for I'd be over his head and on the ground if he did. I still heard the pounding hooves behind me, but now the shouting was gone. I chanced a glance behind me.

The shorter robber, who hadn't spoken to me in the woods, was only a few lengths behind me, the other a few lengths behind him. Seeing me look back, the shorter one shouted, "Stop! I'll shoot."

I didn't see a gun, nor did I expect his riding shooting would be accurate. But mostly, I'd made up my mind to take his co-conspirator at his word that they were not murderers and had no designs to hurt anyone.

Fisheye was lathering where the reins rubbed against his sweaty neck, forming foam that gathered on his black coat and flew off behind us in little white clumps. His breathing was growing ragged, but he could see the horses behind him, and he knew his job. I clucked in his ear, and he rushed forward with more strength in each leap.

But we had so far to go. The distance to the jail was miles longer than any race run at the track, yet we were galloping as if it were a sprint. I didn't urge Fisheye anymore. I only kept checking behind me, making sure the others were just out of reach. The little man was applying the whip to his sweating horse, who was breathing like a steam engine. But still, the horse did not gain. My own heart pounded in my chest, and I gasped for breath.

The sturdy horses galloping after us were no racing horses. They were shorter, stockier. They had speed for a burst, and now it was dwindling. Fisheye was clearly pulling ahead. I kept him running, promising him oats and green pastures if he could get us into town.

We crested a little hill, which took a disconcerting toll on Fisheye's pace, and there was the jail below us.

I started yelling, only realizing then that my throat was parched from the wind. I was panting like a dog, and the wind whipped my words away as soon as they'd parted from my lips.

"Robbers! Jailbreak! Lookout!" I yelled. I don't know if anyone could hear above the pounding hooves, but I hoped the pounding, iron-shod hooves would be enough to wake the guard if my words were not.

We sped past the jail and continued towards the town. 'Twas only another mile or so, but Fisheye needed all the urging now. I whistled in his ear and waved my hands in front of his face, wishing I'd brought along a riding crop.

I glanced behind me. The robbers had pulled up their horses and were already fading behind us into the darkness. This worried me, but I urged Fisheye on.

Fisheye stumbled, but he righted himself and continued running. We ran into the outskirts of town, approaching the first old farmhouse with only a yard and not a full field out front. We crossed a cobbled patch in the road. Fisheye slipped and threw up his head. I fell onto his neck and then clung to the reins as he lifted his forefeet off the ground.

"Robbers!" I yelled. "Robbers!"

An old woman ran out of her house.

"Robbers! Over the hill! They're getting away!"

"Well tell the Sheriff about it," she said, reproachfully. Her husband appeared in the doorway. "Robbers?" He disappeared and returned a moment later with a rifle.

"Ye'll not go after 'em. That's a young man's job!" the old woman said.

"If not I, who else?" the old man said. "Give yer horse to the missus. Looks like he's 'bout ready to fall over. Run along to the barn now."

I jumped off, my legs nearly giving way and my feet protesting loudly when they hit the hard ground. I pulled the reins, which were drenched in Fisheye's sweat, over his head and gave them to the old woman, who took them obligingly and looked at my poor, heaving, and shaking horse sternly.

"Thank ye, ma'am," I said. She only waved me away. I ran after the man, who was already running towards his barn.

"I only got the one nag," he said. "Go wake the rest of the street."

I switched course and began running down the street. The next house was a couple hundred paces from the first. I reached it and began pounding on the front door, yelling robbers and the like.

The commotion at one door yielded four or five folks from surrounding houses, and they were all quick to saddle their horses and tote their guns and ride back out of town. I didn't know what they'd find, if anything at'all, on account of the scant direction I gave. Nor did they wait for more. They set out like minutemen, galloping up the hill a few hundreds of paces in between each. Dogs ran after them and some men simply grabbed their guns and ran after the rest on foot.

Finally, I saw the Sheriff on Champlain, galloping towards me on his way out of town. I saluted him, he returned the gesture, and I figured that was my duty done for the night. I considered the matter handed off to the care and custody of the Sheriff, and I was well pleased.

Chapter Twenty-Four

I made my weary walking way back to the first farmhouse, the one right on the edge of town. I meandered to the little lean-to out back. The old woman was there, throwing another bucket of sudsy water over Fisheye's back as he stood, calm as a carthorse, looking on with weary eyes.

"Ye sure did run him good," the woman said when she saw me.

"Aye," I agreed.

"Walk him out a bit. I'll go mix up a warm mash," she said. I took up the lead rope and walked off. We plodded around like a couple of old folks until the woman called me back. She put a pail of warm mash on the ground, and Fisheye put his nose in the bucket and began eating.

The woman looked on approvingly and then motioned me to follow her. I tied the rope loosely to the lean-to wall and followed her into her house. She put a steaming bowl of porridge in front of me, probably the same as she'd served Fisheye, and I tucked into it with matching gusto.

"Thank ye very much," I finally remembered to say. She waved my thanks away and took to tidying up the kitchen, and I continued eating the porridge with relish.

I was scraping the bowl with my spoon—I would've licked the bowl had I not been in a stranger's house—when the farmer walked in abruptly.

"That boy in here?"

"Aye," the old woman and I said at once.

"He's in here," the man called to someone outside.

Sheriff Hoogkirk appeared in the doorway, his spurs clinking against the wood-plank floors. I jumped down from the stool, my legs protesting again, ashamed to be caught enjoying a meal while the rest of the male inhabitants of the town were off seeking justice.

"We caught a couple of boys a little ways out of town. What were you saying they did?" the Sheriff asked.

"Planning a jailbreak. And they were the bank robbers."

"You're saying ye recognize them? I know ye've got better eyes than I do. I could see it. One scrawny. Both white. Riding horses."

"Nay, I can't be sure I recognize them. But they admitted to doing it."

"My, that's gold. Ye don't get that all too often. Well come along, now, ye've got to make the identification."

I followed the Sheriff out, only remembering at the last moment to bow to the woman of the household.

The Sheriff walked like he was worried the men would get away. But when we arrived, me slogging along with wavering legs, we found the robbers bound back-to-back, patrolled by no fewer than ten people, old men and boys, toting rifles or old muskets or carrying knives or hatchets in their belts.

"Oh, I must tell ye," Sheriff Hoogkirk said, "the men we've got may be not at all connected with what you witnessed. In the interest of justice, it's most important that you take an honest and non-prejudicial look at these men and tell us truthfully if you can make an identification. So, take a look. Are these the men you're accusing of robbery and attempted jailbreak?"

I looked at them and had no doubt in my mind that these were the two I'd talked to in the woods. Yet they looked at me with such pitiful expressions. They'd only been trying to free an innocent man from execution when they'd confessed their crimes to me. 'Twas only an accident, and I hated to be involved in such an accident. But I had been, and I'd given up lying, so I nodded, not breaking eye contact with the man who'd promised he wasn't a murderer, and who had been true to his word.

"Are you sure?"

"Aye. It's them who I talked to."

"Let's take 'em into custody, then folks," the Sheriff said. The folks were most eager to help, but not quite sure how to do that. They eventually picked the prisoners up to set them on their feet. The lads were still bound back-to-back, their hands bound between them. They had to hobble and totter, shuffling sideways. And such a long walk they had, too, to the county jail. 'Twas a comical sight, despite their being accused of a capital crime. I was delirious from fatigue, and it was all I could do to stifle a laugh.

I wasn't free, either. The Sheriff carted me off to the Judge's house for a warrant.

The Sheriff bounded up the front stoop steps, all energy and excitement, and I followed slowly, climbing the steps with my hands on my knees like an old man. Sheriff Hoogkirk had to ring the bell thrice before a servant came to the door.

He opened the door just a crack, just enough to show one of his bleary eyes squinting out at us.

"What is it?" he asked.

"We need a warrant from the Judge," Sheriff Hoogkirk said.

"Not at this hour, ye don't."

"Aye, 'tis precisely at this hour that we do."

"Don't neither."

"Do too, and if ye don't let us in, I'll be asking for a warrant for your own arrest next. Obstruction of justice will do, I think."

The servant shut the door with a snap. Sheriff Hoogkirk hesitated a moment, as if waiting for the servant to draw back the chain and open the door for us, but there was no movement from inside the house. Sheriff Hoogkirk drew back his hand and pounded on the door.

"I'll wake the Judge and bring him out here myself if you won't!" he shouted at the closed door. I wanted to melt away into nothingness, but I was too newly afraid of the Sheriff to even shrink back from the doorway.

The door opened mid knock and Sheriff Hoogkirk nearly fell inside.

"Do quiet down. Most uncivilized. If you will be such a dunce about it, I will show you inside, but you must act civilized."

The Sheriff clapped the servant on the shoulder and walked inside, and I squeezed in after him.

"Lawless behavior. A lawless sheriff. What have we come to?" the servant mumbled, loud enough to impress everyone with his displeasure.

"Right, go run along now and bring back the Judge," Sheriff Hoogkirk said.

The servant shook his head and grimaced. He gesticulated at the chairs in the parlor as he walked away, probably indicating we could wait there. He did no running, though. I do believe he dragged his feet and walked slowly as he could out of spite, for he was middle-aged, not yet old, yet he walked as though he'd been walking for a hundred years, and his body was quite worn out from the exertion.

The Sheriff didn't sit in the parlor, though I wished he would have, for I thought a chair would do nicely, though I'd prefer to stretch out on the parlor floor. 'Twas ages and ages before the servant came back, and then it was only him alone, walking very, very slowly, a triumphant grin spread across his face.

"He says to come back in the morning. There's no reason to need a warrant this late at night, for you can hold a man two days without one, and he will not entertain such inconsiderate behavior, and he wonders what on earth you were thinking, showing up and waking the entire household at such an hour."

"Well, we'll sit and wait in the parlor for his Honor to awaken. Would you bring us some coffee and biscuits, sir?"

"Absolutely not. You will leave and return at a reasonable hour, if you must."

"I believe you are forgetting your manners. We will wait in the parlor."

I nearly died at hearing this from the Sheriff, for I wanted nothing more than sweet sleep at that moment, but I could no more leave the Sheriff than barge into the Judge's private bedchambers.

The Sheriff sat down in the parlor, and I followed suit. The servant watched us with angry incredulity, and then he shrugged and walked away. He did not bring us coffee nor biscuits.

I kept drifting off to sleep until my chin drooped down, and then I'd jerk awake again, with a crick in my neck and no feeling of refreshment.

'Twas a relief to me when the parlor grew dim and gray. The Sheriff was snoring, slumped in his chair, and I felt crooked as a dog's hind leg and envious of the Sheriff's sleep. The maid bustled in before there was true sunshine streaming through the windows. She put a pot on the stove and started bustling around before she caught sight of us in the parlor—I haven't the faintest idea how it took her so long to notice the Sheriff's snoring—and screeched.

That woke the Sheriff with a start, and his foot hit the ground—it'd been resting on a footstool—with a bang.

"What on earth?"

"Waitin' on the Judge. Do pardon, ma'am."

"What are ye doing waiting in the parlor at this hour?"

"We've been waiting for a good many hours, to tell ye the truth. Yer butler wasn't so keen on us."

"Well I can hardly be keen on ye sleeping there, either. My, didn't the Judge wake for ye?"

"As a matter o' fact, he did not," Sheriff Hoogkirk said, rather proudly, I thought.

The kettle whistled and we all startled again.

"Well you'll have some tea, and a hot breakfast in a moment. My. To think ye spent the night in a parlor. Terrible. 'Twasn't always like this."

The Sheriff nodded solemnly, and I frowned from embarrassment. The housemaid brought us hot tea and biscuits and I stood, stretched, and nibbled and felt almost cheerful.

The Judge kept us waiting a long time. The housekeeper frowned and mumbled that the eggs were going cold, and the Judge was usually down by that time. Even the servant bowed and grumbled that the Judge was seeing to his affairs and would see us in a moment. I was feeling as grimy as I'd ever felt, and the dear housekeeper was not making me feel any better by her nervous dusting all around us as we waited in the parlor.

Finally, the servant announced that the Judge would see us in his office. The Sheriff rose calmly and walked with such poise that you'd've thought he had all day—that he'd arranged for a meeting and was a few minutes ahead of schedule himself. I followed behind slowly, my legs feeling like dead weights.

"Good morning," Judge Mason said, when the servant announced us and let us in the door.

"Good morning to ye," the Sheriff replied. I don't know where his chipper response came from, but I admired it.

The Judge raised his eyebrows. "Do you have something for me?"

"Yessir. We need a warrant to hold a couple o' men."

"On what grounds?"

"On the grounds that this man here heard these two men we've now got in custody confess to those two bank robberies."

"Is that true?"

"Confess may be rather too strong of a term," I said. "It's more like they didn't deny it when I accused them."

"Oh that's a confession, all right. There's loads of common law on that," the Sheriff interjected.

"Kindly don't instruct on the law," the Judge said. "That is my job."

"Absolutely right, sir," the Sheriff said.

"Thank you, Mr. Hoogkirk. Glad to have your approval."

"Yessir, and I'd be glad to have your signature on a warrant, sir."

"I don't know that I can trust this man's credibility. He was rather upset about his friend being convicted for the same crimes."

"It's the truth, I promise," I said.

"Oh, you promise, do you? No one's ever lied to a judge before, so I suppose that's good enough for me."

"They were caught running, your Honor," the Sheriff said.

"Running is no evidence of guilt."

"Oh yes it is, sir," the Sheriff said.

"Well what else do you have?"

"What else? Three men in custody for a crime that by all accounts was committed by two."

"What else in evidence? I can't lock these men up on this man's word alone."

"First of all, yes ye can. All you need until trial is probable cause, which this man's word can give ye."

"Kindly refrain from instructing on the law."

"And second of all, they ran like they were running from the law."

"Anything else?"

"Ye don't need anything else!"

"I do think I recognized the horses. Did you, Sheriff?" I asked.

"As a matter o' fact, I do. Those same horses. Big, sturdy, light-colored, nothin' fancy."

"Alright, well that's something else. Anything else?"

"Ye don't need anything else!"

"If there's anything else I would surely like to know it."

"One was short-ish."

"I reckon you don't have anything else?"

"I know ye don't need anything else."

"Very well, though, Sheriff, you are risking being held in contempt of court."

"And you're risking being arrested for—"

"That's quite enough. Good day to you," the Judge said, returning the Sheriff's proffered sheet with his signature in ink, still damp.

The Sheriff took the arrest warrant, and we left without ceremony, stopping by the dining room for another biscuit on the way out.

The Sheriff dismissed me offhand, thanking me for my good work on behalf of the citizens of our town as an afterthought. I was happy to be on my way, so I took off with more sprite than I felt. I walked back to the farmhouse on the edge of town and loitered in the front yard, torn between going straight to the barn to retrieve my horse and taking leave of the woman of the household.

I decided 'twas only proper to take leave of the woman and thank her for her kind care of my horse, so I meandered up the steps and knocked on her door.

"Yer horse is in the barn, ain't he?" she said, before I could get out a greeting.

"I expect so, ma'am. I only wanted to thank you kindly for your hospitality."

She waved me away. "You boys. Best be careful ye don't run that horse into the ground."

"Yes ma'am," I said, and I backed away. She snapped the door shut. I turned and continued to the barn.

Fisheye was there, contentedly munching on hay. His flanks were smooth and shiny, washed and dried the night before. I threw the saddle over his back, tightened the girth despite his angry ears, and pulled his head away from the hay long enough to get the bit in his mouth and the headstall over his ears.

For once, Fisheye was content to walk away, after I mounted, and we walked the entire way back to the barns. It did make for a long journey, but it was pleasant enough.

When we reached the barns, Fisheye hadn't even broken a sweat. I pulled off the saddle and shooed him into his stall. I threw some hay in behind him and checked the water bucket. It was half full, with a few flies floating in circles around the surface of the bucket. I left it there, Fisheye went straight to his hay, and I went to my own stall. I stripped off my dust-covered shirt and crawled into my bed, the noon-sunlight streaming through the rectangular, cut-out windows in the old barn, illuminating the dust that floated on the still air.

Chapter Twenty-Five

I dreamt of Rebecca. She was standing somewhere. In a busy street, perhaps, though I don't think I saw anyone else. I only got the sense that she was looking around, shifting right and left to allow people to file past her, distracted and unable to see me. I tried to call to her, but I couldn't make a sound. I tried to approach, but I couldn't lift my feet. She turned from me, as if to walk away, and simply dissolved into the air. I awoke and then dozed off again, almost immediately.

***

I woke again to that lad—Mr. Worthingham's clerk—pounding at the stall door. I reckon he'd been knocking politely for a time and had found it futile. He was pounding rather loudly, loud enough to get a "let him in, for cryin' out loud, go shake the fellow," from Mr. Bean's pipe-damaged voice.

I'd forgotten the lad's name, but I didn't even recognize this oversight at the time. It never occurred to me to call him by his name. I haven't wondered until I sat down to write this, and finally it came to me—his name is Simon.

I opened my eyes and rolled over.

"Eh, Chester! I'm after you!" he said.

I rubbed my eyes. "Hello," I croaked.

"Mr. Worthingham would be pleased if you could make your way down to the office for an interview. You seem to be the star witness again."

"Now?"

"Yes, now. It's hardly an irregular time."

"What time is it?"

"Three past noon."

"It's only noon?"

"Nay, it's three hours past noon."

I wondered who on earth accounted for time in such a manner, but I chalked it up to me being still disoriented by sleep. Upon cool reflection, as I recount it now, I still find it irregular.

I managed, finally, to get out of bed and don an unclean shirt, under the watchful gaze of the clerk. I walked out into the aisle without looking at him, and then I followed him out of the barn, head down and squinty-eyed, and to the cart.

I felt as ashamed as if I were being questioned regarding my own crimes. It only struck me at times like these that I ought not sleep in a barn, perhaps. That I ought to wash my shirts before re-wearing them, and comb my hair, and build a tidy house on a small plot. I ought to put away money for a rainy day, perhaps in a bank rather than in a bag beneath my pillow.

We trotted along to town, me shading my face the entire way because I'd forgotten a hat. The clerk kept glancing at me, some sort of wonder in his face.

"I can't believe they confessed to you," he said. "Did they really? I reckon half the time the Sheriff says he got a confession he makes it up."

"I did not make it up," I said. "But they didn't quite confess. They just didn't deny it when I put the confession to them."

"You mean you told them what you thought they did, and they didn't deny it?"

"Aye, that's exactly right."

"Adoptive admission," the clerk said, looking rather pleased with himself. That's as good as a confession. It's admissible hearsay, you know."

I didn't know it, and I didn't think the clerk had any right to think I knew it, so I didn't respond.

I did my best to shake the dust off my shirt when I arrived, but I reckon the dust was more closely woven into my shirt than the threads themselves at that point. 'Twas no longer a white shirt, and I dimly hoped no one would know it had once been white.

The clerk left the cart and pony standing, unattended, and ushered me inside, through several sets of doors, and then presented me to the prosecutor, Mr. Worthingham, after knocking loudly at the office door and being met with a "come in."

"Mr. Carter. Good to see you again," he said. "Although I regret the circumstances in which we always meet. Although, of course, our meeting sets the wheel of justice rolling, the only remedy to crime, in my opinion."

"Aye, sir," I said. I didn't mention the injustice which had been done to Berton, not in so many words, at least, but I did continue: "will Berton be released soon, do ye think?"

"About as soon as he can appeal based on new evidence, so long, of course, that we have a legitimate case against these two fools you picked up last night. Which, of course, is why I asked you to be here."

"When can he get an appeal?"

"I don't know. I'm no defense counsel. Really, though, let us please focus on the task at hand, which involves you being a witness in a case involving these two men arrested last night." I said nothing, so he continued. "I believe you know the process by now. You'll have to tell me everything."

I don't reckon I knew the process very well for the amount of urging and coaxing I required to get out the story he wanted to hear. He sent me through it backwards and forwards, and then back to the very first robbery again. Then he wanted to know about all the details I might have forgotten and everything which might be important, which put me at an absolute loss for words.

Then he tasked me with writing the story. "Everything," he told me. "Write it all down, even if you're not sure if it's important. I'll sift through it and decide what's important. It's much better than missing those final facts."

He gave me a stack of paper, and a dip pen, and a few bottles of ink, which I accepted, a touch abashed. As soon as I got home, I went back to sleep, and then I fed and watered Fisheye and changed his bedding. He'd started fidgeting again, so I saddled him up and took him out to the track for a ride. It must've been the first track workout I'd put Fisheye through in ages, and we both enjoyed ourselves thoroughly.

Then, when my stall mates had settled down to play cards, I begged leave of their game to attend to my clerical duty. They didn't believe me until I showed them my stack of papers and let on that I needed to fill every sheet with writing. They looked at me with deep pity, made a few joking remarks, and left me to my work.

I started writing then, and I wouldn't have come up with half so many words as I did had I not had witnesses to my writing there in the room with me. The story tumbled out so profusely I fancied myself a playwright and perhaps added more flair than desirable.

The later it got, the more fanciful my writing became. It's all true, mind you, at least as true as my memory, down to the last detail.

So ends my account.

Epilogue

I enjoyed the writing well enough, so I thought I might continue. Plenty of folks keep journals, and I reckon they come in handy every now and again.

Concerning my initial account, I wrote through the night and into the morning, up until it was time to exercise the horses, and then I rode and collapsed into bed afterwards, still covered in mud and too tired to care.

The writing gave me clarity, which sleep helped me see. I awoke feeling filthy. Too filthy to be cleaned with a rinsing of soap and water. It was all I'd been doing, the dust of my new life clinging to me regardless of how much I rinsed and lathered and repeated. I saddled my horse, stuffed my extra shirt in a bag and affixed it to the saddle, and said my goodbyes to Ronnie, Mr. Bean, and anyone else I happened to see in that old barn on my way out. I mounted my horse, stack of papers in hand.

I rode away from the barn, Fisheye trotting nicely, not intending to return, and not minding.

We passed the jail on the way. I would've called on Mr. Ernet, for the sake of Rebecca, of course, but I was newly unemployed and habitually filthy, so I pointed Fisheye for home.

I could've cried when I saw the chestnut trees that lined the way, laden with spiky pods. Suzie, in a light frock and shawl, stooped to pick up the fallen chestnuts and throw them in her bag one by one, looking like a giant chicken. She dropped her bag when she saw me and ran up to greet me.

Fisheye wasn't yet tired enough to resist the lightness in his front end which overcame him at the sight of Suzie hurrying towards us. She laughed.

I might've scolded her, or the horse, but I was light enough myself to jump down and scoop my sister in a big hug.

"Take my horse, will ye?" I asked her.

"Oh, ye can't pass yer ill-trained horse off on me. He's an imp if I ever saw one."

So, I walked my own horse to the barn, unsaddled him in twenty seconds, and turned him loose in the pasture.

He acted like he'd never seen a pasture before, and I reckon he'd been without one for most of his life. He made up for lost time, snorting and galloping and tearing to and fro.

"He's not going to jump in with the mares, is he?" Suzie asked. She'd followed me along, chatting most pleasantly, sparing no extra thought for the bag of chestnuts she'd left behind on the road.

I hadn't thought of that, but a few rows of fencing separated him from our two cart mares, so I answered in the negative.

'Twas nearing dinner time, and Pa and Tim were walking to the house right when I was.

I waved.

"Is that Chester?" Pa asked Tim.

"Aye," I said.

"Have ye come to help with the harvest?" Pa asked.

"Aye."

"Well, then, it's good to see ye." Pa laughed, and hugged me, and clapped his hand on my shoulder.

Ma appeared and hugged me. "Mr. Carter!" she scolded, over my shoulder.

"He knows I'm only joking," Pa said. "Of course I'm happy to see him for whatever reason he visits, and I have a feeling it's not to help with the harvest."

"'Tis to help with the harvest," I said. "I reckon my time at the pleasure gardens is done."

"Oh thank heavens," Ma said.

"Why?" Tim asked, but Ma was entertaining no talk of the gardens at her dinner table, though we'd not yet processed inside, and I didn't feel like answering Tim anyway.

***

I helped with the harvest. I was covered in dirt and dust from the dried stalks. It made me itch and sneeze, but it was a cleaner dust than at the barns.

Ma washed my shirts and ironed them out, and I took a proper bath after dark and before supper, and I felt positively fantastic by the day's end.

I was so busy I could only fill in my narrative bits and pieces at a time. Eventually, I delivered my written account to Mr. Worthingham, who teased me mercilessly on my verboseness.

I testified in court again, a few weeks later. The Jury convicted the two men I'd seen in the woods. 'Twas a capital crime, but I led a convoy out to the governor, and we secured a pardon, on account that they'd spared my life where they would've done well to shoot me.

Simeon wasn't charged, nor Mr. TenEyke, the elder. I spoke my piece against them to Judge Mason, but he wouldn't entertain my complaints. He said Berton was the only one with standing to get Mr. TenEyke disbarred, if he chose to make the claim. I relayed this to Berton, who was released and now thinks he holds free license to race mules all he wants. I don't reckon Berton cared to make the relevant claim. For all his faults, Berton is not one to harbor grudges. He spoke with me as courteously as ever, after all.

Not long after the second trial, I had a most lucid dream. I wrote a little story with it, about horses, robbers, and Injuns. I showed it to Suzie, who found it so amusing I submitted it to the paper. They bought a few more little stories off me, after that. They hardly brought in much, those stories, but it led to a post at the periodical and a few novels from my studies at night.

The best part of all was that Rebecca enjoyed my writing, and she still does, so she says, after all these years of hearing them round the dinner table. She dug out my old, true, and written account of the robberies, and I don't know if she fell in love with me over again or wondered at how she'd ever ended up with a man with such an impetuous youth.

And that's enough of a remark on the story, I suppose, for I'm wearysome and have been only succeeding at slipping into reverie as I muse on the time gone by. You'll take from this what you will, I suppose, and I trust you to the guidance of Counselor Worthingham's opening admonition.

Signed most truly,
Chester Carter

About the Author

Elaine Mary Griffin works as an attorney and was involved in criminal trials for the St. Louis City Prosecutor's Office. A lifelong equestrian, she owns a retired racehorse and worked as the horse identifier for two seasons at a racetrack. This is her first novel.

Note from Elaine Griffin

Word-of-mouth is crucial for any author to succeed. If you enjoyed *Shadows in the Pleasure Gardens*, please leave a review online—anywhere you are able. Even if it's just a sentence or two. It would make all the difference and would be very much appreciated. Also, please connect with her through her website and blog at elainemarygriffin.com

Thanks!
Elaine Mary Griffin

We hope you enjoyed reading this title from:

www.blackrosewriting.com

Subscribe to our mailing list – *The Rosevine* – and receive **FREE** books, daily deals, and stay current with news about upcoming releases and our hottest authors.
Scan the QR code below to sign up.

Already a subscriber? Please accept a sincere thank you for being a fan of Black Rose Writing authors.

View other Black Rose Writing titles at www.blackrosewriting.com/books and use promo code **PRINT** to receive a **20% discount** when purchasing.